M000087957

BEARING WITNESS

This book is a work of fiction. Names, character, places and incidents are the product of the author's imagination or are used fictitiously. Any resemblance to actual events, locales, or persons, living or dead, is coincidental.

Printed in the USA

ISBN: 978-0-578-77584-5

Cover design: Mary Anthonis

This book is dedicated to my amazingly supportive children

Kate and Ben,

and always to my husband Mick.

Also by Ann Travers

His Brothers Eyes

Bearing Witness

by

Ann Travers

Chapter 1

Twenty-three years ago

Emmalise walked purposefully down the dirt road. She was ten years old. She wore too-short jeans and a faded blue tee shirt with a barely visible cartoon whale on the front. Her big toes peeked out of her dusty white tennis shoes; her feet were bare. She was small and thin with her long, chestnut hair pulled into a ponytail that hung to the middle of her back.

She was thinking about her name for at least the millionth time, because Larry Pritchard had decided to make fun of it again at school yesterday, calling her "Mona Lisa", even though he didn't know that the Mona Lisa was the most famous painting in the world. She ignored him, and hoped he would forget on Monday, or have someone else to pick on. Mama had named her Emma Lisa, because of Mama's sisters having those names, and they had both died a long time ago. Luckily, her big brother Frank slurred the pronunciation to Emmalise, and pretty soon, everyone followed suit. Even luckier, Mama wrote it out the way it sounded, as one word, when she enrolled Emmalise in kindergarten. Jerks like Larry still made fun of her name sometimes (his worst was Emma Lice the month her class suffered from that affliction, probably brought in by Larry himself), but there were at least three other unusual names in her class, so she didn't suffer alone. Penelope Jones was Loopy Juice; Imogene Slattery was Sluttery; and the worst was poor Hugo Faulk, which Larry turned into You Go Fuck way back in first grade. None of the bad names were used within teacher earshot, but were whispered on the playground or yelled away from school. Larry himself had earned the name Prick Turd, but not to his face or large ears. Larry was the biggest kid in fourth grade, and had two mean buddies, Ralph and Craig, to back him up.

Emmalise sighed and forgot about Larry as she neared her destination. A narrow track branched off from the road to her right, and she followed it through tall grass. Her objective was a derelict wood barn that stood about a quarter mile from the road. It didn't look like it was in use, but a padlock held the big doors firmly closed. The little girl easily pushed aside a loose board on the nearest side wall and slipped inside. The farmer who owned the barn used it for hay storage upstairs and had two full hay racks parked downstairs. The barn smelled wonderful from the rich alfalfa/timothy mix. Emmalise closed her eyes and breathed in the clean smell.

She quickly climbed a ladder leading to the haymow. The hay was stacked in a criss-cross pattern with the taller piles in back on the wall, gradually becoming lower toward the front edge with about one foot of space left to walk. Emmalise climbed to a three-bale-high stack and sat quietly. Within a minute, five small kittens scampered toward her, followed by a tabby female. The kittens clung to her pants legs and jumped onto her lap. She held them, rubbed their heads and tummies. The mother cat watched from a distance, and Emmalise told her that it was OK. Eventually the little girl lay down, so the kittens wouldn't have to dig in so sharply to climb all over her. It was an unusually cool day for mid-September, but warm in the barn, especially upstairs in the hay. Ten minutes passed, and Emmalise and the cat family were asleep.

She woke to a dimmer barn, feeling very warm. Opening her eyes, she saw the mother cat resting by her shoulder, her gold eyes looking back at Emmalise. The kittens were cuddled on her chest and stomach, still sound asleep. Suddenly a loud metallic snap sent cat and kittens flying back into the hay. The barn doors opened with loud screeches. Emmalise crawled further back into the bales, until she found a hole that would hold her. Down between the bales, she saw a tunnel where she could stretch out on the floor, so she slid quietly down. Through a crack on the floor, she could see a small area of the ground floor and the edge of a rack loaded with hay. She hoped it was just the farmer, and he would only be there to take out a rack of hay.

"This way, sir. I hid it over here." The man's voice was low and deep.

"Why in God's name would you take it out? Why didn't you just give it to me at the house?" This voice was slightly higher, a lot louder, and agitated.

"You weren't home, sir. I didn't want anyone to see it."

A black man in overalls and a faded blue shirt walked underneath her, then disappeared. A white man in a suit and hat stepped into her view, and backed out again.

"Where did you find it?"

"On a shelf in the old tool shed. In a cigar box. I was looking for some needle-nose pliers, and that box rattled like it had some small tools in it."

The black man still sounded calm and reasonable, but Emmalise could barely hear him. She could imagine him bending over behind the rack to retrieve whatever he had hidden.

"Here it is, Mr. ——." His voice dropped at the end, and she couldn't understand the name.

The black man walked underneath her again, and held out something that looked like a dark red box. She saw the white man's hand take hold of it.

"You shouldn't have been snooping, " said the white man, his voice shaking, his words followed by a loud crack. The black man fell back into her view, a red hole in his forehead, his eyes wide open. For a few seconds, she saw blood trickle down the side of his face, but a lot more was pooling under his head. Suddenly the head and upper torso moved, and was dragged out of her sight. She heard some grunting and a thud, then a wheel rolling across the floor. The barn door creaked open. A minute later it closed with a squeak. Emmalise was frozen in place. She started to breathe again, until the barn door reopened. Footsteps paced the floor; then white hands threw a bucket of water over the blood spot, which thinned and spread under the rack. She could see the man's hat, arms in suit sleeves and hands as he pulled loose hay off the rack and onto the floor. She heard him walk back and the door did its noisy open and shut.

Emmalise waited, barely breathing. She had no idea how long she stayed hidden, but she didn't want to see what was happening outside. Eventually, she noticed that her whole body was trembling, and she couldn't stop. She put her head down, closing her eyes. She thought she heard a car engine start up, but far away. Then she heard a tiny mew, and one of the kittens popped up by her face. Another plopped onto her back, then another. Soon all five, varicolored kittens, plus the mama, were around her arms and hands, crying for pets. It must be safe, thought Emmalise. Carefully, she pulled herself out of the hole and dislodged the kittens.

"Sorry, babies," she whispered, "I have to go. Mama, keep them safe."

Emmalise was still shaking as she crept down the ladder and hurried behind the hay racks to the loose board in the wall. She pushed it aside a couple of inches and peeked outside. Nothing. No one. Just the sun low in the sky beyond the golden fields. She squeezed through the opening and walked with weak legs down the dirt track. Suddenly she noticed a black snake curving its way slowly through the short dry weeds and grass beside the path. She stopped for an instant, staring at it. She wasn't afraid: knew it wasn't poisonous. But it seemed to light a fire inside her and she took off running as fast as she could for home. Her legs pumped. Her arms pulled at the air. Her hands were in fists. She sucked in breaths and blew them out in perfect rhythm with her legs. Her head was up. Her eyes filled with tears that spilled down her cheeks and then dried in the breeze her running made. She ran past fields of yellow wheat and brown corn; past farmhouses and barns; past pastures with black fences and brown horses; past small wooden houses, a few trailers; and finally tore up the dirt and gravel lane to her family's old, gray house, set well back from the road. She ran up the steps, across the porch, threw open the wooden door with its peeling paint and dusty glass window, ran past the living room, up the stairs, and into her bedroom. She slammed the door and threw herself on her bed, breathing hard. She wasn't crying anymore.

No one came. No one knocked on the door and asked her what was wrong. Her mother was at work. Dillon, her fifteen-year-old brother, was working too. At the same roadside diner as Mama, Hank's Burgers and Shakes. She was a waitress; he was a busboy. Frank would have taken their brothers and sisters into the diner for their one free ice cream a week. Emmalise hadn't gotten home in time for supper or ice cream. She wasn't hungry anyway, and was glad no one was home. She couldn't tell them, especially Mama. Maybe Dillon, but Mama would freak out. She wouldn't let Emmalise go anywhere alone again. Dillon might not either, but he wasn't around that much. He might know what she should do, who she could tell. That white man had to be caught. You couldn't kill another person, except in self-defense, and the black man hadn't attacked him. She hadn't seen a weapon. Maybe he'd had a knife or gun too, but it looked like he was just handing something to the white man. She couldn't see everything. Couldn't see much of anything. Thou shalt not kill. That was in the Bible. The preacher didn't even talk about that commandment much, because everyone knew it. People hardly ever did it.

Never around here. Well, not that she remembered. Some kids at school said Mr. Thomas killed Mrs. Thomas, but other kids said she ran away from home. This was different. She had heard the shot, and seen the small hole in the black man's forehead and the blood spreading out on the barn floor. She wondered if he felt it. His eyes were open, but he didn't make a sound. Except the thunk when he hit the floor. She held her hands over her ears and squeezed her eyes shut, but only for a moment. She rolled over and stared at the fine lines that spider-webbed the ceiling of her room. She had to tell the police. But she was just a little girl. They wouldn't believe her. She needed to take someone with her. Who could she trust? Who would take her to the police and make them believe her? Miss Tippet. Her teacher. She was the safest person Emmalise knew.

Chapter 2

Lorraine Tippet was surprised by the soft knock on her front door Sunday afternoon. No one had called to ask if he or she could call. She opened the door, then looked down as a quiet voice said, "Hello, Miss Tippet."

Standing on her front porch was Emmalise Pine, her long hair hanging down her back, and held off her face with a plastic headband. She wore a purple and yellow flowered dress that hung below her knees and scuffed black Mary Janes. Probably her church outfit.

"Why, hello, Emmalise," Miss Tippet smiled, "Would you like to come in?"

Emmalise stepped inside silently, looking around. The room to her right was light with a floral pattern on the couch and arm chairs. She saw yellow and pink and green, like a spring day. Emmalise thought it was the most beautiful room she'd ever seen.

"Sit down with me, Emmalise," said Miss Tippet, "Would you like a drink?"

"No, thank you," answered the girl. She sat carefully on the couch, continuing to look at the room's walls, which were covered with photographs.

"There I am," Emmalise said, pointing at a black and white photo next to the fireplace.

It was a candid shot of Emmalise climbing the monkey bars on the playground, standing tall on the top rung, her right arm reaching for the first horizontal bar, her face intent and confident.

"Yes," said Miss Tippet, smiling.

"They're all kids from school," added Emmalise. She looked at Miss Tippet, and made her decision.

"I saw a murder," Emmalise stated. Then her throat filled with a lump, and she didn't think she could talk any more.

"Oh, no," answered Miss Tippet, reaching for Emmalise's hand, "I'm so sorry, Emmalise. Would you tell me what happened?"

Miss Tippet looked concerned, but not doubtful or irritated, like most adults, when you told them something important. What mattered to kids didn't always matter to grown-ups, or they thought you were "telling stories" (as in fibs).

"You believe me?" Emmalise asked.

"Well, yes," Miss Tippet looked serious, "You wouldn't say something like that lightly."

Emmalise told Miss Tippet everything: the barn, the kittens, falling asleep, hiding when the men came in, what they said as closely as she could remember, hearing the shot, seeing the black man fall, and seeing the blood. Miss Tippet didn't speak or interrupt her.

Near the end, Emmalise choked out her words, and tears filled her eyes. When she finished, Miss Tippet squeezed her hand.

"I'm so sorry, dear. That is a terrible thing for anyone to see. Did you recognize either man?"

Emmalise shook her head "no."

"Did you tell anyone else?"

"No," said Emmalise, "I can't tell my Mama. I thought you could help me tell the police. They won't believe just a little girl."

Miss Tippet looked thoughtful. She patted Emmalise's hand.

"I know who to call. Deputy Sheriff Dade. Is it alright if I call him now and ask him to come over?"

Emmalise nodded. Miss Tippet reached for a phone sitting on the end table and pulled a thin phone book out of the table's drawer. While she talked quietly, Emmalise continued looking at the photographs of children, recognizing most of them. Then on a table in front of the large front window she saw a photo of a young man with dark hair and kind eyes. He was in a uniform. Next to it was another photograph of the young man with his arm around a pretty blonde lady who was laughing up at him. They were both wearing jeans and different long-sleeved plaid shirts, leaning against one of the black fences that were everywhere in the country. Suddenly Emmalise realized the woman looked like Miss Tippet. That must be her boyfriend. They were much younger. Where was he?

Just then Miss Tippet said, "The deputy is on his way over. Let me get us all some ice water."

Emmalise could hear Miss Tippet in the kitchen. Now she just stared at her hands, wondering what it would be like to talk to a real deputy. Soon Miss Tippet returned with a tray with three glasses of water, putting it down on the coffee table in front of the couch.

Emmalise picked one up and took a long drink. Miss Tippet got up again and went to the bookcase along the wall behind the couch. She had to lean over to look at the titles. They were all fairly thin on the lower shelf, so Emmalise thought they were children's books.

Miss Tippet came back with a book that had a boy flying over housetops at night on the cover. The title was "Peter Pan." Emmalise had heard the name, but had never read the book. She'd never seen it at the Belleriver Library or at school.

"Shall we read this to each other?" asked Miss Tippet.

Emmalise nodded and her lovely teacher began reading. Miss Tippet's voice changed with what was happening in the story, making it all come alive. They took turns reading one page each, and had just reached the part where Peter told Wendy, Michael and John about mermaids and pirates, when they heard a firm knock on the front door. Miss Tippet left the book in Emmalise's lap, and answered the front door.

A big, dark-haired man stepped into the room. For an instant, Emmalise thought he was the soldier in the photos, then she realized he wasn't much taller than Miss Tippet. Plus he was big in the chest and arms and legs, not fat, but husky. He was dressed in regular clothes, tan slacks and a blue shirt, not a uniform. He smiled at her.

"Emmalise, this is Deputy Sheriff Dade," Miss Tippet introduced them, " Deputy, this is Miss Emmalise Pine."

"Hello, Emmalise," said the deputy, stretching out his big right hand toward hers.

Emmalise gave him her small hand, which was engulfed when they shook. She had felt cold when she heard the knock, and when he first came into the room, but his hand was warm, and his eyes looked kind.

"Parker, why don't you sit on the couch with Emmalise?" said Miss Tippet, sitting in one of the armchairs flanking the fireplace. She was still close enough to touch Emmalise.

"Lorraine here, er, Miss Tippet said you saw something terrible that I should know about," the deputy's voice was deep and quiet.

"You can tell him just what you told me," said Miss Tippet.

Emmalise did, looking back and forth between the two adults. Deputy Dade listened quietly, just like Miss Tippet had, but he frowned when she told about the shooting and the blood. She looked down at her hands again, when she finished.

"When did this happen?" asked the Deputy.

"Yesterday afternoon. I probably got to the barn about 3:00 and the sun was setting when I left. I got home around 7:00. Missed supper."

"OK. That's very good, Emmalise. You did the right thing talking to me about this. Can you tell me where the barn is?"

"Yes. Do you know where I live? On Orchard Road?" she began, and the deputy nodded, "You go to the second road, turn right and follow that road about a mile or so.

You'll see a dirt path through some trees and behind them is an old, white barn. It's locked, but I went in through a loose board on the side. Just to see the kittens. I didn't break anything." Emmalise had suddenly realized that it was probably not legal for her to go in that barn, but the deputy smiled at her again.

"It's OK, honey," he said, "but please don't go back there. Even to see the kittens. I'll take a look in the barn, and check on the kittens myself. "

Chapter 3

Present day

Deputy Sheriff Sam Kincaid noticed the woman in front of the reception counter as soon as he walked into the office. She was tall, close to six feet, with long, streaked chestnut hair pulled into a ponytail, but still hanging down her back almost to her waist. Her voice was low, and she spoke quietly, yet he heard every word clearly.

"I need to see Sheriff Dade as soon as possible," she said, "It's urgent."

"Yes, ma'am," answered Ida Masters, one of the Sheriff's receptionists, "I still need your name and an idea of what your business is. Sheriff Dade is in a meeting, and I shouldn't interrupt him."

"It's about a murder!" said the woman firmly.

"Today? Where?" asked Ida.

"Around Belleriver. But no, not today," the woman looked rueful, "Look. Deputy Dade knows about it. I need to talk with him. I have a lead."

"I still need your name, ma'am, " said Ida, "I'll send the Sheriff a note."

Ida Masters remained calm. She had a kind face that was usually reassuring to the public; but she was a firm guardian of Sheriff Dade's time. Sam knew Ida well enough to guess that this was trying her patience, but she didn't let it show. Ida had not looked at him, probably trying to keep him out of it. The tall woman broke first.

"Emmalise Pine," she stated, "e-m-m-a-l-i-s-e."

Ida wrote on a sticky note, obviously a little more than the woman's name. To the woman, she said, "I'll check with the Sheriff. Be right back. You can take a seat, if you like."

The woman remained where she was. Sam slipped through the door to the deputies' large office space, and went right to his desk. He was curious, but Sheriff Dade would let him know if he needed Sam's help. He looked at a small pile of concealed carry applications, picked up the one on top and began to read. Right away he thought he recognized the name as someone who shouldn't have bothered to apply. He probably carried anyway, and one day, they would catch him. Sam hoped someone wouldn't have to die for that to happen.

Just then, Ida called his name. Sam looked up.

"Sheriff wants you in his office," Ida smiled at him, then went back to the front counter.

When Sam walked into Sheriff Dade's office, he saw that Emmalise Pine had preceded him. The sheriff stood behind his desk. He was a big man, broad-shouldered and a little over six feet tall. He was barrel-chested with a belly to match, but he looked hard with arms that could lift and toss a barrel, if it came to that. His head was large, too, with a craggy face, and brown and gray hair cut short around his bald dome.

"Sam Kincaid, this is Emmalise Pine," the sheriff introduced them, "She grew up in Belleriver, but now lives in Lexington."

"Hello, Deputy," Ms. Pine reached out her hand and they shook, "Please call me Emmalise."

"Hello, Emmalise," answered Sam. Now that he could see her face, he saw that she was about 30 years old with a thin face, strong cheekbones, dark brown eyes and a wide mouth. She wore no make-up that he could see, and looked fine without it. She wore a green plaid flannel shirt, a dark green windbreaker, jeans and short brown boots. Sam sat down in the only other chair left in the office.

"I'd like Emmalise to fill you in on some history," continued Sheriff Dade, sitting down in his wooden chair, "I first met her when she was ten years old. Do you mind telling Deputy Kincaid what you saw and what happened between us back then, Emmalise?"

"No, sir," responded Emmalise, looking directly at Sam, "Like the sheriff said, I was only ten, out walking on a country road not far from my house. I was headed to an old barn to visit some kittens I'd found there with their mama. It was October, a Saturday in the middle of the afternoon, sunny and warm. The barn was locked, so I went in through a loose board in the outside wall. I climbed up in the haymow and the kittens came right to me. There was lots of hay up there, so we played in the hay. Then I lay down, petting them and their mama and I fell asleep. The creaking of the barn door opening woke me up. I kind of rolled down in a crack between two bales and the kittens ran away. I figured it was the farmer coming for a rack of hay, but I heard two men talking. They came in almost right under me and I could see them a little through a crack between the floorboards. I could see parts of them, their hands in particular. Their voices were quite different. The black man was soft-spoken. The white man was upset, and talked fast. The black man told the white man that he had something for him. Said he found it in an old shed."

"The black man went over behind a hay rack underneath me, and dug around for something. When he came back, he said, "Here it is." and handed a red box or book to the white man. I couldn't tell what it was. His hand moved too fast. Then the white man said, "You shouldn't have been snooping around." and shot him. I heard a bang and saw the black man fall with a hole in his forehead and blood coming out. It was horrible. His head fell out of my view, but he had a nice-looking face, gentle, except for the hole and blood."

She paused momentarily, looking into the distance as though she was seeing it all again. She looked at Sheriff Dade, and then at Sam. They waited in silence.

"I saw the black man's body moving, like the white man was dragging him. I could see a puddle of blood on the floor and streaks where he was dragged. I heard other noises. I think the white man put the body in a wheelbarrow and took it out of the barn somewhere. The doors creaked open and closed, then open again, a while later. I heard him walk across the floor. I saw him throw a bucket of water over the blood, then pull loose hay off the rack over it. He had on a gray hat with a brim, a fedora, and a black suit. At least it looked like the sleeves and legs of a suit. I couldn't see his face. Then I heard him walk out and close the doors. I thought I heard a car start, but I'm not sure. It didn't sound like it was near the barn. I don't know how long I waited, but eventually the kittens came back, so I thought it would be safe to leave. I ran all the way home."

Emmalise paused again and sighed, closing her eyes for a moment.

"You have a remarkable memory," Sam said.

"Yes," she answered firmly, "I don't remember every moment of my life from birth, but I remember a lot, particularly that day. I don't think it's eidetic or photographic, closer to hyperthymesia, like that story on *60 Minutes*, but I haven't been tested."

"I wasn't doubting," said Sam.

She cocked her head and gave him a small smile, "Maybe a little. I know how it sounds. I'm surprised Sheriff Dade believed a ten-year-old girl."

"It helped that Miss Tippet introduced us," said the sheriff.

"I'd never question her," agreed Sam, "Was she your teacher?"

"Yes," answered Emmalise, "I went to see her the next day. I thought I couldn't tell my family. It would have scared my mama. I knew a lawman had to be told, but I trusted Miss Tippet first, and I was right. I told her my story, and she called Sheriff Dade."

"I was a Deputy then," he said, "I did believe her story and was convinced when I went to the barn and found the blood stain. It was mostly washed away, but we found some splatter that the water didn't reach. Unfortunately there was no match in the system and we never found a body. We talked with the barn owner and he had an ironclad alibi. The lock on the barn had been broken. No fingerprints. The farmer gave us the few names of people he knew that knew about the barn, but really anyone in Belleriver could have known, just like Emmalise did. Don't worry; I did tell Mrs. Pine, and she handled it better than any of us expected. We kept the case open for years, but no missing persons matched the victim. No bodies found since then have matched. I felt terrible letting Emmalise down, but there were just no leads."

Sam looked at his boss.

"Well, what's happened?" he asked.

Emmalise shifted her weight in her chair, sitting up even straighter.

"I know who the murderer is," she said.

Chapter 4

Sam and the sheriff looked at each other, then back at Emmalise.

"I heard him on television," she explained. "Well, I saw him too, but I heard his voice first. Gideon Printes. He was on the news two nights ago. Some reporters caught him coming out of the District Courthouse in Lexington. They asked him if he was running for the Court of Appeals."

The two men looked at each other again, but their faces remained stoic. Emmalise bent over, picked up her purse, unzipped the top and pulled out a folded piece of paper.

"I wrote what he said, but I remember it as well," she said, handing the paper across the desk to Sheriff Dade. He opened it and read, while she recited.

"Reporter: Mr. Printes, we've heard rumors that you may run for the Kentucky Court of Appeals. Is that true?

Printes, smiling and using a back-off motion with his hands: I'm not sure where you heard that, because we are just in a research stage. I would be honored to serve my district in the Kentucky courts, but I have not made a final decision. Since the word is out that I am considering a run, I will announce a press conference as soon as a decision is made.

Mr. Printes walked through the reporters and climbed into a waiting black SUV. He was still smiling. That's it," she finished, looking up at them.

"I can see that this has upset you," Sheriff Dade said quietly.

"I'm angry. He's lived all these years, risen to prominence, and now he might run for an appellate judgeship," Emmalise responded. "Now that we know who he is, maybe we can do something about that."

Sheriff Dade started to speak, but Emmalise hurried on, "I know it's not enough to arrest him, but he himself is a clue. We can find out what black people worked for him back then to start with."

"Not 'we', Emmalise. Me or my deputies," said the sheriff, "You have to stay out of this. We don't want to make him suspicious. I certainly can't interview or accuse him at this point. It's just your word against his. You don't have a tape of his voice at the scene, so there's nothing but your memory to identify him. That won't hold up in court."

"I know all that," Emmalise answered irritably, "but I can't forget it. I promise I won't contact him or his family. I'm sure you can do more than I can anyway. That's why I came here."

"Please be careful, Emmalise," he said, "If you talk to anyone, rumors will start. Be very careful."

"I will, Sheriff," she answered, "Thank you for listening. It means a lot to me that you believed me back then, and now."

"Where are you living now?" asked Sheriff Dade, "And what are you doing?"

"I live in Frankfort," she said, "I work as a veterinary technician at the Wags and Purrs Animal Hospital."

The sheriff smiled at her, "More kittens."

Emmalise grinned back at him, "Yes, and puppies, birds, parrots and turtles. Dr. Dunnigan takes in all kinds. We do large animals too. She just hired Dr. Grantham this year to help with that. He does most of the traveling."

Suddenly, she turned to Sam and said, "Did you know Sheriff Dade helped me find homes for those kittens? He took them in, had the mother spayed, and kept her."

The sheriff was bright red, but he said, "That was all my wife Clare. She named her Charlotte and we had her for fifteen more years. She was a sweet cat."

Sheriff Dade stood and handed a notepad to Emmalise and asked her to write down her address and phone number.

"I'll let you know if we find out anything," he said, "Just leave it to us."

Emmalise wrote a few lines, then stood and handed him back the pad. They shook hands. Emmalise shook hands firmly with Sam as well.

"Good-bye, Sheriff, Deputy," she said, nodding slightly to each of them.

Sam nodded back, and the sheriff said good-bye. She closed the door softly behind her.

"What do you think, Sam?" asked Sheriff Dade.

"About her," Sam paused, grinning, "or her story, or the great kitten rescuer?"

The sheriff smiled back and said, "Her first, then the story."

"It's OK to be an animal lover, sir." Sam continued, "It's a sympathetic trait in a lawman."

"Emmalise Pine," the sheriff redirected him.

"She seems bright, straightforward, blunt" said Sam, "a woman who knows her own mind, believable. Was she like that as a little girl?"

"Absolutely. First I had Lorraine Tippet's opinion to recommend Emmalise, but after we talked, I just believed her. Then, as I said, we found the bloodstain and splatter. We still have the sample and can do a DNA test, if we ever have anyone to test it against. What do you know about Printes?"

"Not much," said Sam, "he's with some big law firm in Lexington and he and his family live just outside Belleriver. They've got that big old Southern style mansion on Turtle Creek. His mother lives with him, and a sister and brother-in-law. I believe the sister works in an office, and the brother-in-law runs an antique store in Frankfort, only opened about a year ago. I haven't met any of them personally."

"I've met him. Wasn't impressed one way or another," said Sheriff Dade, leaning back in his chair, "He doesn't do criminal law, just civil, and estates and wills."

The sheriff leaned even further back in his chair, so far that Sam thought it might flip over. The big man's head was tipped forward with his chin on his chest and his large hands were laced together across his belly. All the deputies knew this was the sheriff's thinking position, and to just be quiet and wait. Eventually, he sat up, pulled his chair forward, and looked at Sam.

"You find as much as you can about him and his family on the Internet," stated Sheriff Dade, "while I check out County Records. We should be able to find plenty, but whether it leads us anywhere is something else. Just you and me on this for now."

Chapter 5

Emmalise drove her bright yellow Mazda slowly back to Lexington, not because she was basically a careful driver, but because her mind was moving so fast, she couldn't share the speed with her foot. After a few cars passed her, two of their drivers blaring their horns, she shook herself, and sped up to her usual five miles per hour over the speed limit. When she first sank into the driver's seat outside the Woodford County Sheriff's Office in Versailles, she felt relieved and ready to head back to work. She had taken the afternoon off, but had spent less time with the Sheriff than expected. With her identification of the killer, she was sure Sheriff Dade could solve the long ago murder.

As she took highway 60 through Frankfort, questions began popping into her head. What resources did the Sheriff have that wouldn't alert Printes? Like most politicians, did he have eyes and ears everywhere in local government? What records would there be of the Printes family's employees, especially house servants? Maybe the family hired "under the table," so there weren't any taxes or Social Security forms to mess with. Besides, even the Sheriff would need a warrant for taxes and bank accounts. Would bank employees keep quiet, when one of their best investors was being investigated? Would the Sheriff know whom he could trust? Was there any way she could help? There it was. She didn't want to leave it in anyone else's hands. As foolish as it was, Emmalise wanted to investigate.

After she crossed the Capital Avenue Bridge, she took W. 2nd, instead of heading south to the clinic. She ended up on Devil's Hollow Road, then turned right on Meadow Lane, and drove all the way to the end. Her rental house was a two story, old farmhouse, covered in white siding. It sat on about two acres with just a few trees and a separate two-car garage. Emmalise had the upstairs two-bedroom apartment with a back-door entrance and an inside staircase.

She had really lucked out on the downstairs tenant. Kellon Fairs had moved in about a year ago, after the former tenants, an elderly couple, had left (the husband to a nursing home and the wife to their son's home). Kellon was an EMT with two dogs, both rescues. He usually worked the second shift, 3:00-11:00 pm, so Emmalise had the house to herself most evenings. Not that he was loud when he was home, and the dogs rarely barked. She liked the quiet of the country, but, truth be told, she liked Kellon too. She felt a little safer if she was awake and heard his Dodge Ram pull into the drive, and then into the garage. The dogs were a comfort too. One was a gray pit bull and the other was a mix with a Labrador body and brown and white spots. Kellon was meticulous with their training, so they were friendly with her, but excellent guard dogs.

She pulled into her lane, climbed out to open the left door of the garage, got out, locked her car, and lowered the door manually. As expected, Kellon's side was empty, since it was after three. Emmalise let herself into the back door and climbed the steep wooden steps to her apartment. The dogs knew her sounds by now and weren't barking, but she could hear loud meowing from upstairs. She opened the door to two expectant faces, one gold and white, and one black and orange tortoiseshell. They stopped crying, as she took off her jacket, dropped her leather purse on the kitchen table, and headed for the living room. As soon as she sat on the blue, green and yellow plaid couch, the two cats jumped on either side, and she began petting them. The long-haired golden tiger settled on her lap, while the tortoiseshell, also a longhair, curled up beside her.

"Hello, babies," Emmalise spoke in a natural tone, not baby talk. "How was today? Did any mice show up, Lance? They will be coming in soon. Did he let you get any sleep, Guinnie? Are you glad I'm home early?"

The two cats purred and pushed against her hands now and then. Emmalise smiled and relaxed. She closed her eyes and focused on her breathing, gently stroking the cats' heads and backs. After about ten minutes, she slowly extricated herself and headed for her laptop, which sat on an end table. She plugged it in and returned to the couch, putting it on her lap. She pushed off each short boot with the other foot, leaving them as they fell. The cats settled in again, on either side of her, purring continuously.

First she set up a Word document to take notes. Then she began to search: Google, Facebook, LinkedIn, Twitter, and Instagram. Gideon Printes wasn't on Twitter or Instagram at all. His Facebook site was actually his firm's, with only an introductory page and no posts. In fact almost everything she found was related to his firm: Kirkendall, Printes and Bibb, Attorneys-at-Law. She found his alma mater on LinkedIn: the University of Kentucky, as well as the fact that he had always worked at the same firm. It was

Kirkendall and Masters when Printes began in 1970. He became a partner in 1977, and there was no Masters or Bibb included then. After two hours she stopped with a list of background check sites. Did she want to spend $30 or $40 to find out what more she could online? She closed her laptop, put it back on the end table, and stood up, stretching, and disturbing the cats.

"Time for some exercise," she said, looking down at her buddies, "and I'll have dogs for company. Sorry, but you don't want to go for a 2-mile run."

Lance and Guin seemed to agree, curling up together on the warm spot she had vacated. Emmalise grabbed her boots and headed into the bedroom. She threw her jeans over an armchair and hung up the plaid shirt. She quickly changed into gray sweatpants, a green Keeneland tee shirt, a gray hoodie, white cotton socks and turquoise Nike running shoes. She slipped her keys into the hoodie's front pocket. She ran down her stairs, locked the outer door and stepped into the downstairs screened-in back porch and unlocked Kellon's back door. The two dogs were waiting just inside the door. Archer, the gray pit bull, sat patiently with his head cocked to one side, while Mugsie with his brown and white splotches, quivered in excitement, and began jumping as soon as Emmalise stepped inside. He didn't jump on her, but went straight up and down as if he were on a spring. She attached their leashes, and headed back out. She walked at first, pulling up on Mugsie's leash a few times, like Kellon had shown her, until the dog walked beside her. Archer was no problem. Kellon said he'd been easy to train not to pull, in spite of his great strength. It was dusk, getting dark rapidly, but Emmalise wasn't worried, since the dogs were with her. They had reflective collars, and she had reflectors on the heels of her shoes, but she took the less traveled side road.

They ran a mile at a steady pace, her ponytail swinging from side to side, while the dogs loped with happy grins and tongues hanging out. They stopped for a doggy sniff and potty break along the edge of the road. Both dogs only peed, to Emmalise's relief, since she had forgotten the plastic bags that Kellon insisted she use to clean up after them. She understood cleaning up the yard, but along the road seemed a stretch in neighborliness. Of course, she would have been the one of the people stepping in it, so she should be grateful. They ran back faster for the next half mile and jogged the rest of the way home. No cars passed either way. She took the panting dogs back into Kellon's apartment, made sure they had water, and headed up to her place.

Emmalise loved her apartment, her job and her sunny yellow car. They all meant independence, her own world. She loved her family too, and saw most of them often, but she preferred living on her own. It felt like such luxury, even though everything was second-hand, except most of her clothes (and they were purchased on sale).

Her apartment was old and came unfurnished. Her landlord said she could paint, if she paid for it, any color but black. She had taken her time buying furniture at garage sales and antique stores, just picking what she liked, not worrying about everything matching. Most of her curtains were made from sheets or inexpensive fabric. (Mama had let her use her old sewing machine.) The entrance was into the kitchen, which was painted red with white woodwork, and had 1950's white appliances that actually worked. Her small kitchen table was painted royal blue with four yellow chairs. The blue and white flowered curtains covered the bottom half of the two windows with matching valances on top. The cupboards and drawers were white wood with flowers painted on the knobs. One door led into her bedroom; the other to the living room. Hardwood floors ran throughout.

Her bedroom was fairly large, about fifteen feet by eighteen feet. It was also painted red with white woodwork, bookshelves and a white closet door. Her bed was queen-sized and covered in a multi-colored quilt her mother had made for her out of scraps from her childhood clothes and curtains. In the center was a patchwork cat curled up sleeping. When Emmalise was in college and her siblings were getting older, Mama began quilting in the evenings to pass the time. At first she mastered old techniques and styles, but eventually she was sewing pictures in her quilts. Since most of her work was done by hand, the area craft shops loved them. She could now support herself with her quilt making, some done on commission. Emmalise's quilt was an early picture quilt and she treasured it. The one window was covered in white dotted Swiss curtains, and a window shade on which she had begun doodling animals, designs, and quotes or sayings that she liked in magic markers. Another door connected to her turquoise bathroom with its claw-foot tub and shower with a surround shower curtain of green and blue plaid. It had a white pedestal sink, basic toilet, white woodwork and built-in cupboards. The next door led to the living room, her main space.

Emmalise spent most of her home time in the living room, which was large and painted royal blue with white trim. She brought the couch from her mother's home, and had it reupholstered in a soft burgundy fabric that the cats loved to claw, but seemed indestructible. Above it hung a long Japanese style print of a hunting tiger that she found in an antique store for only thirty-five dollars, black wood frame and all. Unmatched end tables in dark wood sat at either end with equally unmatched lamps. She had a naturally distressed coffee table in front of the couch, covered in books and her laptop. Two armchairs, one taupe and one gray, faced the ends of the coffee tables. A worn Oriental rug extended from under the coffee table out into the room, so she had something soft for yoga. On the opposite wall were two windows, a used flat screen television sitting on a small cupboard and, in between, two identical three-shelf bookcases, completely filled with her personal library. On one short wall were her stereo turntable, a CD player, and crates of records and CD's. The other held framed photos of her family and the door to her kitchen.

Cat toys were scattered throughout the apartment. A kitty condo stood in one corner of her bedroom. The litter was hidden under a cartoon-covered box in the bathroom. A rough-barked log stood in one corner of the living room, their favorite scratching post.

Emmalise fed the cats and reheated some leftover chicken and noodles for herself. She read a Richard Jury mystery while she ate at the kitchen table, gently removing Lance when he jumped up to inspect her plate. Guinnie lay at her feet, futilely hoping for scraps. Soon she finished, hand washed the dishes and returned to her laptop.

She spent two more hours searching for anything useful on Printes. She had less than a page of notes on a yellow legal pad. Tired and frustrated, she decided to watch some TV.

Flipping through the channels, she clicked on "Romy and Michele's High School Reunion". It had been a favorite of her high school best friend, Amy Winstead, who now lived in Denver. They kept in touch, but hadn't seen each other since their ten-year high school reunion. Emmalise flopped down on the couch and the cats climbed up with her.

She had only watched for half an hour, when she sat bolt upright, startling Lance and Guin. She knew where to get more information on Gideon Printes. She smiled, lay back down, and patted her abdomen for the cats to join her again.

Chapter 6

Sam drove slowly up the gravel lane toward the house in the hill. He still couldn't believe it was his…theirs. Young oak trees were planted at intervals on either side of the lane and two much older oaks stood in the yard. A long green lawn spread out on either side of the lane and just past the big trees. About forty feet of gravel surrounded the three walls of a log home that extended out of the low hill and two garage doors were set further back to the side. The log house had a heavy, rough-hewn front door and two tall windows on either side. More windows filled the side walls, until the house disappeared into the hill. Sam clicked the opener and the garage door on the right slid quietly up. He pulled his Honda in next to Mac's Jeep Cherokee.

Mac was his wife. Mackenzie Field Kincaid. He'd met her almost two years ago on a horse-shooting case that turned into a murder investigation, which Mac helped solve, partly by being kidnapped. She also helped Sam find and rescue her; and one year later, they were married. Mac was a painter, mostly portraits of show and race horses. Her father owned the ranch down the road and had given them twenty acres of it for their wedding present. Sam had sold his small house in Versailles, so that income, plus Mac's savings, had financed most of the cost of building their log home in a hill, as well as a small barn on the opposite side of the hill.

Sam walked into their kitchen, which along with a bedroom and bath, was the only somewhat-finished room in the house. Wood floors ran throughout, and walls were painted a creamy white. They were still shopping for some of the furniture, rugs, and art. Even though half the house was under the hill, the living room in the front with its many tall windows made the house seem light and open to the outdoors. Sam wandered into it and looked up at the two-story entryway with its wood and beam ceiling. Half way over the room was a balcony, which enclosed their master bedroom. He didn't bother to call out, knowing Mac might be too focused to hear him, let alone answer. He walked through the living room, down a hall past two smaller rooms and up a stairway. The second floor held their bedroom, a large bathroom and Mac's studio. Sure enough, she was in there, painting.

"Hey, gorgeous!" Sam said from the open doorway, smiling at his beautiful, auburn-haired wife. Mac looked back at him and returned his smile, although she had to remove a brush from her mouth first.

"Hey, handsome!" she said. "What do you think?"

"Honey, it's beautiful," Sam hugged her from behind.

"I mean the painting," Mac leaned into him.

"I know," Sam answered, glancing at it over her shoulder at the painting of a mare and foal. "It is beautiful. Finished?"

"Not quite," she said, "but I can't figure out what's missing."

"Well, dinner, for one thing," said Sam, "guess it's my turn to cook again."

"Sorry," Mac put the brush in a jar of turpentine and turned around to face him.

They kissed. Sam pulled her tightly against him and Mac jumped up, wrapping her legs around his hips.

"Not in here," Mac mumbled against his lips.

They both smiled into the kiss. Sam carried her into their bedroom and they dropped onto the bed.

Dinner was leftover vegetable beef soup, wheat rolls, and salad at an old oak table big enough to seat eight. Mac and Sam sat close together at one end.

"Any luck finding a couch?" asked Sam.

"I don't like shopping online for furniture," Mac answered, "Let's go to Lexington or Frankfort on Saturday and look."

"I heard about an antique store in Frankfort we can check out," said Sam, dipping a roll into his soup broth.

"I don't want an antique couch," Mac said adamantly; then she looked at her husband skeptically, "Since when do you talk about furniture or antiques at work?"

"It's part of a new case," Sam replied, shoveling in a forkful of salad.

"OK. That's enough teasing. What new case?"

"It's actually a cold case," said Sam, "but new to me."

As they ate, he told her what he knew about Emmalise Pine's story. Mac listened intently without interrupting him. Sam did not always talk to her about work, partly because so much of it was tedious. He knew that for most law enforcement officers it was better not to talk to anyone outside a case about that case, even other deputies. With Mac, though, he felt safe. They met on a murder case; then the killer kidnapped her, but Mac's wits had led Sam to rescue her before she was a casualty. Sam learned it was better to trust her and let her be his sounding board. Mac didn't gossip, and she stayed somewhat isolated because of her painting. She wouldn't even confide "work talk" to her best friend Sarah, who was married to Mac's brother Connor, or to their dad.

"Wow," Mac said when he finished, "So what have you found so far?"

"His family moved to Belleriver in the 1920's. Came with money and made more, mostly in tobacco. His father gradually sold off the farms—they were all over the state—and lived off the proceeds. Young Printes was smart enough to take a different route. Got his undergrad and law degrees from the University of Kentucky. He's been with the same law firm since he graduated: Kirkendall and Masters then, Kirkendall, Printes and Bibb now. He has a sister, Faye. She went to Kentucky also, but married right after graduation, and works as an office manager. Her husband is Luther Wynn, who currently owns that antique store in Versailles."

"Ah ha! The connection," she smiled.

"Yeah, "Sam nodded, "They all live with his mother in that old house on the southern edge of Belleriver on Turtle Creek. Lots of acreage left. No one else lives within a mile. Can't find anything about the mother after the father died. There was an old newspaper article about Oscar, the father. He claimed they were distant relations to Judge Roy Bean."

"Well, we might be able to find out about the family from Aunt Tina," said Mac, "She can ask her friends. We can talk to Miss Tippett"

"If I do, it has to be without them know why, or talking about it," said Sam, "We really don't want Printes hearing that we're investigating him or his family. Although Miss Tippett already knows the first part and she's trustworthy."

"True," Mac answered.

"What I really need to find out is if and when that family had any employees, especially a black man, who no one missed after he was killed." Sam continued, "The Sheriff not only didn't know the shooter at the time, but they never found a body, and no one was reported missing. He didn't have a starting point."

"Did they get blood samples? I know they didn't do much DNA testing then, but if he has any blood, they could test it now," Mac offered.

"I suppose he could, but there's nothing to match it with—no body," said

Sam,."Anyway, I'll bring it up in the morning when we compare notes."

"It's strange," said Mac, "you're working backwards. It seems like it should be easier, since you know the killer, but it's not at all."

"Plus, Emmalise could easily be mistaken," said Sam. "She sounds positive about the voice recognition, and the sheriff trusts her, but we know how unreliable eyewitness testimony is. Why would hearing be any better?"

"Did you look into hyper-whatever-it-is? I saw that "60 Minutes" segment and those people were amazing."

"Yes, I did. I watched the *60 Minutes* show too. Hyperthymesia. It's a little easier to remember Superior Autobiographical Memory. Unlike people gifted with that talent, I won't remember the names for long," grinned Sam. "What I don't know is whether the hearing aspect is part of it, or it it's primarily visual. I suppose if we ever got to the trial stage, we could have her tested."

"On "60 Minutes", they mentioned that sometimes people with that condition have trouble with personal relationships. Like other people don't like being corrected, and not being able to argue with a perfect memory," said Mac. "Did you see any evidence of that in Emmalise?"

"No," answered Sam, "but I didn't get to talk to her for very long. I can ask Parker. She does well enough to have a job, as a vet tech. Having a memory of a murder might not make her inclined to confide in people. She didn't strike me as attention seeking. If she didn't tell other kids when she was a child, I doubt she'd tell anyone now. But she did seem confident—in herself and in the sheriff."

"You definitely need to talk to older people, probably older black people, to find out any Printes family secrets," Mac said. "I'm not sure you can go in officially, if you want to stay under the radar."

"I know," sighed Sam. "This one is tricky."

"We can visit that antique store on Saturday," said Mac. "We might find something for the house, and maybe we can meet the brother-in-law."

"Maybe," answered Sam, "I'll let you know."

"I'll clean up the dishes," said Mac.

"I'll see what's on TV tonight," Sam offered.

"You know that TV is not staying in the bedroom after the living room is fixed up," Mac looked at him sternly. "It leads to nothing but trouble where it is."

"I don't think it matters where it is," Sam laughed. "You're just too much of a distraction!"

Chapter 7

Ida informed Sam that Sheriff Dade had meetings all morning, so Sam decided to take Mac's advice and visit Lorraine Tippet. He called the retired schoolteacher first, and she sounded delighted at the prospect of his visit.

"Hello, Sam," Miss Tippet greeted him at her door. "How is your beautiful bride?"

"Hello, Miss Tippet. She's just fine."

The tiny woman led Sam into her spring-like living room. Sam smiled at the photographs of children covering the walls. Lorraine Tippet had taught at Belleriver Elementary School her whole working life. She had helped Sam with the sniper case two years ago, and had set up the "stakeout" that had initiated Mac's rescue. She had lived in Belleriver all of her life, except for college at the University of Kentucky. She didn't look old enough to be retired, but Sam thought there were more white streaks in her chestnut hair, than when she'd been at their wedding.

As though reading his mind, Miss Tippet commented," I don't think I've seen you since your wedding. How's the new house coming?"

"It's getting there," Sam smiled. "If we ever get it furnished, we'll have you out for dinner."

"That would be lovely," Miss Tippet handed him a glass of iced tea. "Now, how can I help you?"

"I need to ask you some questions about a local family, and I need for this conversation to remain between us."

"No problem, Sam." Miss Tippet looked back at him steadily. "Ask away."

"You were there at the beginning," Sam continued, "and you brought in Sheriff Dade, although he was a deputy at the time."

"Emmalise Pine," said Miss Tippet softly.

"Yes," answered Sam, "She's been to see us recently and we're looking into the murder again, as quietly as we can. Emmalise heard Gideon Printes speaking on television. She's sure his is the voice of the murderer, so we need to get information on the Printes family at that time. Who lived there, who worked for the family, anything you can remember."

Miss Tippet frowned slightly. She looked at the fireplace, but wasn't seeing it; her eyes were focused on memories.

"The murder was in 1993, when Emmalise was in fourth grade. Gideon Printes would've been a grown man, but he lived at home with his mother. His father had already passed. Gideon drove to that law firm in Lexington every weekday. I'm sure his sister and her husband were not living there yet. I really did not know Gideon. He would have been in 8th grade or high school, when I began teaching. His sister was in middle school, so I didn't get to know her either. I saw his parents at town functions, knew them by sight, but not well. Oscar and...uh...Athena. What a name, poor woman. My mother thought she was a snob. I don't know. She was quiet, unobtrusive, possibly shy. She let her husband have the limelight. He was more outgoing, friendly. I'm sorry. I don't remember much at all."

"You're doing fine," said Sam. "Anything may help. Do you know if they had servants?"

"They were wealthy, the richest family in town, according to Mother. I'm sure they had help, a cook and housekeeper, probably. Maybe a yardman. I doubt they were live-in, but I'm not sure."

"Would the help have been black?" asked Sam.

"We had a small black population back then," said Miss Tippet. "Come to think of it, we still do. Less than five percent. About one hundred people. A lot of my black students' parents did that kind of labor—housekeepers, cooks, yard workers, mechanics."

They sat without speaking for a few minutes, drinking their tea. Miss Tippet's eyes were still looking back in time.

"Oh, I know someone," she said abruptly, "someone who might help. Did you ever meet Judge Turner?"

"He retired before I became a deputy, but I heard about him," Sam acknowledged.

"Probably most of what you heard is true," Miss Tippet smiled. "He's a corker! He was a District Judge, then a Circuit Judge. He's close to Mrs. Printes in age, and he would've known the family. I believe he retired to Frankfort. Let's see where he is."

Miss Tippet lifted up a New Yorker magazine from her coffee table and pulled out an iPhone. She continued talking as her thumbs moved quickly over the tiny keyboard.

"You don't have to worry about Wainwright telling anyone about our visit. He dearly loves a secret. He did some of his best judging privately, outside the courtroom; then all parties would show up in court for the settlement. Most of his punishments were common sense, too, rather than jail time. Don't think judges can do that anymore. I suppose his way could be dangerous with the wrong person, but it worked for him and people around here. Once two farmers were arguing over a pig. Judge Turner used the old Solomon trick and told them to butcher the pig and share the pork. The real owner loved that pig as a pet and refused, while the other farmer agreed to the slaughter. So Wainwright knew whom to award the pig. Oh, here he is. Yes, he's in Frankfort. Should I give him a call?"

Sam was dumbstruck, but nodded.

Twenty minutes later, they were in Sam's Honda Civic on highway sixty heading to Frankfort. Before they left, Miss Tippet insisted that he call her Lorraine, "especially after all they'd been through." The rest of the trip she was mostly silent, for which Sam was grateful. He was going over the questions he could ask without giving the case away.

When they pulled up in front of the whitewashed brick bungalow that was Judge Turner's home, Sam was debating the wisdom of this decision. He got out and offered Miss Tippet his arm as she stepped out of the car.

"Don't worry, Sam," Lorraine Tippet said. "Just follow my lead."

The short, but upright gentleman who opened the door did not look like a "corker" to Sam, except for his sparkling blue eyes. He was bald on the top of his head with a ring of long, fine gray hair flowing behind his ears and covering the back of his head. He had dark horn rim glasses and wore a crisp, striped blue and white shirt and khaki pants. Lorraine introduced the two men, and Judge Wainwright Turner took her arm, patting her hand and led them into his living room.

"Lorraine," said the judge, "it's been far too long since I've seen you."

"I agree," she smiled. "That's why I was so glad to have an excuse to call you."

Judge Turner walked to a grouping of a brown leather couch with two dark green leather armchairs at either end. A tray of glasses and a pitcher of iced tea and a plate of oatmeal raisin cookies sat on a wooden coffee table. The rest of the room was almost entirely books. One wall was made of filled bookshelves. A long table on another wall held piles of books and more were stacked on the floor under it. Books lay on each end table and on the coffee table around the tray. A newspaper lay under the tray. At a glance the books looked old or at least well read. Sam didn't see any obvious law books, but the titles or authors' names that he could read were eclectic: Kafka, *Centennial* by Michener, *Gravity's Rainbow* by Pynchon, Stephen King, *The Rise and Fall of the Third Reich*, John Irving, and Dick Francis.

"Sam," he heard Miss Tippet's voice, "have some tea."

He looked back at her, and took the tea with a smile. She and Sam settled next to each other on the couch with the judge in an armchair facing them.

"To old friends," Judge Turner said, "and to lovely ladies." He lifted his glass to Miss Tippet.

Then he added, "And to enterprising law enforcement." He looked intently at Sam over his glass, while they all drank. Sam was at a loss for words, so remained silent.

"Sam here is a new old friend, Wainwright," began Miss Tippet. "As I told you, I helped him out a little on that sniper case in Belleriver. He has become interested in the history of the area, primarily Belleriver, where his wife grew up, and I thought you could help him. He might actually write a book, and I would like to assist, because I don't know when he'd have time. I don't think there is any written history, do you?"

"No," said Judge Turner, listening with one corner of his mouth turned up in a skeptical smile, "I have one question first."

"Yes," said Miss Tippet.

"Does this young man speak for himself?"

Sam flushed, but answered, "Yes, I do, sir. I would appreciate your help, if you're willing."

"Well, I am," said the judge. "Although I suppose we'll have to continue with the subterfuge of a book. I'm sure you cannot tell me the real reasons, but this is the most interesting consult I've had since I retired. Please assume that our conversation will be private and confidential, since we don't want anyone stealing your book idea."

Judge Turner had been frowning as he spoke, but now he beamed at them. Miss Tippet smiled back at him, and Sam sighed in relief.

"Thank you, sir," Sam said. He hesitated, not sure where to begin.

"Sam is particularly interested in the influence of some of Belleriver's early and wealthy families," said Lorraine helpfully, "I believe he is currently trying to research the Printes family. I told him what little I knew of Oscar and Athena."

"There you go again, Lorraine, speaking for the young man," Judge Turner frowned at her playfully.

"Sorry, sir," said Sam, "I'm just a bit star struck."

The judge looked surprised, then let out a laughing snort.

"All right. All right," he chuckled. "That's better. I knew the Printes family fairly well, at least Oscar. I'm not sure that anyone knew Athena very well. She was a quiet hostess, listening more than talking. That was good for Oscar, since he was gregarious and loved to tell stories. I believe his family came from Virginia and Athena's from North Carolina. I have no idea how they met. Oscar's father was a tobacco farmer and Oscar decided to farm in Kentucky. He would start a farm, get it producing and running smoothly, then leave it with a caretaker and move on to another farm. He became quite wealthy, in spite of all the ups and downs of that industry. He did well during World War II and, shortly after that, he came to Belleriver. He dabbled in horse racing and was part owner of a few thoroughbreds. He didn't have a tobacco farm here, but ruled his other properties from afar. He would go on tours of his holdings a few times a year. He was interested in politics, and all the politicos catered to him. He and Athena would have grand parties in their home. Apparently he considered me to be influential, even though our beliefs were quite different, so I was invited. Sometime in the '70s, he sold all of his tobacco holdings, and more or less, retired. I believe he encouraged Gideon to become a lawyer and to eventually manage the estate. Oscar died in the early '90s of heart failure. Gideon was quiet, like his mother. There were no more big parties after Oscar passed. Actually they ended in the '80s, when Oscar didn't get out and about as much."

The judge paused and took a long drink of tea. He picked up a cookie, took a bite, and passed the plate to Miss Tippet, who also picked up a cookie and handed the plate to Sam.

"Can you describe one of the parties?" asked Sam, taking a cookie.

"It's a good thing they have a large home," Judge Turner resumed, "I'd say there were close to one hundred people who came and went during an evening. Most of the guests were from Versailles, and a few from Frankfort. Locally, it would be anyone of wealth and/or influence: doctors, lawyers, a mayor or two, town councilmen, the district attorney, and judges. State congressmen and senators often came. Movers and shakers with their wives or lady friends. Dressy affairs—sometimes tuxes and evening gowns.

I would just wear my best suit. Didn't and don't own a tux. I also came alone, so that I could observe freely."

"To the loss of the females of Frankfort," smiled Miss Tippet.

"I should have brought you, Lorraine," answered the judge, "but I didn't know you well then. You were much younger, but you would've been a good partner in…."

"Crime?" she asked.

"Surveillance would be the more accurate term," Judge Turner laughed, "although I don't know to what end."

"Was there a large staff at the parties?" interjected Sam.

"Oh, yes. The Printeses had a wonderful cook, housekeeper, and gardener, but they hired extra people to bartend, serve and wait on guests."

"Were they all black?" Sam asked.

"Yes, the Printeses maintained many fine Old Southern traditions," stated the judge, sarcastically, "including using only black service staff. The children even had a black nanny, until Faye finished third grade. She was the cook's daughter, a lovely young woman, who went to college after she left their service, and became a teacher."

"Do you remember her name or any of the staff?" Sam watched the judge squint his eyes and look past them. They were silent long enough for Sam to wonder if the judge had forgotten the question.

"The cook was Serafina Washington and her daughter's name was Malayna," Judge Turner said triumphantly. "I knew they were unusual names. Took me a minute to recollect."

"Do you know if either of them still lives around here? Could Serafina Washington still be working for the Printeses?" Sam responded.

"I have no idea. I doubt it. Mrs. Washington was in her mid-thirties at the time. My visits were during the '60s for the most part. We are talking a long time ago. I think I'm feeling my age," Judge Turner pressed his thin lips together and raised his eyebrows in an expression of puzzled scrutiny. "I haven't thought about being in that house for a long time. For some reason, it brings a feeling of melancholy. I'm not sure why."

"How did you happen to know or remember Mrs. Washington and her daughter?" Miss Tippet asked quietly.

"I remember one night in particular," said the judge. "It was a smaller group, about twenty people. We were served such a delicious meal, particularly the apple tarts for dessert, that I went to the kitchen to thank their cook. Of course, most people wouldn't do that for a servant, but I felt like it. Mrs. Washington was quite startled, of course, but she beamed when I complimented her. Malayna was there with the children, having their desserts. Two servers were there, both young women, putting away clean dishes. I introduced myself, and Serafina introduced the other women, her daughter, and the children. Gideon looked to be about seven or eight, his sister Faye a few years younger. He stared at me openly, but just said, 'Hello, sir.' And Faye hid her face in Malayna's side. Malayna was lovely with big, dark eyes and very short hair. It fit her head like a curly cap. She spoke with a strong voice, saying, 'Thank you for appreciating my mother's work.'

I said, 'You're most welcome.' I took my leave, because they all obviously wanted to get back to what they'd been doing. After that, I always made a point of thanking Serafina for whatever she had cooked."

"That puts Serafina in her '90s and Malayna about my age?" said Miss Tippet.

"You've given me some other people to talk to," Sam stood and put out his hand, "Thank you for your help and time."

"You're welcome, young man," Judge Turner also stood and shook Sam's hand, "It was pleasant to have company. You can certainly come again, especially if you bring the beautiful Lorraine."

"Good heavens, Wainwright, act your age!" Miss Tippet grinned at him.

Chapter 8

Emmalise pulled up Magnus's file on the computer and smiled at his owner, Jerry Johnson, a tall, thin, boy with an acne-spotted face. The dog was huge, fitting his name, part Mastiff, part Great Dane. He was standing on his hind legs with his front end on the examining table, panting and drooling.

"What's bothering Magnus today?" she asked.

"I don't think anything ever bothers him," answered Jerry, "but his farts bother me."

Right on cue, the Magnus let one go, and a pungent stench filled the small room.

"Oh, Magnus! Yuck!" Jerry backed away from the big dog, who seemed to be grinning from ear to ear.

Emmalise backed up too toward the door, laughing and waving one hand in front of her face.

"Yep, that would bother me too," she said, slipping through the door. "I'll just get Dr. Dunnigan to help you."

Emmalise hurried to the back of the clinic, where she found Dr. Dunnigan in her closet-sized office. Dr. Dunnigan looked at her expectantly.

"We have a putrid pooch in room three," smiled Emmalise, "Jerry Johnson is here with Magnus who has a terrible flatulence problem."

Dr. Dunnigan smiled and got up, all five feet of her.

"Maybe I should get a face mask," she said.

"Definitely," agreed Emmalise.

In fifteen minutes, with Jerry and Magnus out the door, it was time to close the clinic.

Usually, Emmalise was in no hurry, but today she had an extra errand. She had made an appointment with the librarian at Woodford County High School, who said she would stay late, if Emmalise could be there by 5:00. With the clinic closing at 4:30, she could make it easily.

At 5:01 she was waiting at the front door of the high school, when a young woman with shoulder-length brown hair, and a pretty face with red-framed glasses pushed open the door.

"Hello," she said. "Are you Emmalise?"

"Yes," Emmalise answered. "Thank you so much for waiting for me."

She slipped past the woman, who let the door close, and stuck out her hand.

"I'm Becky Lester," she said. "Please call me Becky."

They walked through the halls past student lockers and classroom doorways. Emmalise wasn't sure how she felt, being back. High school had been kind of a mixed bag for a tall, smart girl from the "poor side of town".

"Did you go here?" asked Becky, as if reading her mind.

"Yes, a long time ago," said Emmalise.

"Not many people ask to look at old yearbooks. What years were you interested in?"

They had reached the library, and Becky opened the door for her.

"Late '60s, early '70s," answered Emmalise. "How late can you stay?"

"I'll be here until 7:00 or so," said Becky.

Becky Lester led the way to the furthest row of shelves and back into the corner of the large room. She pointed to the second highest shelf and said, "Those are the '60s. We've tried to keep two or three copies of each year, but haven't been able to do that every year. Some have been lost. Anyway, help yourself. These do have to stay in the library."

"No problem. I appreciate this." Emmalise reached for a volume marked 1968 on the binding. It was white with "Jacketeer" in black letters. She sat at the nearest table and turned to the listing in the back of student names and the pages they were pictured. She found Gideon Printes's class picture, a square-jawed young man with short black hair combed neatly to the side and black-framed glasses. His only other picture was with Science Club. He was unsmiling in each photo. He wore button-down shirts in both shots, like the other boys. All of the girls had skirts and blouses. Emmalise typed a few notes on her phone's notepad, then put the yearbook back, and pulled out the next three years.

In the 1969 yearbook Gideon had dropped Science Club, but added Debate Club and Wrestling. He still looked scrawny and serious in all of his photos. Emmalise began taking pictures of Gideon's yearbook photos with her phone. She didn't know if it was legal, but she figured that as long as she didn't put them on Facebook or any other social media, she was OK. She wrote down names of other people in the club and on the team. She didn't recognize any names, but thought Sheriff Dade might.

The '71 cover was an anomaly: white with green lettering and the title was misspelled "Jacketteer." Emmalise was surprised to learn that the official school colors were white and black, not gold and black, like she and everyone else assumed. In 1971, students were still wearing "nice" clothes. Girls' skirts and dresses were above the knee, but no jeans. Apparently the style prevalent on college campuses hadn't filtered down to Kentucky high schools. The yearbook contained more candid shots, so she went through the books page by page. Gideon had remained in Debate and wrestling his junior year, but the '72 yearbook showed that he had dropped wrestling his senior year. He was wearing a dress shirt and slacks for the Debate photo and his senior picture. The '72 book had the colors and title corrected, but even Gideon's senior picture looked similar: serious. He even had on a tie with his pale button-down shirt. She only found one casual photograph of Printes, but it was a good one. He was not the main subject, who was a boy in a Yellow Jacket costume, worn for Homecoming Week. Other students wore the yellow and black (adapted) school colors (according to the caption) and were cheering around the costumed boy in a school hallway. To one side, a pretty girl with long, dark hair, dressed in a dark sweater and short skirt, was leaning against a locker, her head cocked and a crooked smile on her face. On the far side of the hall stood Gideon in jeans and a light sweatshirt, his eyes riveted on the girl. His expression was obviously that of a smitten Romeo. No one in the photo was named, so Emmalise went through the '72 book again, and found the girl in chorus and her junior class picture, bright-eyed and smiling that crooked smile. Her name was Gretchen Sawyer.

Emmalise grabbed the 1973 yearbook. Printes was graduated, of course, but Gretchen should have been a senior. No name in the index. What happened to the girl who was probably Gideon Printes's first love?

When Emmalise was sitting in her car, she debated whether to call Sheriff Dade or not. She was kind of excited about the dark-haired girl, and she had a long list of names for him to possibly identify. She pulled his card from her purse and saw that he had printed his home phone on it. That seemed like permission to bother him at home, so she added it to his contact info, and called. Four rings, then a message to leave a message.

She did, then drove home.

As she pulled into her driveway, she was a little surprised to see another car parked behind Kellon's side of the garage. It was a sporty red Fiat, almost as flashy as her little Mazda, she thought. She drove into her side of the garage, closing the big door and walking out the side door. As she headed for the back entrance, Kellon and a slim young man turned the corner, leading Archer and Mugsie. Both dogs perked up when they saw Emmalise, but before either could jump toward her, their handlers lifted the leashes slightly, then relaxed, and the dogs relaxed too. Emmalise smiled, partly in relief; she had forgotten it was one of Kellon's off days, and he wouldn't need her to walk the dogs. She was also impressed at how well trained he kept the dogs, and his friend seemed to know what to do, as well.

"Hi, Kellon!" she said. The men and dogs had reached her, so she bent over to pet the pups.

"Hi, Emma!" grinned Kellon. "This is my friend, Jake Williams. Jake, this is Emmalise Pine, the wonderful neighbor I've been telling you about."

"Hi, Emmalise," said Jake, reaching out to shake her hand.

Emmalise was glad Kellon had given his friend her full name. Kellon was one of the few people she allowed to shorten her name. She noted quickly that Jake's jeans were tighter than Kellon's, and his black tee and open long-sleeved white shirt looked pretty stylish, as did his expensive tennis shoes. Kellon was his usual clean, but casually dressed self.

"Looks like Archer and Mugsie are just barely restraining themselves," Emmalise commented. "Have a good run."

On cue, the men and dogs took off at a trot. Kellon gave her a wave. Emmalise laughed and shook her head at herself, as she climbed the back stairs. Both cats climbed her legs and stretched as soon as she was in the door.

"Hello, babies. Your mom just escaped making a world class ass out of herself!"

Lance and Guennie looked at her expectantly, almost as if that was normal. Emmalise smiled as she spooned out their wet cat food and put it on the floor. She straightened up and watched them wolf down their slightly late dinner.

"Guess what I just figured out? You know that nice man who lives downstairs and takes care of you sometimes? Kellon, yep, that's his name. You know how I was wondering if I should ask him out, and how I wasn't sure I wanted to ruin a good friendship. It's a good thing I didn't. He's gay."

She sat down at the kitchen table and continued talking.

"I know, I know. I thought he was kinda cute, and I knew he was nice, and an animal person, which is a big plus. But I never felt hot to trot around him, or felt anything like that from him, so I kept putting it off. Good thing I did. That could have been seriously embarrassing. His friend running the dogs with him is actually beautiful. Well, I'll just have Kellon up for dinner sometime, and we can relax. Maybe I'll have both of them, if the new guy hangs around."

First Guennie, then Lance came over for pets, their bowls licked clean. Emmalise gave them some rubs and butt scratches, then got up.

"Speaking of dinner, I need to eat," she said.

Just then her phone rang, Aretha's "Respect." She looked at the screen and saw that it was Sheriff Dade.

"Hello, Sheriff," she answered.

"Hello, Emmalise," said the sheriff. "What did you find?"

He sounded hesitant, concerned.

"Don't worry," she tried to reassure him. "I just looked through the yearbooks from when Gideon Printes went to Woodford County High School. I'd like to give you a list of names, and show you some pictures."

"Do you have the yearbooks?" Sheriff Dade definitely sounded alarmed.

"No, no, I just looked at them at the high school, but I took pictures with my phone."

"Who else was there? Never mind," said Sheriff Dade more calmly. "Let me call Deputy Kincaid and see if we can meet tomorrow."

"Oh, I don't want either of you to have to work on your day off," objected Emmalise.

"Goes with the territory. I'll call you back, when I get hold of Sam."

"OK," Emmalise answered and ended the call.

She fixed herself tomato soup, a grilled cheese sandwich and a small salad. She brushed her cats, and watched *The Amazing Race*, which had been on earlier, but she had set it to record.

"I wonder if Kellon and Jake like *The Amazing Race,"* she wondered.

Her phone rang, and she paused the show.

"We can meet tomorrow morning in my office," said Sheriff Dade without preamble. "How's 9:00?"

"That's fine," said Emmalise. "Thanks, Sheriff."

"Good night," he answered.

"He might be a little irritated with me," Emmalise said to the cats. They looked back at her, as if that was to be expected.

Chapter 9

The Sheriff's office was nearly empty. Ida Masters stood behind the counter as though she was on guard. Today she looked as tough as when she'd worked construction, but now she was a tough grandmother. Her face was tan and lined from the sun, her steel gray hair was pulled back in a braided bun, and her shoulders were held back straight, ready to take all comers. She nodded briskly, as Emmalise walked in and opened the swinging gate to the area in front of the sheriff's office. Sheriff Dade was in his office, and waved at her to enter. Sam Kincaid was already seated in the far chair, and he said, "Good morning, Emmalise," with a smile. She took the second chair, holding an accordian folder in her lap.

"Looks like you've been busy," Sheriff Dade commented. "Sam, would you close the door? And you and Emmalise switch chairs?"

Emmalise could see that if she moved, she wouldn't be visible through the window in the office door. As Sam closed the door, she took his chair.

"What do you have?" The sheriff looked pointedly at her folder.

Emmalise opened the accordion file and pulled out several papers. She had typed up all of the names with the accompanying photographs. She handed the top sheet to Sheriff Dade.

"This is Gideon Printes's freshman photo," she began, and passed him the second paper. "This is the Science Club, which he was in that year, and I typed the members' names underneath. Do you know any of those names?"

Sheriff Dade had passed the photo of Printes to Sam, and was staring at the Science Club picture.

"Heck, yes," he said, "I was only a year ahead of these kids, so I remember most of them. I don't know where they all are now, but the ones who stayed in Versailles or around here…."

His voice trailed off, and he shook his head and grinned at old memories.

"OK, Sam, would you mind taking notes for now?" Dade spoke again, handing Sam a legal pad, "I'll just go in order. Mike Reynolds is President of the Community Trust Bank here in town. John Farmingham teaches economics at the University of Kentucky. Mary Leonard teaches science at the high school. Jennifer Gray married a boy from my class, Jim Pagel, raised their four kids, and volunteers a lot. Jim is a lawyer here in town. Phil Crater is President of our Chamber of Commerce. This kid, Lester Maynard, I don't remember, so he must've moved away. We can check if he's in any of the next yearbooks. Patrick Goins is retired, but he was Chief of the Fire Department for many years. Randall Mason I remember, but not where he is now. He was on the baseball team with me for a couple of years. And last, Larry Arnold—I believe he's still in prison for embezzlement or fraud, if he's not dead. The teacher was Mr. Archibald, who is deceased."

He looked up at Emmalise, and gave her a nod.

"Good job. This is an interesting group. We'll have to think carefully about who we talk to, or if we do. Some of these guys might still be in touch with Printes, if not friends, associates. They might even be on his campaign committee, assuming he has one."

He passed the sheet on to Sam, who had been writing quickly on the legal pad. Luckily, Sheriff Dade had paused between every name, giving Sam time to finish.

Emmalise had given him three more pages.

"The top one is his class picture, obviously," she said. "The next one is the Debate Club and the last one is the wrestling team."

The Sheriff continued the same process of reading the names and identifying the people if he could.

"Mitchell Harney. He's a lawyer too. Moved up to Lexington years ago. Arthur Bishop. Looks like he was the only black kid on the Debate Team. He runs that natural-foods grocery that sells a lot of local produce and organic food. He is also the President of the Black Historical Society. I think he's in the local American Legion, so I might be able to talk to him that way. Phil Crater. In Debate and Science Club with Printes. Good. Mary Leonard, also in both clubs, and the only woman in Debate. Jackson Blevins. Don't remember him. Malcolm Winters. Deceased."

The Sheriff paused and looked up at Sam.

"Remember that multi-car pile-up on sisty-four that winter a few years back when we had that heavy snowstorm? Malcolm was one of the casualties. I believe he worked as a tour guide at Liberty Hall. Doesn't matter, I guess."

Sam nodded and said, "I have a source to add, who I've already talked to: Judge Wainwright Turner. I went to see Miss Tippet and she thought of him right away. Took me over to meet him."

"I know him," said the Sheriff. "Had some cases in front of him. Knew the law, but used common sense too."

"He knew Gideon Printes's family," continued Sam. "He mentioned a Serafina Washington, their cook, and her daughter Malayna, who was the kids' nanny for several years. I thought they would be good sources for other employees."

"That's good, Sam. Could you also approach Miss Tippet and the Judge about the people we have on the list Emmalise brought us? Maybe they can give us an idea who we can talk to about Printes without it getting back to him. I have an American Legion lunch meeting on Monday, so I'll talk to Art Bishop."

"What about me?" Emmalise asked.

"You've been a big help," said Sheriff Dade, "but we have to handle it now."

"Miss Tippet and Judge Wainwright are citizens," Emmalise pointed out.

"They are sources, not active investigators," said the Sheriff, "I know you're involved, but you aren't law enforcement. I don't want to put you in danger."

"Sheriff, I hardly think we're at the dangerous stage yet," Emmalise forced herself not to roll her eyes, "I can help you talk to people. I didn't have to give the librarian an excuse to look at the yearbooks, but I'm sure I can make up back-stories easily. Also I know Miss Tippett, so I could talk to her and get info on all of the yearbook people. It also might be easier to talk with the cook and her daughter with a woman along."

Sheriff Dade leaned back in his chair, chin down, arms crossed over his chest, glowering at Emmalise. Sam looked down at his notes, trying to hide the smile pulling at his mouth.

"Sam, what else did you learn from the judge?" He asked.

Sam reviewed Judge Turner's description of Gideon's parents, the parties at the Printes home, and the story about thanking Serafina Washington for her cooking.

"I think the main point is that the local gentry were at those parties, so we need to figure out who they were and if any of them are still alive. If Miss Tippet doesn't know, I may have to visit the judge again. The peers of Gideon's parents may not be as relevant as his own friends and acquaintances. After all, he was a middle-aged man when he allegedly shot that black man."

"True," Sheriff Dade was still in his thinking pose, but no longer looked irritated. "Emmalise, go ahead and visit with Miss Tippet. See if you can get any information on

Printes's high school friends. Or anyone he's involved with in town. Just, please, do not talk to anyone else until we meet again."

Emmalise had frowned in surprise when Sam said "allegedly," but smiled at the sheriff's directive.

"Sam, I think you need to work on identifying the victim," the sheriff continued, "It will help to make a case, if we at least have a name. Maybe that can lead us to his body. Right now that's Serafina Washington and her niece."

"They're both elderly," said Sam, "but I'll give it a shot."

"Let me go with you," begged Emmalise. "They might be more willing to talk with a woman."

"What about your job?" asked the sheriff, and when she looked frustrated, he smiled a little, "Emmalise, you can see Miss Tippet on your own time, and let me know what she says. You don't want us to try to do this investigation only during your down time, do you?"

"No," she sighed, "but please call me if I can help elsewhere. Besides, this is a cold case, and you both have other work to do."

"My findings aren't helpful so far," said Sheriff Dade, "Printes owns the house and about forty acres. His father had huge tobacco land holdings in the state, but sold it all many years ago. Taxes paid in full. He's squeaky clean; of course, he's a lawyer and would know how to avoid problems. At any rate, I think we're done for today. Just report to me when you get more information."

The sheriff shook hands with Emmalise, who smiled, squeezed around the desk, and shook hands with Sam too. As Sam got up to go, Sheriff Dade watched Emmalise leave the building, then remarked, "Think she'll stay out of it?"

Sam looked directly at his boss and shook his head.

Chapter 10

Ten minutes later, Sam walked out of the Sheriff's office and his heart jumped when he saw Mackenzie leaning against her Jeep Cherokee. Auburn hair falling past her shoulders, a blue gingham shirt, long legs in jeans and Western boots. She looked up and smiled at him.

"Ready to go?" she asked.

"Sure am," Sam answered. "Where to first?"

"I think we have time to hit the Wynn's Antique Emporium before lunch," said Mac.

"Good," said Sam, opening the passenger door of his Civic for her, then walking around to the driver's side.

"Before you came out, I saw a very tall woman with a looooong ponytail come out of the office," commented Mac. "Was that Emmalise Pine?"

"Yep," said Sam.

During the rest of the drive to Frankfort, he caught her up on the latest in the investigation.

"You know, I can really understand why Emmalise wants to be involved," said Mac. "She witnessed the murder and now she thinks she's identified the killer."

"Of course you can," Sam looked at her with a grin. Almost two years earlier, Mac had been involved in the identification of a sniper-killer in the area. The sniper had taken a practice shot at a horse that Mac was painting and Sam had been the deputy who responded to the call.

Mac slugged Sam's arm lightly.

"I did help identify him," she insisted.

"With some scary results," said Sam. The sniper had kidnapped Mac and held her in his attic for several days.

"If you'd listened to me, that might not have happened," insisted Mac. "You need to listen to Emmalise, keep her close."

Sam started to object, looked at his wife's earnest expression, and nodded.

"You've got a point," he said.

They found the Wynn Antique Emporium in a three story brick building on a side street not far from Main Street's colorful tourist shops and galleries. The large picture windows were full of old furniture and home-goods, definitely from before 1950. Sam found a parking spot right in front.

"Just furniture shopping, right?" said Mac.

"But we can use help, especially if it's the owner or his wife," said Sam. "A little friendly, nosy conversation."

They walked in together, Sam holding the door and Mac's hand. At first they seemed alone in the sprawling store crammed with furniture, cases of jewelry, coins, stamps and any item an antique lover could envision.

"Let's start at that far aisle and work our way back," suggested Sam.

As they reached the aisle, they saw a double doorway leading into another equally packed, large room. They looked at each other and headed inside. As they began walking to the far end, they heard footsteps behind them, and turned.

"I'm so sorry," drawled a small man, dressed in a brown suit that looked like an antique itself. "I like to greet my customers at the door, but I had a phone call. My name is Luther Wynn. Welcome to Wynn Antiques Emporium."

He stretched out a small hand to Sam, and shook with a firm grip. Then he extended his hand to Mac as well, but bowed over her hand and brushed it with his lips. Startled, she tried not to pull back too quickly. Mr. Wynn's smile exuded charm, or was meant to, but seemed overdone, perhaps because his mouth was wide and his lips full, partly covered by a thick mustache. He was a little below average height, shorter than Mac by at least an inch. His shoulders were narrow, his arms lanky and thin, the rest of his body equally so. His best feature was his warm, brown eyes, under black eyebrows, and alongside a long, Roman nose. His hair was dark brown with streaks of gray, and thinning in front, giving him a high forehead.

"Normally this is a busy time," Mr. Wynn continued, "but since it's not today, would you mind if I showed you around my establishment? You haven't been here before. I would have remembered."

"No, we haven't," said Sam.

"Are you looking for anything in particular?" asked Mr. Wynn.

"We just built a new house," said Sam, "so we're in the process of furnishing it."

"New house, but old furniture?" Mr. Wynn stood straighter at the thought.

"Oh, yes," Mac jumped in. "We love antiques. Older furniture seems so much more comfortable and homey. We would love for you to show us around."

Mr. Wynn led the way, and Sam grinned at Mac over Wynn's head. She hooked her arm through his, and squeezed. They followed Luther Wynn up and down the narrow aisles, while he kept up a steady monologue. If either of them commented on a piece, Wynn would tell them its history. Mac was interested, but Sam doubted that all of the stories were true.

Finally Sam asked, "Where does your merchandise come from?"

"Mostly estate sales," answered Wynn, "from Kentucky and bordering states. Actually most of it is from around here. That's how I can be so sure of the provenance."

"The what?" said Sam.

"Provenance," said Wynn. "The origin of a piece, its history, background. For some pieces I know the style, and approximately how old it is, and that's all. For others, I can tell you all about the family who owned it. For instance, this armoire comes from a local family."

They had slowly made their way to the main room of the store, and were looking at a huge oak wardrobe with double doors. Mr. Wynn opened the doors, and they could see that half of the armoire held several drawers, while the other side was open with a rod across the top for hanging clothes. It was large, sturdy, and simply made.

"This came from my mother-in-law's home over in Belleriver," said Luther Wynn. "My father-in-law used it for years, and claimed it was handed down in his wife's family, originally used by Judge Roy Bean before he went West. I don't know if that's true, but Father Printes loved to tell people that."

"The Printes family?" said Sam. "Don't they live in that colonial out on Turtle Creek?"

"Yes, my wife and I live there too," volunteered Wynn. "Mother Printes gave me several old pieces after her husband died. She didn't even want them on consignment. Just gave them to me to help fill the store."

"Well, that was nice," said Mac, "and this wardrobe is magnificent, whether it was Judge Roy Bean's or not. I think it may be too big for our place."

"I think that's why it's still here," mused Wynn. "I've lowered the price, but it's rather massive."

They continued the tour, and Mac mixed in personal questions with furniture comments.

"Do you know why Mrs. Printes was willing to part with her family furniture?" Mac asked.

"There was just too much," said Wynn. "She asked Faye, my wife, and her son, Gideon, if they wanted any of it. They chose what they wanted to keep. The house is still full. It's big, but some of the rooms are smallish, especially bedrooms, so we really didn't need all of it. In fact some of the pieces were stored in the barn. Bringing that wardrobe here really opened up Father Printes's bedroom, which became Mother Printes's sitting room after his death."

"It must be fascinating for you living in the family home," said Mac. "It's an antique in itself, and large enough for several people."

"Yes, it is a beautiful old place," Wynn looked thoughtful, "and we get along tolerably well. My wife and I have our own set of rooms, as does Gideon, and Mother Printes."

He paused, and then asked, "Did you see anything you liked?"

"Oh, yes," Mac sighed, "but we are on a budget. Do you mind if we look around on our own for awhile?"

"Good heavens, no," Wynn smiled. "Please do."

He turned on his heel, and walked back toward the checkout counter. Mac and Sam wandered through aisles, looking primarily at furniture.

When they got out of earshot, Sam whispered, "I'm starved."

"Me too," said Mac, "but I actually like an old desk back here. And that dining set."

After Sam examined the roll top desk thoroughly, they decided to buy it, but to wait on the dining room table and chairs. They asked about the provenance, and were relieved that it came from a large estate sale in another county, not from the Printes family. They arranged with Mr. Wynn to pick up the desk the following week.

"Let's go to the Coffeetree," said Mac. "It's not quite noon, so we should beat the rush."

The café was less than a two-block walk, so they left the Civic and strolled through downtown Frankfort.

"What did you think of Mr. Wynn?" Mac asked.

"He's from another era," said Sam. "If he weren't married, I'd think he was gay."

"That's how some people hide from being gay, or hide that they are," said Mac, "but I don't think he is. He's trying to be an old Southern gentleman. Maybe he thinks it fits the furniture."

At the restaurant, they were pleasantly surprised to find a small empty table. Mac ordered the cranberry and walnut chicken salad, and Sam got the black bean salsa wrap.

"Do you think you got anything useful from Wynn?" Mac asked, while they waited for their food.

"Not that I noticed," said Sam. "He mentioned Gideon, but not as a candidate. And he didn't namedrop any family friends or relations."

"Except Judge Roy Bean," Mac smiled.

"That should help Gideon get elected!" Sam chuckled softly.

"If nothing else, we've met Wynn. He's a contact," said Mac.

"And he knows us," said Sam.

A smiling waitress brought their food, and all conversation stopped. Sam finished first, and watched Mac piling her salad into her mouth as fast as she could.

"Good grief, woman, slow down! We can get you more food."

She glanced up at him, chewing. She straightened, and wiped her mouth with her napkin.

"Good," she said, "let's split the triple layer chocolate cake."

"Whoa!" Sam grinned. "I'm not sure I'm that hungry."

"Don't worry. I'll eat most of it," said Mac, scraping the last bite of chicken from her plate.

She was as good as her word. Sam had a few bites of cake and Mac finished the rest slowly, savoring the last chunk with closed eyes and a sigh.

After Sam paid the bill, and they walked back to the car, he asked, "Which furniture store do you want to hit next?"

"Hmmmmm," said Mac,. "Which one has cribs?"

"Cribs?" Sam stopped walking. "Like baby cribs?"

"Exactly like baby cribs," Mac stopped too, turned toward him and smiled, her green eyes shining.

Sam grabbed her, pulled her close, and hugged her tightly. His face was buried in her hair, and he whispered, "Oh my God! Oh my God!" in her ear.

Chapter 11

Faye Wynn closed her eyes, slipped off her high heels, and leaned back in the soft armchair in her and Luther's bedroom. She bent one leg, resting her foot on her other knee, and began massaging her toes. She was glad to be home, but marveled for the umpteenth time that she was still living in her childhood home. She smiled just a little, thinking, "Athena." Faye called her mother "Mama", but always thought of her as "Athena." After her father died, it didn't seem right to leave Athena alone. True, Gideon was living in the big house, too, but he didn't seem to be much company for her mother. Luther agreed. Within six months of Oscar Printes's funeral, they had moved into their own set of rooms in Athena's house. That was a total of over thirty years, plus the eighteen of her childhood. She had had other plans as a child. World traveler. A photographer for *National Geographic*. A writer for a travel magazine. Cruise ship entertainment manager. Tour guide in Paris, or London or Madrid.

That small smile remained as she switched legs, and rubbed her other toes. Somehow, none of those careers had materialized. She had drifted through the University of Kentucky; her only definite decision was not to follow Gideon into law school. She took a job as a secretary at a Louisville law firm, was obviously overqualified, and switched to a paralegal position at her boss's insistence. She met Luther at a half-marathon, running into him at the finish line, where he was bent over dry heaving. She knocked him flat, apologized profusely, and he asked her out for dinner that night. They married four months later, over Oscar and Gideon's warnings. Athena had liked Luther from the beginning, just as Faye had. He had finished college in three years, was four years younger than Faye, and had a solid job as a CPA. Those facts, and his sometimes flamboyant mannerisms, worried her father and brother. But Luther was funny, intelligent, quirky, and unexpected, and he adored Faye. She was crazy about him too. And they traveled.

Once a year they went somewhere overseas, planning their own itinerary, staying in hostels, or less expensive bed and breakfasts, going to small towns, and less often to big cities. Their second vacation would be in the United States, usually driving, and stopping wherever caught their fancies along the route. They had taken Athena with them several times, when she was younger, staying in nicer hotels and bed-and-breakfasts. When she got past 80, she said it was "too much fuss and bother," even though she still got around very well. Faye knew Athena felt she held them back, so they shared photos and stories when they came home.

Faye stretched her back, and went to their walk-in closet to switch her heels for comfortable flats. She would keep on her soft taupe slacks, and striped blouse for dinner.

Just as she closed the closet doors, Luther walked in and smiled at her.

"Hello, sweetheart!" he said, slipping his arm around her waist, and giving her a gentle kiss.

"Hello to you too," Faye replied, leaning into him.

"How was work?" they asked simultaneously.

He paused and waited for her to answer. Faye was now the office manager at the same law firm, which paid considerably more than her former paralegal position. She was very good at dealing with the different personalities among the lawyers and clerical staff, and kept the business running with rarely a hitch. She often had funny stories to share with Luther and Athena, but never with Gideon. He did not approve of talking about people from work, whether clients or staff. Fortunately, he worked at another firm in Lexington, while Faye was in Versailles. Also Gideon frequently worked late, and was only home for dinner on weekends.

"Hmmmm," Faye pretended to think hard. "Carolyn is getting braces, those new clear ones, and she is mortified."

"Because she's the receptionist?"

"Yep. Always in the public eye. Plus she's over 40."

"Well, she shouldn't worry. They're not very noticeable, and it's the new in thing for adults."

"That's what I told her. Also, we won the Murphy case!"

"That's fantastic! I'll bet Hatcher is relieved."

Luther hung up his suit coat, and changed his slacks for khakis. He sat on the bed and tied up dark brown tennis shoes. Faye leaned against the wall, looking out a sheer-covered window at their lawn, sloping down to the river.

"I had a good day," announced Luther. "I sold that big roll-top desk to a nice, young couple."

"That's great, honey," Faye looked at him with a smile. "Anyone we know?"

"I didn't before today," said Luther. "Sam and Mac Kincaid."

Faye shook her head.

"I googled them, of course," Luther added. "Sam is a local sheriff's deputy, and Mac is Mackenzie Field, the horse artist."

"Oh, I've heard of her," said Faye. "One of her paintings is in the library, and it's quite good. We'll have to ask Mama if she knows them, or their families."

"I could smell roast pork when I came in," Luther said. "Let's go down."

Athena was already sitting at the table, when Faye and Luther came into the dining room. With all of its leaves, the walnut table could sit twelve, but Athena had Luther remove all of them, so the three (or four) of them could sit within comfortable conversation distance. Gloria, Athena's caregiver for that day, was placing a partially sliced platter of roast pork on the table. Faye had offered to help once, years ago, but Gloria wouldn't hear of it. She was a plump, pretty Hispanic woman in her forties, and had worked for Athena the longest of her caregivers, about twelve years. At seven o'clock, the night worker, Pam, would arrive, clean up the kitchen, and help Athena get ready for bed.

Athena sat very straight in her tall-backed wooden chair, and smiled at Faye and Luther, as they took their seats. Faye thought her mother was still beautiful, and it was clear that she once had been strikingly so. Her narrow face was wrinkled, but her dark eyes were bright, her lips still full and smooth, and her short, white hair was swept away from her face in soft waves that curled behind her ears.

"How was your day, Mama?" Faye asked.

"Gloria and I took a long walk this afternoon," answered Athena. "Around the house and back to the apple orchard. Two more of the trees are dying, so I'll have to get someone to look at them."

"It was a beautiful day for a walk," said Luther.

Gloria placed two more serving dishes on the table, one filled with yams in brown sugar and butter sauce, and the other with green beans.

"This looks delicious, Gloria," said Athena. "Thank you. Just let me know when you're leaving."

"Gracias, Senora," Gloria smiled, and slipped quietly back into the kitchen.

Plates were passed to Faye, who always served. The pork was so tender that Athena had no trouble cutting her own, and feeding herself. They spoke about the warm fall weather, news from work, or at home. Athena and Gloria had seen a possum out in the apple trees, and it had played possum at their approach. As they turned back toward the house, it had waddled quickly toward the river. Faye explained the outcome of the Murphy case without using names, since Athena knew the families involved. Not that Athena would gossip with anyone, but Faye knew clients should be protected.

Athena listened to her daughter talk, and watched her, thinking how elegant Faye looked, and how intelligent she was. Faye had been a daring child, and Athena had expected her to leave home for New York City or Paris or London, and had encouraged her fearless child to go where she wanted. She was secretly pleased that Faye seemed to have found enough adventure in her job, her unconventional husband, and their travels.

"I met an interesting couple at work today," Luther said. "They bought a huge, old roll-top desk for their new house. Mac and Sam Kincaid."

"I don't know that name," said Athena.

"He's a Woodford County Deputy," Luther continued. "She is MacKenzie Field, the racehorse artist."

"Oh, yes," Athena brightened, "I've seen a few of her paintings. They're beautiful! Her father is Gabriel Quinn, who trains horses and raises beef cattle. Lives on the south-east side of town."

"Oh my, I just realized!" gasped Faye. "MacKenzie is the woman who was kidnapped by the sniper killer a few years ago!"

"That's right," said Luther. "How did I not remember that? It was in the papers. Deputy Kincaid rescued her from the killer's attic!"

"Then they ended up getting married," smiled Faye. "Happy ending."

"The sniper was from Belleriver, too, a new family" Athena said. "I didn't know them, but it was a sad story. I just don't remember the details."

"I can look it up online, if you'd like, Mama," offered Luther.

"Not on my account, Luther. I've lived through so many sad stories; I don't need to hear another one."

"Well, they seemed very nice," her son-in-law continued, "and they're a very handsome couple. I hope they come back and buy more furniture for their new house."

"That desk was a good sale," said Faye. "Not many homes are large enough for an old roll-top like that. Didn't it come from a lawyer's office?"

"Yes, an old family firm in Louisville that moved offices, when the patriarch retired. There are still a lot of roll-top desks made, but they're not as large or beautiful as that one."

The conversation followed the line of old furniture being far preferable to new.

They lingered over blackberry crumble and coffee, discussing some area news, and the books each was reading. They had been together for so long, they were comfortable with long silences as well. About 7:30, Faye and Luther rose to go back to their part of the house, each kissing Athena on her cheek, and wishing her a good night. Pam was a tall, sturdy woman with a broad pink face, and broader shoulders, who accompanied Athena up the stairs and watched her settle in a comfortable armchair in front of the unlit fireplace.

"Call me if you want anything, ma'am," Pam said with a smile. "No need for you to make an extra trip."

"Thank you, Pam," Athena smiled back at her caretaker. She was happy that she still got around so well, slower, but with good balance. There was an intercom system throughout the house, just in case, and to reassure Athena's grown children that she was safe. But she wanted to take care of herself for as long as possible, to retain her privacy.

She dreaded having someone help her dress, shower and use the toilet, and hoped she would simply die in her sleep before it came to that.

"I'm lucky," she thought to herself, as she put on her wire-rimmed glasses and picked up the top book on the table next to her. She opened *I Know Why the Caged Bird Sings,* but the words were blurred at first, and she had to blink away tears before she could read.

Chapter 12

The Printes family was gathered in Athena's parlor after dinner on the following Sunday afternoon. Traditionally, the big meal was at noon on Sunday, followed by coffee and conversation, and reading the Sunday papers in the living room that Athena and Gideon shared. Faye and Luther had their own library and television room on the second floor. They also had a small kitchen that they rarely used, that had been a transformed from a bedroom, when they first moved. Athena had expected them to want a truly separate apartment, but Faye wasn't much of a cook, and they quickly developed the habit of having meals together.

As usual, Gideon and Athena sat in armchairs on one side of the fireplace, and Faye and Luther shared the gold-colored couch on the other side. Luther sat at one end, while Faye lay on the couch, her stockinged feet in Luther's lap. They all wore their dress clothes, even though they hadn't attended a church service. In fact, Gideon was the only one who went to church with any regularity, but he was not a member of a particular parish. He simply attended when and where he felt like going. When the children were growing up, Athena took them to the small Baptist Church in Belleriver, or the bigger one in Versailles. Oscar went with them, when he was at home. When Faye and Gideon were both at the University of Kentucky, and came home for their first break, they learned that their parents were no longer attending church, and they were given no explanation. They were puzzled, but didn't mind; college provided enough distractions. Gideon began his sporadic church visits after he started working as an attorney. Faye gradually became an agnostic, and Luther also had his doubts about God. He told Faye that either way, he thought you should live your life by helping others when you could, and doing your best at anything you did for whatever time you had.

"I'm a positive fatalist," he said. "We don't know what comes after death, but I think life is better if you're both kind and productive. If you and I can be together, I'll be crazy content!"

Several months after Faye and Luther moved into the family home, Faye asked her mother why she left the church. They were walking by the river without either Luther or Gideon at home. Athena looked at Faye and sighed.

"The Lord and I have parted ways," she answered. "We don't seem to have an understanding anymore. You don't belong to a church, so does it bother you that I don't?"

"No, I guess not," said Faye, drawing out the 'no', "but you used to have such a strong faith. I wondered what changed."

"I began to see the world differently. So much pain, and evil. Why does God allow it? And I wasn't finding any answers or comfort in church, so I left. Why don't you go?"

"Partly I'm not sure there is a God, partly for the same reasons you mentioned. And it also bothered me that a truly loving God required worship from us. Wouldn't an all-knowing being be above that? It seems narcissistic or arrogant."

They never talked about it again. Neither of them asked Gideon why he wandered from church to church, or what he believed, and he didn't ask them, or invite them to join him. They might discuss religion in the news, or local church activities, but not their personal beliefs.

So on this Sunday, each of them had a section of a newspaper, either the Lexington Herald-Leader, or the Louisville Courier Journal.

"Oh, Gideon!" said Luther abruptly, "the Journal has a photo of you from the day you were on television. Good picture."

He held the paper up, so that they could all see the photograph.

"How do they get such a long article out of you saying you haven't decided whether to run or not?" Luther rolled his eyes.

They all smiled, even Gideon.

"Are you going to run?" Athena asked, her tone mild, but she looked over the paper at her son with concern.

"I still haven't decided, Mama," said Gideon. "Would you rather I didn't?"

Athena didn't answer. She lowered her paper to her lap.

"John Francis approached me. He's a bigwig in the Republican Party. He seemed to think, and he said others did as well, that I have a successful record as an attorney, good background, that I'd be a good candidate for the Appeals Court. There are a lot of advantages in being a judge, rather than staying a lawyer until I retire."

"What does he mean by 'background'?" Athena wanted to know.

"I've always been a Republican. Graduated from the University of Kentucky. Respectable family. Organizational memberships, like Rotary. Things like that." Gideon looked at his mother. "Is there something bothering you, Mama?"

"I'm wondering how much the press or the party will be looking at our family," Athena responded with a small frown. "I like my privacy."

Gideon smiled, "I don't think you need to worry. There isn't usually a lot of publicity for judgeships, even if a Democrat runs against me."

"You were on television," pressed Faye, "and in the papers. Will they care that I vote as an Independent? Actually, I have voted Democratic quite often."

Gideon looked at his sister with an exasperated smile.

"Really, Faye, that TV spot was a fluke. How often do you hear anything about judges in the news, unless they make some controversial decision?"

Faye wrinkled her nose, and grinned at him, "Well, we know you wouldn't do that!"

"What are the advantages?" asked Luther seriously.

"Mmm…better hours. Similar pay, with a preset calendar. A good pension plan."

"Why would you want to be an appeals judge?" Faye was serious, too. "Do you have goals? Do you think you could do some good for the legal system?"

"I can't predetermine what cases I would have," answered Gideon, "but, of course, I would want to be a fair judge. Follow the rule of law, and the Constitution of Kentucky."

"Now that sounds like a good, political answer," said Faye, laughing softly. "Don't worry, brother, I'd vote for you! At least I know you're honest."

They all went back to reading their papers. Athena still had two faint worry lines between her eyebrows, and Gideon kept glancing at her.

Chapter 13

Emmalise trotted to her car, hopped in, rolled down the front windows, and searched for Lorraine Tippet's phone number on her smart phone. She realized she should have asked Sheriff Dade for it, but didn't want to go back, and possibly have him try to cut her out of the investigation again. She hoped the deputy would call her to visit Serafina Washington and her niece with him, but she was anxious to get started now. The phone rang four times, and a recorded voice asked her to leave a message.

"Miss Tippet, this is Emmalise Pine. I know you've talked with Deputy Kincaid about my case. Well, I feel like it's my case. Anyway, I have some names and pictures to show you, so could you call me back when it's convenient?"

Emmalise left her cell number, and hung up. Frustrated and disappointed, she debated what to do next. Deciding to go home and clean the apartment, she backed out of her parking space, looking over her shoulder. Just then her phone rang. She pulled back in and grabbed it out of the cup holder.

"Hello," she answered, expecting to hear Miss Tippet's voice.

"Hey, Lise. It's Jana," said her sister. "I was just at Mom's. In fact, I'm out front. Could you come over? Things are getting worse."

Emmalise's heart sank, and she felt guilty. She hadn't been by her mother's in almost two weeks.

"Yeah, Jana, I'm on my way," she said, and put the phone down.

Jana was a year younger than Emmalise, shakily married with two kids. The sisters had been close growing up, and stayed that way, until Jana married Mitch. Mitch was undeniably handsome, charming, and had a good job with the Kentucky Power Company. Shortly after their second boy was born, Mitch was injured in a fall from a pole. He was lucky. His left leg was broken in three places, but was repairable, and he had workman's comp. After three months off, he was able to go back to work. During those three months, Jana had three babies to take care of, if she counted Mitch, which she did. She'd had eight weeks maternity leave, but had to ask for an extension from her boss at the Ford dealership, where she was the bookkeeper. He was not happy. Neither was Jana. Baby Pete was colicky, and three-year-old Mikey was very energetic. Mitch was almost no help, even complaining about folding laundry or rocking Pete, and drinking beer all day and evenings too. Jana was worn out. She had told Emmalise that things were better, since she and Mitch both went back to work. Grandma Pine took care of the boys two days a week, and they went to daycare the other three. Emmalise had offered to babysit, but Jana hadn't asked. She said she and Mitch were too tired to go out. Seeing her sister's life, Emmalise felt lucky not to be married or have kids.

When she pulled up in front of the house, Emmalise felt a little relieved to see Jana sitting on the porch swing, pushing it slowly back and forth with her foot. Jana gave her a small smile, and patted the empty space next to her on the swing.

"Sorry, Lise. I guess it's not an emergency," Jana emphasized that last word and pushed a loose strand of blond hair off her forehead. She looked tired, her hair pulled back in a ponytail, no make-up, and dark circles under her gray eyes.

"It's OK," said Emmalise. "I missed visiting last week. It's not Mom, is it?"

"No," Jana looked down and shook her head, "Mom's fine. She's in there reading to Mikey, and she got Pete down for a nap, which is a miracle. I don't see how she does it after raising the seven of us."

"Practice," said Emmalise with a smile, "So what's up?"

"It's Tara," Jana said, her voice getting shaky. "I'm pretty sure she's using again. She's up in bed now, passed out. Which means she missed work, and will probably get fired. She hasn't been paying Mom any rent, or helping out at all."

"What's Tara on?" asked Emmalise.

"I don't know." said Jana. "I just think she's using."

"For how long? Has she been going to church?"

"I don't know!" Jana said loudly, "I'm not her keeper!"

Then she burst into tears, and Emmalise hugged her tightly.

Beautiful, shining Tara, who loved to dance, had a strong singing voice, and wanted to be an actress, had fallen off the stage, literally, in a high school musical, because she was high on cocaine and alcohol. Sadly, that was the first time her family had known she was drinking and using drugs. She was a junior, embarrassed and heartbroken. She swore that was it. She would never drink or take cocaine again. She hadn't been using long, but she found it impossible to give up. The next time Mama noticed sooner, and sent her to rehab. Tara managed to stay clean long enough to graduate from high school, but her grades were B's and C's, and her ACT scores were average. There were no scholarships. After that disastrous musical, she wouldn't even sing in the school choir. She'd lost the flamboyant need to sing and dance and act. At eighteen, Tara floated from salesgirl jobs to waitressing jobs, and got high in her off-hours. Mama sent her to rehab facilities three more times, using up her savings. Finally, when Tara was 26, the fourth place seemed to work. Tara had been living at home, paying low rent, working the cash register at a feed store, and singing in the church choir at a small Baptist church in Versailles. A young man she met in AA had taken Tara to his church, although he and most of the congregation were black. Tyrone picked Tara up faithfully every Sunday for church. She had fallen in love with the music there, and singing in the choir had been her saving grace for almost a year. The family suspected she and Ty were dating, but no one knew for sure.

"I'll go talk to her," Emmalise said, giving Jana a squeeze. "Try to relax while you can."

Emmalise walked past the living room and up the stairs. She could hear Mom reading softly to Mikey down the hall. She tapped lightly on her sister's bedroom door, but there was no answer. She and her sisters had shared that room for years, three roommates, then two, now one. Emmalise knocked again.

"Come in," came a muffled voice.

Emmalise stepped into the dim room, saw clothes on the floor and chair, and rumpled, lumpy covers one of the three twin beds squeezed in front of the windows. The lumps moved and Tara peeked out from under a violet quilt.

"Hey, Tara," said Emmalise, turning on a floor lamp by the clothes-covered armchair before she sat on the side of the bed.

Tara yanked the quilt over her head and groaned.

"Please, Emma," she begged in a rough voice, "I'm sick. Let me sleep."

"No, Tara," Emmalise put her hand gently what she thought was her sister's shoulder. "This won't wait."

Tara pulled the covers down, and rolled over on her back. Her face was flushed and her brown hair clung damply around her face. She was the only one of her siblings with blue eyes like their daddy's; now hers were red and dark-ringed.

"What's wrong?" she croaked.

Emmalise felt her heart break. Tara looked as bad as she had at her worst on drugs.

Emmalise didn't know whether to cry or hit her sister, so she shook Tara's shoulder hard.

"Tara, you can't do this again!" she cried. "God damn it! You can't!"

Tara sat straight up in bed, pushing Emmalise's hand away.

"I'm not, Emma. I'm not," she knew exactly what Emmalise thought. Tara wasn't angry; she knew it was only fair that her sister would suspect her of relapsing.

"I swear. On the Bible. On Daddy's grave. Anything you want," Tara went on. "I'm just sick."

"What about church?" Emmalise demanded. She'd heard the "I'm sick" excuse before.

"I missed last Sunday, " Tara admitted. "My throat was sore then, and I knew I couldn't sing. I doubt I'll go tomorrow either."

"Did you call in sick today?" asked Emmalise, more calmly.

"Yes," Tara lay back down.

"Have you been paying rent?" Emmalise said, remembering Jana's other suspicion.

"Yes, but I'm late this time," Tara said. "I've been so tired, I just forgot. I'll get up right now and write the check, if you'll leave me alone."

Emmalise looked into Tara's eyes and laid her hand on Tara's forehead.

"You're burning up!" she said, quickly changing gears. "Did you take any ibuprofen?"

"No," sighed Tara, "I just want to sleep."

"I'll be right back," said her sister.

When Emmalise came back, she had to wake Tara again to make her take two ibuprofen.

"Does Ty know you're sick," asked Emmalise, as she took back the cup of water.

"He's on a mission trip," said Tara, "but I called the choir director last week, and I'll call him later, if I don't feel better. Oh, and I went to AA every day, except today."

Emmalise crossed to the light, and turned it off. As she was closing the door, she heard Tara whisper, "Sorry I scared you."

Emmalise brushed tears from her eyes and hurried downstairs to relieve Jana of one worry.

Chapter 14

Emmalise stayed at her mother's for lunch, whipping up some turkey and cheese sandwiches served with leftover potato salad for everyone except Tara and the baby, who both slept. She cleared up the misconceptions about Tara with Jana, while Mary Ellen Pine indignantly said she hadn't been worried about the rent at all, she knew Tara was sick, and how could Jana be so suspicious?

"I think she's given everyone cause to worry before," commented Emmalise, "but I'm glad it's just the flu this time."

"Big ears," said Jana, glancing at Mikey, who was eating the turkey, cheese and bread of his sandwich separately.

"Who has big ears?" he asked on cue.

"You do!" said Emmalise, grinning and pulling gently on his ears.

"Do not," Mikey smiled at his aunt and went back to rolling up strips of turkey and popping them in his mouth.

"Does she have health insurance?" asked Emmalise. "She needs to see a doctor."

"Not yet," said Mom. "Maybe in another four months, when she's been at the feed store a year, if they get her hours up to full-time. If she's not better tomorrow, I'll make sure she goes to one of the free clinics in Lexington on Monday."

"Mikey, are you going to eat that potato salad?" Jana asked. He was pushing a piece of potato around his plate with his finger. He looked at his mother, but didn't answer, just gave her a little smile.

"It's a potato puff looking for a hungry hippo to eat it!" said Emmalise. "Where is the hungry hippo?"

She looked around the room, put a piece of potato on his fork, looked under the table, all the while waving the fork in front of his face, and asking, "Where is a hungry hippo?"

Mikey tried to catch the potato with his mouth open wide, finally yelling, "I'm a hungry hippo!" Finally Emmalise popped it into his mouth, and handed him the fork.

"Can the hungry hippo find his own potato puffs?" she said. It seemed that he could.

Jana looked exasperated, but nodded at Emmalise.

"You're good with him," she said, a little sadly. "I can't even get my own kid to eat."

"It won't work next time," Emmalise said. "I just got lucky. And I'm his aunt, not his mother."

"Put it in front of them, and no alternatives except what's on the table," said Mary Ellen firmly. "It'll work, or it won't. But they won't go hungry."

Jana and Emmalise looked at their mother incredulously. After their father died, they'd been lucky to have food on the table, and all seven of them had known it. They had eaten a lot of spaghetti and casseroles, food that could be stretched to fill them up.

"Well, look at the bunch of you," continued Mary Ellen. "No matter what I fed you, some were picky, and some of you would eat anything. You're still that way. I've got a fast food junky, a vegetarian, a would-be chef, and everything in between!"

The sisters laughed, and started naming which sibling had which eating style. Suddenly someone's cell phone played "Dueling Banjos."

"Not mine!" said Jana and Mary Ellen together. Upstairs baby Pete began crying, and both women pushed back their chairs to go get him. Mary Ellen nodded at Jana to sit back down with Mikey, and she left the room.

"Hello," Emmalise answered her phone.

"Emmalise, this is Lorraine Tippet. I just got your message. Would you like to come over this afternoon?"

"Hello, Miss Tippet!" responded Emmalise. "That would be great."

She glanced at her mother's kitchen clock. It was 1:15 p.m.

"Would two o'clock be OK?" she asked.

"Perfect," said Miss Tippet.

Emmalise stayed another half an hour to fuss over Pete, who was a beautiful baby. At ten months old, he had dark, curly hair, blue eyes, and was pulling himself up on furniture to walk. Everyone thought he was trying to keep up with Mikey. Watching the brothers play with wooden blocks on the floor, she rethought not wanting Jana's life. It was messy and exhausting, but the kids were priceless. She hugged her sister and mother good-bye, again offering to babysit for her nephews. Jana smiled and said she'd talk to Mitch about it.

Promptly at 2:00 p.m., Emmalise pulled up in front of Miss Tippet's narrow, two-story brick home. It had been an unusually cool April, but plenty of rain had brought out white spirea blooms around the house, and patches of colorful tulips at the bases of oak trees in the yard. When Emmalise started up the sidewalk, she saw Miss Tippet waving at her from the front door.

"Your yard is beautiful!" called Emmalise.

"Thank you," said Miss Tippet, smiling. She stepped out on the small porch and hugged Emmalise.

"You look beautiful yourself, Emmalise. It's been much too long since I've seen you. High school graduation, I believe."

Miss Tippet followed her students from a distance, attending the Woodford High School graduation annually, to see how many of her former fourth graders accomplished that goal. After that, she was always available to any young people who sought her out. Many asked to be her "friend" on Facebook, and her feed was filled with their college, first job, wedding and children photos. Emmalise was part of that group, but hadn't provided too many photos.

"Your car is delightful," said Miss Tippet, "bright and quick, like you."

Emmalise was surprised by that comment. She knew her Mazda 3, painted a glowing yellow by a former owner, was noticeable, and fun to drive, but she didn't think of herself in those terms. She smiled at her teacher, who seemed to see all of her students in the best possible light. She followed Miss Tippet into her summer garden living room and they sat on the floral patterned couch together. Two glasses of ice water sat on the coffee table.

"What are you doing now?" asked Miss Tippet, "I know you work at Wags and Purrs, but what do you do there?"

"I'm a vet tech, " answered Emmalise, "and at least at our office, I get to do all kinds of things. I like direct contact with the animals the most, even though they're scared. I mostly work with Dr. Dunnigan with small animals, but someday, I'd like to help Dr. Grantham with the large animals too."

"You know, I have a stray cat that has taken to hanging around," said Miss Tippet. "He started coming into the back yard and watching me. I asked around the neighborhood, and no one claims him. Of course, I made the mistake of feeding him, so I think he's here to stay. He has been rubbing on the trees or chair legs, whatever I'm close to, but when I try to pet him, he shies away."

"Do you want him to stay?" asked Emmalise.

"I never had a pet before. I felt it wasn't fair when I was teaching, that I wouldn't give an animal enough time or attention. Then I got used to living on my own," she paused, looking at the photos of her students on the walls, "but, yes, I think I'd like him to stay. He's a big, gray fellow, lots of scars on his head, probably not neutered. I'd at least like to get him fixed, so he can't procreate, and maybe he won't get in so many fights."

"Well, just be patient. He'll eventually let you pet him. Then you can scoot him into a carrier and take him to the vet. If you're in a hurry to get him neutered, use a live trap. Once he's neutered, he'll be even friendlier."

They continued talking about cats for awhile, including Emmalise's two. Miss Tippet had seen Lancelot and Guinevere on Facebook, and said they were beautiful. Abruptly, Miss Tippet changed the subject.

"Let's get to what you came for," she said, "I believe that you recognized Gideon Printes's voice as that of the man who shot the black man years ago."

"Yes, I'm sure it was the same voice," insisted Emmalise.

"I'm not doubting you, dear. You have an incredible memory. What did you want to talk about with me?"

Emmalise had made copies of the names and photo she had give Sheriff Dade, and had laid the folder containing them on the coffee table. Now she picked it up, and handed it to Miss Tippet.

"These are photos from the Woodford County High School yearbook, when Gideon Printes went there. He was in the Science Club, Debate, and wrestling, so I have the team photos and names of members. Sheriff Dade went over them, and now we want you to look at them. See if you can tell us anything about the people now, whether it would be safe to talk to any of them about Printes."

Miss Tippet looked at the photos and read the names carefully, a slight frown of concentration on her face. After a few minutes, she sat back and sighed.

"Mary Leonard is someone you could approach," she said, "She teaches at the high school now, and is very level-headed. You can't tell her why you want to know about Printes, though. I wouldn't think she was a gossip, but we have to be careful not to start rumors. I'd think Sheriff Dade should talk to Patrick Goins, Randy Mason, and Art Bishop, because he knows them. Reynolds, Farmingham, and Crater were untrustworthy when I knew them, and are the kind of men who would back Printes in the election. They came from money, and they all have it now. Self-centered, and arrogant as boys, self-important and manipulative as men. I would think talking to the black women who worked for Printes, the cook and nanny who Judge Turner told Sam and me about, would be your best bet."

"I agree," said Emmalise, "I'm hoping Deputy Kincaid will ask me to go with him when he interviews them. For now, I'm following the sheriff's instructions. He said he was going to talk to Art Bishop. I'll ask him about Goins and Mason."

"Would you like me to introduce you to Mary?" asked Miss Tippet. "Also maybe you and I should go talk to Judge Turner, find out if any of his peers who attended the Printes's parties are still around."

"That would be wonderful!" said Emmalise. "What did you and Deputy Kincaid tell the judge for an excuse?"

"That Sam was writing a book of the history of the Belleriver area, where Sam's wife grew up," Miss Tippet laughed softly. "Of course, he saw right through that! But he promised to keep our visit and questions to himself. Don't worry. I've known him for years. You could tell him the whole story, and he wouldn't tell anyone. In fact, he could be very helpful."

"OK," said Emmalise. "When can we start?"

"You give me your work schedule, and I'll call Judge Turner and set up an appointment. We'll have to think about how to approach Mary Leonard." Miss Tippet noted that Emmalise had moved to the edge of the couch, her eyes sparkled with excitement and her hands were clasped tightly on her knees, "Emmalise, I know you're probably very hopeful of solving this and giving justice to that murdered man, but we may never be able to prove anything. And looking into this could be very dangerous."

"I know, but I'm not going to knock on Printes's door and accuse him!"

"I didn't think you would. I just don't want you to be too disappointed, if we can't prove Printes guilty."

Emmalise simply liked the sound of that "we."

Chapter 15

When Mac and Sam were back in the car, Sam asked if she knew how far along she was.

"I just peed on the stick this morning, so not definitely," Mac said, smiling. "Two, three weeks. A month. I'll make an appointment with Dr. Matthews next week."

Sam couldn't stop grinning, as he drove to Lexington, or as they walked through furniture display rooms. After two stores, and no luck, they decided to head home. Mac said, "Let's look online. We can at least get some ideas."

"Fine with me," Sam agreed.

Mac's phone pinged a text message notification.

"It's Sarah," she said. "She apologizes for the short notice, but they'd like us to come over for supper."

"Sounds good, " said Sam. "What time?"

"Sixish, she says. That's a couple of hours. So I'll say 'yes'?"

"Sure."

"Sam, could we not tell anyone for awhile? Wait until I'm three months or so?"

Sam glanced at her, and Mac smiled reassuringly. He knew why she wanted to wait.

Mac's older brother Connor and her best friend Sarah were married about seven months before she and Sam. Sarah got pregnant right away, but at eleven weeks, she lost the baby. The miscarriage had been devastating for them. Having the whole town of Belleriver know had not helped. People were sympathetic, but there was too much of "it's for the best."

"If the doc says everything is OK, can we tell our families?" asked Sam.

"That might be kind of tough on Sarah and Connor," Mac said.

"We have to tell them eventually. They'll be happy for us."

"Let me think about it," answered Mac, "but nothing tonight."

Sam nodded. He understood, but he didn't want to feel sad today.

Sarah and Connor lived in Connor and Mac's childhood home with Gabriel Quinn, their father. Connor wanted to continue to work the ranch with his dad, and Gabe had put the home in their names as a wedding gift. He had offered to move into town, but Sarah and Connor thought that was foolish. So far, the arrangement worked. Sarah had confided in Mac (before her miscarriage) that she liked the idea of her and Connor's kids growing up with their grandpa in the house.

When Mac and Sam walked into the old farmhouse, they saw that Aunt Tina was there too. She was setting the table, while Connor and Sarah worked in the kitchen. Gabe was sitting in the living room, reading a newspaper. He put down the paper, and got up, when he saw Mac and Sam.

"Looks like it's all under control," said Mac, hugging her aunt, then her dad. "I guess we don't need to volunteer."

"Nope," said Sarah, walking in from the kitchen with a basket of rolls and a butter dish. Her face was flushed, and she looked happy. She and Mac hugged. It had been over a week since they'd all been together.

"Dinner is ready," announced Connor, bringing in a platter of fried chicken. Aunt Tina and Sarah added mashed potatoes, gravy and last summer's home-grown green beans to the table.

Conversation was sporadic, since everyone was hungry. Gradually, plates were emptied and stories began. Connor and Gabe told about a two-year-old Quarter Horse that kept getting himself in trouble.

"This week he got stuck in a water trough," said Connor. "It's tall. The sides reach his belly. I don't know how he got his front half in, but he couldn't get back out."

"What did you do?" asked Aunt Tina.

"Luckily, he just stood there, splashing with his head, until we showed up," Gabe answered. "Put a halter on him. Emptied out more water with buckets. Connor tipped the trough sideways, while I told Scooter to back up, and he did! Good thing we've been working on that command."

"He got caught in one of the pasture fences, too," Connor added. "He put his left front and left hind between the rails, but stopped there."

"Wow! Sounds like he could have hurt himself," said Mac.

"Yep. He's very curious, but stays calm when he's in a predicament," continued Connor. "We don't know exactly how long he was stuck, but it could've been three or four hours."

"He let us lift his legs back through," said Gabe, "And he hasn't tried that maneuver again."

"Sounds like he'll be a good horse when you finish," Mac commented.

"If he doesn't kill himself with curiosity before then!" Connor smiled, shaking his head.

"How's your house coming?" Aunt Tina asked Mac and Sam.

"Well, we bought a roll-top desk today," answered Sam.

"Where will that go?" Sarah said.

"Not sure," said Mac. "We still have that big living room to fill. I'd kind of like the desk to be near a window, so we can look out, while we pay bills!"

They discussed couch styles, and furniture stores in the area.

"Sam," said Connor, "why don't you just let Mac decorate the house? She's the artist."

"I didn't think I'd care, until I had my own place," Sam answered. "I'm not a decorator, but I found out I had opinions. I wanted to feel comfortable when I came home. I bought a new mattress and couch, but everything else was used. Garage sales. Antique stores."

"I'm a painter, not a decorator," Mac put in. "I like picking things out with Sam, although it takes longer."

"Hey, Connor," Aunt Tina looked at Connor with arched eyebrows, "did you even ask Sarah if she wanted to redecorate this place?"

"Uh, no," Connor looked perplexed. He glanced at Sarah.

"It's OK, honey," Sarah said quickly, "I love everything here. Sam's right. I like 'comfortable.' I've always felt at home in this house."

Connor looked relieved.

"Anyone ready for dessert?" he asked. "Aunt Tina's blueberry pie!"

"You bet!" said Sam, standing up with Mac. "Let us clear."

Connor joined them to get plates and cut the pie. In a few minutes, everyone had a piece of warm blueberry pie and coffee, except for Mac, who preferred cold milk. The three women and Sam savored their pie, while Gabe and Connor wolfed theirs down. Gabe pushed himself back from the table with a groan of pleasure.

"You did it again, Tina!" he said.

Everyone agreed. Mac noticed Sarah reach for Connor's hand, and they smiled at each other. Connor spoke quietly.

"Everyone, we have some news," he began, pausing briefly. "Sarah is pregnant and doing great!"

"I'm four months along," Sarah added, "The doctor says everything is going well, a completely normal pregnancy."

The others hurried around the table and joined Sarah and Connor for hugs and cries of "Congratulations!" Mac decided to save her questions for when she and Sarah were alone. She knew that despite their excitement, Connor and Sarah couldn't help but worry.

Mac hoped it would be for nothing.

"Which room will be the nursery?" asked Mac.

Gabe and Connor grinned.

"Yours!" they said together.

"We already redid my room for Sarah and me," added Connor. "Yours is right across the hall. We'll start working on it soon."

Mac smiled back at them, "Perfect!"

As Sam and Mac drove the short mile home, Sam looked over at her and said, "I'm glad we didn't tell them our news tonight."

"Me too," said Mac.

"You do realize that our kids will be in the same grade in school?" Sam grinned.

"I do," Mac smiled back. "Same class, possibly the same teams…."

Sam reached for her hand. They rode the rest of the way home in silence, smiling.

Chapter 16

When Emmalise pulled into her driveway, Kellon and Jake were playing Frisbee with the dogs in the large back yard. Mugsie was racing frantically between the two men, jumping at and missing the Frisbee. Archer sat on the sidelines, his big head moving back and forth, his eyes never leaving the florescent green disc. Emmalise walked back and watched the game for awhile. Suddenly Archer crouched and leaped, catching the Frisbee at the perfect midpoint of Kellon's throw. Then he took off, running in a big oval around Kellon, Jake and Mugs, a big doggy grin on his mouth with the Frisbee in it. Emmalise laughed. Kellon waved at her; and he and Jake walked over to her.

"He gets it every time," grinned Kellon, "and apparently Mugsie hasn't learned his trick. She just runs herself to exhaustion."

Mugsie was lying in the grass, watching Archer run. Finally he dropped beside her and laid the Frisbee in front of Mugsie's nose. She nudged it; then laid her head in the grass and closed her eyes.

The three people smiled at the dogs and each other. Emmalise started to turn toward her door.

"Hey, Emma," said Kellon, "We're going out for karaoke tonight. There's a great bar in Lexington and we're meeting some friends there. Want to come with?"

Emmalise paused, and said, "I've never done karaoke."

"You don't have to sing, if you don't want to," said Jake, "I didn't at first. But it's really fun!"

Emmalise hesitated. Her initial reaction was to stay home, but that's what she always did.

"OK," she answered, smiling, "Thanks!"

"Great!" said Kellon, "We'll meet down here at 6:30, go somewhere for dinner, and hit the bar about 8:30."

It took Emmalise the next two hours to get ready. She had a discussion with the cats about what to wear, finally settling on her black jeans, a black shirt with red snaps and simple black flats. She put on some mascara, and wore her hair down with a narrow black headband holding it off her face. She fed Guinnie and Lance, then headed down the back stairs.

"Wow!" Kellon greeted her.

"Lookin' hot!" agreed Jake, grinning.

"I don't know if I've ever seen you with your hair down, Emma," said Kellon. "It's beautiful."

"Thanks, guys!"

They decided to drive separately, so Emmalise could leave whenever she felt like it. They ate at a Chili's, taking their time. Emmalise enjoyed watching Kellon and Jake together, and getting to know Jake better. Turned out he was a freelance computer engineer (programmer) who worked mainly for companies in Lexington and Louisville, but had done jobs throughout the Midwest. He and Kellon had met when one of Jake's friends had an appendicitis attack, and Kellon was on the EMT team who picked up the friend.

"While my friend Tom was in surgery, Kellon came into the waiting room."

"Well, I'd just finished my shift," explained Kellon.

"Uh huh," grinned Jake, "and the waiting room was on your way home."

"Sort of. I wanted to see if he was going to be OK. Easy enough to ask his friend."

"Yeah, yeah, yeah!" Jake turned to Emmalise and added, "And to ask for my phone number!"

Emmalise laughed. She continued to watch the two young men, who were physically quite different. Kellon was blond with very short hair, blue eyes and a strong, stocky build. She noticed a two-inch scar on the side of his forehead, near the hairline that she hadn't paid attention to before. Jake was slender, a little taller than Kellon's six feet; he had dark, tousled hair, long on top, and brown eyes with thick, black lashes. They all ate for a few minutes in silence, until Emmalise said, "I know Kellon grew up around here. What about you, Jake?"

"Well," Jake dragged out the word, "yes, I was born in Lexington and had a semi-hellish childhood, because I was small, and singled out as a geek at first, then gay. Some tough guy called me "gay" in 4th grade, and I had no idea what he meant, except that it was bad. When I asked my mother about it, she told me never to tell my dad, and rushed me off to karate lessons. Luckily, I like karate, and even liked the competitions. My dad was so proud of the trophies I won. I escaped to Columbia University in New York, and told Dad I was gay before I went back for my sophomore year. Turns out he knew, and didn't mind. I don't know why Mom was scared to tell him. She did talk to him about it eventually, but they never told me. Could have saved me a lot of trauma as a kid, thinking my dad would hate me if he knew."

"Columbia!" cried Emmalise. "Why did you ever come back?"

"Long story short," Jake smiled and shook his head, "I missed Kentucky! I worked for three years in Manhattan after I graduated, and suddenly, I missed my parents, and my old Kentucky home. My folks financed my own tech business, for which I have paid them back with a bonus. I bought that hot little red number we came in, and set out to find some like-minded, or at least open-minded folk."

"How has that gone?" asked Emmalise, "aside from Kellon."

"Great!" said Jake. "You'll meet some people tonight. Mr. Football here has had a harder time than I have, since he never left. He was such a great athlete, it didn't occur to anyone that he was gay!"

"Yeah, I went to University of Kentucky and lived at home," Kellon looked sheepish,."I've been coming out gradually, since I moved into my own place. My folks figured it out, and were upset at first, mostly because of their church. They're OK now. My granny still prays for me at family gatherings, but she loves me. Most people would just as soon forget about it, ignore it."

"Which will be kind of hard with me around!" grinned Jake.

Emmalise thought she'd keep her former assumptions to herself.

At 8:40 p.m., they were walking in the door of Leonardo's, a relatively new karaoke and live music bar in a neighborhood of bars. A group of people, who had pushed three tables together to the right of a small stage, immediately began waving at them. Jake introduced her as Emmalise, Kellon's neighbor, and rattled off six names. Across the table were Les and Jeannie, obviously a couple: both with streaked blond hair, his long, hers chin-length, and nose studs. Next to them was Sally, who had a round face, light gold eyes and brown hair, curling to her shoulders. Beside Sally was Gem, an elegant black woman with her hair pulled up in corn rows ending in a braided bun. At the end of the table sat Whit, a lanky, long-legged man with gray eyes in a tan, angular face and straight blonde hair that was short, but with longer bangs that hung over his forehead. He lifted his chin momentarily, when she looked at him, then returned to peering into his beer. The chair next to Emmalise held Louann, who was Hispanic, beautiful, with a tough set to her mouth and eyes, but she smiled and nodded when introduced. Emmalise pulled out her chair and sat down, looking around the room. It was crowded, a few empty seats, but all the tables taken. The crowd looked to be in their twenties and thirties, but with a few older folks mixed in, including an elderly black couple sitting off to the other side of the stage. A few tables were taken by men or women only, but Emmalise couldn't tell if they were gay. Surely Kellon and Jake would have sought out a tolerant bar. A perky waitress with short shorts and curly blonde hair appeared and took their orders. Everyone at their tables was drinking beer, but Emmalise ordered bourbon and Coke, while Kellon asked for a whiskey sour and Jake got a mojito.

"So how does everyone know Kellon?" Emmalise asked Louann.

"Sally is an emergency room nurse, so she works with him," Louann answered, "but the rest of us are friends of Jake. We're all nerds, either professional or amateur. Well, except Whit here. He and Jake go way back."

Louann looked pointedly at Whit, who was still staring at his beer. She nudged his arm.

"What is with you tonight, man? Tell Emmalise here how you know Jake."

Whit sat straighter, looked at Louann, and then at Emmalise. He smiled gently.

"Sorry, Louann," he said. "Just preoccupied tonight. Lookin' forward to the music, though. Emmalise, Jake and I are cousins. As soon as I knew what gay was, I knew Jake was gay. I didn't care. We grew up together at family gatherings. I took him fishing. He taught me some karate. I showed him how to throw a baseball. We always got along. He had one sister, and I had three sisters, so Jake and I were like brothers."

"Did you go to the same schools?" asked Emmalise.

"Different grade schools. Same high school."

"How was that? Did kids give him trouble?"

"I'm a year older, so when he came to high school, I could show him around," said Whit, "and keep jerks off his back somewhat. I pitched for the baseball team, and tried to get him to try out, but he knew that wasn't his skill set. He kept taking karate, and I spread the word. He is also very smart, and was in all the college prep classes. Those kids were more open-minded, so that helped."

"So, what do you do now?" Emmalise asked.

"I'm a PI," Whit said.

"Wow!" cried Emmalise, then she blushed, when Louann and Whit looked at her oddly, and everyone else at the table turned to look at her.

"Sorry," she fumbled for an explanation. "I never met a PI before."

"I don't think I ever had anyone react with such enthusiasm," grinned Whit.

Just then, a striking Asian woman with long black hair down her back, a silver top and skin-tight jeans jumped on the stage and grabbed a mike.

"Hey, everybody!" she yelled. "I'm Kinsey May, and I'm here to let all of you sing!"

The crowd cheered, applauded and whistled. Kinsey gave them a big smile and continued, "Sign-up's at this end of the bar, for any newcomers. I see I've got a page full already, so let's get goin'!"

She strode across the stage to a computer set on a table next to keyboard, touched the keypad, and "500 Miles" by the Proclaimers poured out of the speakers. The lyrics were on a screen behind the stage and one across the room that singers could see. Kinsey strutted back to center stage, singing in a surprisingly strong voice, and lifting her arms to get the crowd to join the chorus. They did. Everyone with Emmalise was singing boisterously, and she joined in without prodding. Individual singers followed, some good, some drunk and terrible, but all were supported by Kinsey May and the Leonardo crowd. Emmalise danced with the other women in the group to a giggling version of "Girls Just Wanna Have Fun." Then Jake sang Springsteen's "Dancing in the Dark," while Kellon danced with Emmalise, Les with Jeannie, Sally with Gem, and Louann with Whit. Jake sounded and acted a lot like the Boss, and received raucous applause. When Emmalise sat down, she noticed Whit hadn't returned. Turning to the stage, she saw him with the mike in his hand, looking very uncomfortable. However, as soon as the music to Toby Keith's "Should've Been a Cowboy" began, a different person appeared. Somehow he had acquired a cowboy hat that he plopped on his head. He grinned; he moved to the rhythm and mimed the lyrics. He sang in a clear baritone with a touch of twang. He was having a great time, and the crowd loved him. When he finished, he bowed to cheers and whistles, then went over to talk to Kinsey as the applause subsided. He rejoined their table to congratulations and laughter.

Kinsey stepped out on the stage with the mike.

"Folks, we have a newbie tonight, and as you know, I like to give first-timers my support. I know you will too! Come on up here, Emmalise Pine!"

Emmalise was stunned, looking from face to face at her group. Kellon and Jake shook their heads; so did the others, until she looked at Whit, who smiled and nodded.

"You can do it," he said.

"You definitely can," said Louann, giving her a gentle push.

Emmalise rose slowly and walked to the stage on trembling legs. Kinsey handed her a mike, and held on to her own.

"I'll sing with you, if you want," Kinsey said softly, holding her hand over the mike.

"What are we singing?" asked Emmalise.

Kinsey looked a little confused, but said, "Dixie Chicks, "Cowboy, Take Me Away." Isn't that what you picked?"

"That's OK," whispered Emmalise, her mouth dry.

The music began and the lyrics appeared on the screen. She heard Kinsey begin: "I said, I wanna touch the earth..." and she joined softly: "I wanna break it in my hands...."

Emmalise loved the song, and her voice quickly grew stronger. Kinsey stayed with her through the chorus, switching to harmony, but she let Emmalise sing the second verse alone. Even to herself, she thought her voice sounded pretty good. Emmalise couldn't help but look at Whit when she sang: "Except for maybe you and your simple smile...," grinning when he wiggled his eyebrows at her. Kinsey came back in for the chorus, lifting her arms again to bring in the crowd. Emmalise thought her smile would break her face, as the crowd cheered and cheered.

Going back to her seat, she gave Whit a little punch in the shoulder, and then hugged him, asking, "How did you know what song to pick?"

"Just guessed," he answered, smiling back at her, "You're a cowgirl."

She didn't know what he meant, but she was flushed and happy, as she sat down.

"You have a beautiful voice," said Gem seriously.

"Great job, newbie!" said Kellon.

"You can sing!" added Jake.

Everyone else agreed. Emmalise was sure they were just being nice, but she'd had a wonderful time, and was tingling inside. She switched to ginger ale, so she could drive home, and proceeded to enjoy the rest of the evening. The crowd stayed in high spirits, and most of the singing was good, until about 1:00 a.m. After a slow number, Emmalise started to feel sleepy, and decided to call it a night. That feeling seemed to hit everyone else at the same time. They all trailed out to the front of the bar, and said their good-nights. Whit gave her a smile and a little wave, before he turned away to walk to his car.

"I think he wanted to talk to you some more," remarked Jake.

"He was definitely reluctant to leave," added Kellon.

Emmalise smiled, shaking her head.

"Thank you for inviting me," she said. "I had the best time."

"You were fantastic!" said Jake.

"You were!" Kellon insisted, when she scrunched up her face and shook her head again.

"I didn't mean that," insisted Emmalise, "but that was fun too. Unexpected, but fun. Jake, you were wonderful! You could be Bruce in a cover band!"

"Don't give him ideas!" laughed Kellon.

"You have to sing next time, Kellon," Emmalise said.

"Oh, no. I really can't sing," Kellon was shaking his head emphatically.

"He's right," said Jake. "He can't."

They both laughed.

"Here we are," said Jake, stopping by their cars, "Can't miss these."

"Thanks again, guys," said Emmalise, walking around to the driver's door.

"Let's do it again," said Kellon.

Jake pulled out, and both men waved out their windows, as Emmalise followed them.

They must've been going to Jake's place, since the flashy red car turned off before she reached the road home. She felt relaxed, but something warm was thrumming through her. As she climbed the stairs to her apartment, she could hear Lance and Guinevere crying, and she wanted to tell them about her evening. She collapsed on the couch, kicking off her shoes, and the cats jumped up beside her. Just then, her phone rang.

Her first thought was family trouble as she reached for it. It was an unfamiliar number, and she almost didn't answer, thinking telemarketer.

"Hello," she said.

"Hi. Did you get home OK?" She recognized Whit's voice, and smiled.

"Hi. I did."

"Good. Want to go out sometime?"

"Yes."

"Good. Tomorrow afternoon?"

"Sure."

"Do you like to hike?"

"Yes, I do."

"OK. I'll pick you up about eleven."

"That's morning, but OK."

"We can have some lunch."

"All right. Do you know where I live?'

"Above Kellon. See you tomorrow."

"Yes. See you."

She clicked off, looked at her cats, and said, "Whoa!"

Chapter 17

Emmalise was up by 7:00 a.m. to feed her cats, and take Kellon's dogs for a short run. He had texted her the night before to make the request. She almost texted back, "You owe me!" But decided that he didn't. She ate a piece of toast standing up, while talking to the cats about Whit.

"I hope you like him," she said. "You probably don't care that he's very good looking. And funny. He sings well; you might like that."

Suddenly she stopped with the toast half-way to her mouth.

"I don't even know his last name!"

Lance and Guin watched her intently. Or the toast. Any kind of food was fair game, until they smelled it up close, and knew whether they would eat it or not. Emmalise finished the last few bites and downed a glass of cranberry juice. She opened a drawer and pulled out a stick attached to a string with a feathered toy tied to it. For twenty minutes she tempted the cats with the "bird," pulling it across the floor, over chairs, and flipping it in the air. They spent a lot of time watching, but would also run and pounce, or jump two feet off the ground, trying to snag it. Eventually they curled up on the couch and started grooming. Emmalise stroked them each on the head, and went into her bedroom. She pulled out jeans, a long-sleeved rust-colored knit top, socks, underwear and tennis shoes, thinking, "I'm so glad we're hiking and I don't have to pick out date clothes." After showering, she left her hair down, but stuck a hair band in her pocket in case she wanted to pull it up. It was only 9:30 a.m., so she grabbed a Sue Grafton mystery that she was reading and plopped on her bed. In a few minutes, both cats had joined her, Lance stretched out along her side and Guinnie on the pillow next to her head.

Emmalise faintly heard a bell chiming. It rang again. She sat up, shaking her head, and heard her doorbell loud and clear. She'd fallen asleep. She jumped up, and ran to her back door, down the stairs, and yanked open the downstairs door.

"I thought you forgot," Whit smiled at her.

"No," she smiled back. "I fell asleep. I'm not used to late nights, I guess."

"You ready?" he asked.

"Just let me get my bag," she said, starting to turn.

"Well, hello, beautiful!" Whit was bending down, stroking Guin under her chin. Lance was sitting further up the stairs, watching.

"Who are these beauties?" Whit asked.

"Oh, I forgot to close the door! That one is Guinevere, and the guy on the stairs is Lancelot. I'll have to get them back in the apartment."

Whit scooped up Guin, and followed Emmalise up the stairs. Guin was completely limp in his arms. He carefully closed the door and looked around the kitchen.

"I'll be right with you," said Emmalise. "The living room is that way, if you want to sit down."

Whit waited in the kitchen, and Emmalise reappeared moments later, carrying a brown leather purse over her shoulder.

"Hey," she said, "what is your last name?"

"Pierce," Whit answered, smiling. "Whitman Pierce. And, yes, my mother liked Walt Whitman."

Emmalise smiled back at him.

"What about you?" she asked.

"He's good," said Whit, "but I'm not a big poetry guy."

He headed down the back stairs, and Emmalise closed the door carefully behind them.

They headed around the side of the house, and she saw a dark green Camaro parked behind her shiny yellow Mazda.

"Oh, nice car! I love Camaros!"

"Me too," said Whit, holding the passenger door for her, "Are you a car person?"

"Not particularly," Emmalise said, sliding into the seat. "I just know what I like. What about you?"

"Not particularly," Whit grinned at her and started the engine. "Have you ever been to Cove Spring Park?"

"No."

"It's over by Frankfort, not too far," Whit said. "I packed some lunch. Hope that's OK."

"Sounds good," said Emmalise.

Whit revved the engine, grinned at her, then took off sedately. It had a stick shift, which Whit maneuvered easily.

"There aren't too many stick shifts any more," Emmalise commented.

"Can you drive one?" Whit asked.

"I don't know," she answered. "I've always wanted to try."

They rode in silence for awhile. Soon they were on highway 421 to Frankfort.

"Was that really your first time singing in public?" Whit glanced at her.

"Except for choir in high school, and church choir back in the day. Do you sing in public a lot?"

"No," Whit laughed, "only karaoke and in the shower."

"Well, you have a great voice."

"So do you. I think you could sing professionally."

Emmalise felt her face flush, so she looked out the window, watching the fields go by.

"What do you do for a living?" Whit asked her.

"I'm a vet tech at Wags and Purrs Animal Hospital."

"And you have two cats, so I guess you're an animal lover."

"Well, sure. Do you have any pets?"

"I would, but I'm gone so much for my job, it doesn't seem fair to an animal."

"Don't you mostly work in Lexington?"

"Yes, but I keep very long, odd hours. I don't seem to have much free time. Last night and today are exceptions. Is your job fun?"

"Sometimes. It's never boring. It can be sad, or frustrating, but mostly I get to help animals, so that's good. I don't imagine your job is boring."

"Oh, yes, it can be. Long stakeouts. And I mostly see the worst sides of humanity. It's not often that I get to tell a spouse that their partner is NOT having an affair!"

"You don't just do divorce investigations, do you?"

"No. I do lots of business work: employee hiring checks, primarily. Some missing persons. It can be interesting, and it pays the bills." Whit paused, and said, "Do you mind if we don't talk about my work?"

"Sure. That's fine."

Emmalise wanted to tell him about her investigation, see if he had any suggestions, but she knew it was too soon. Naturally, that was all she could think of, so they rode in silence again. At first, it seemed uncomfortable, but after a few minutes, it wasn't.

The countryside was beautiful with lots of farms, especially horse farms, on either side.

"I'd like to have a horse," Whit said.

"What kind?"

Whit grinned, and said, "The riding kind. I don't care what breed, just a good riding horse that can teach me what I need to know."

"Have you ever ridden?"

"Not since I was a kid. My uncle, Jake's dad, breeds racehorses. He kept a few that weren't winners for the kids to ride. Jake and his sister, Jenny, would have my older sister and me out once in awhile. Jake wasn't that into it, but Jenny, Claire and I were hooked. Jenny practically lived in the stables, worked as a stablehand, followed the trainer around. He got her first horse ready for her, and after that, Jenny took a few others in hand. She was five years older than Jake, and we idolized her. She would train horses for us to ride, and teach us, as well."

"Sounds fun. And exciting."

"They were thoroughbreds, but not fast enough to be winners. Still, they seemed pretty fast to me!"

"Can't you still go there to ride?"

"No. My uncle just has broodmares and foals now. Jenny became a trainer herself. Has her own barn. She has her hands full trying to make a go of it. It's a very competitive business."

"You could lease a horse, or share ownership. That cuts down on expenses and with two owners, the horse gets more attention and exercise."

"Really? I haven't heard of that."

"One of our vets does the large animals. He and his wife both lease horses, because, otherwise, they wouldn't get to ride regularly. I can ask him how they went about it, find out where you could find a horse to lease."

"That would be great! Thanks. And here we are."

They were pulling into a parking lot with only a two cars already there. Emmalise saw some picnic tables under a roofed area.

"Want to eat at the tables?" Asked Whit.

"Sure."

He popped the trunk, and they both got out. He pulled a small cooler and a large paper bag out of the trunk. They walked over to the tables and chose the cleanest one in the shade. Emmalise sat down and watched him unpack. First came a loaf of sourdough bread, then a variety of bagels. The cooler held water bottles, four cans of soda, a chunk of cheese, a package of sliced salami, green grapes, a bag of carrot sticks, and napkins.

"Looks great!" said Emmalise, beginning to feel hungry.

"Are you a vegetarian, by any chance?" Whit asked her.

"No. This looks delicious. Are you?"

"I'm not, but I didn't want to take a chance."

"If I were vegan, you'd be in trouble!"

"You could choose not to eat the cheese."

"Um, did you bring a knife?"

"Always," Whit pulled a pocketknife out of his pocket.

Emmalise laughed. Whit began sawing at the loaf.

"Don't worry," he looked up at her under his cocked eyebrows, "I washed it recently."

She laughed again.

"How recently?"

"Oh, since the last time I used it."

"I am not going to ask how you used it."

"Good idea."

The knife didn't cut the bread that well, so they both tore chunks off the loaf. Whit began cutting chunks off the block of cheese, which worked better. He laid the cheese, salami, grapes and carrots on napkins.

"What's the cheese?" asked Emmalise with a piece in her hand.

"Sharp cheddar."

"Good. My favorite."

They both began eating, chewing, and smiling at each other. Emmalise noticed that Whit ate one kind of food at a time, while she mixed it up. She remembered that her older brother Dillon was the only other person she knew who ate food one kind at a time, saving his favorite for last. When they finished, Whit packed up what was left and put it all in the cooler, and threw away the trash.

"Want a water for the trails?" he asked before he took the cooler back to the car.

"Are they strenuous?"

"Depends on which you take, but on the whole, not very."

"I'll be OK."

Emmalise pulled a pack of peppermint gum from her pocket, offered it to him, and put it back, when he shook his head 'no.' They spent the next two hours hiking a couple of simple trails, not talking much, except to comment on the woods, the meadow, the waterfalls, or the sculpture of the playing children. It was surrounded by bricks that bore the names of children that families had lost.

"I think it's supposed to be hopeful in some way, a memorial," said Whit, "but it just seems sad."

Emmalise wondered if he was thinking of a particular case he'd had, but he headed on down the trail, so she didn't ask. They saw a tower and a dam, the remains of old waterworks for the town. They talked a little about the "old days," how hard it would've been to live back when Kentucky was first settled.

"Do you like camping?" Whit turned to look back at her on the narrow trail.

"I haven't gone camping," admitted Emmalise, "and I don't like not having a bathroom."

Whit chuckled, "Yeah, me either."

"Speaking of which, are there any outhouses around here?"

"There are honest-to-goodness bathrooms back near the entrance. Want to head back?"

"If the trail takes us back, we can just keep following it."

They continued in silence, listening to their feet crunching on the leafy path, and to the small daytime sounds of the woods. Abruptly, Whit stopped and put a finger to his lips.

Emmalise stopped too. Faintly, she could hear grunting and panting, and wondered what animal would be so noisy in the daylight, or anytime. When she realized what it was, she slapped her hand over her mouth to keep from gasping. Whit turned, grinning, and they hustled back down the path. In twenty yards, they were both laughing out loud.

"Wow! Out in public! In the daytime!" Emmalise said breathlessly.

"Never ran across that before," Whit commented, "They must've been seriously overcome!"

"Teenagers with no place else to go," suggested Emmalise with a smile. She knew her face was bright red, and hoped the laughter covered it. Then she glanced at Whit, and saw, to her delight, that he was blushing too. He looked back at her, grinned, wiggled his eyebrows evilly, and that started the laughter all over again. They headed back to the entrance, the restrooms, and the car. As they drove to Lexington, Whit said, "I can beat that one."

Emmalise turned to look at him, and said, "OK, let's hear it."

"It was one of my first jobs. A pretty young wife hired me to follow her husband. She was sure he was cheating on her. She said that if I saw him with someone else to take pictures. I followed him for two weeks. Nothing. Just work, errands, home. Once he had drinks with a buddy at a bar, but went home early. I called her and said I felt guilty taking her money, but she said to work one more week. Two nights later, he went into a hotel, a nice hotel. I followed him up to a room, where a gorgeous brunette opened the door with nothing on. As instructed, I took pictures. I was pretty far away, of course, but I got lucky. They left the hotel together, and I got better pictures. I reluctantly showed the wife, who was a blonde, by the way, and she cried a little, took the photos, paid me, and thanked me. The next day, a big, good-looking guy came into my office and threw the photos on my desk. I recognized him. It was the husband. 'Are you trying to ruin my life?' he yelled at me. I can take care of myself, but I'm thinking, 'Oh shit! I don't want to fight this guy!' He leaned over my desk like he was coming after me, then he started laughing. The blonde who hired me was his crazy ex-girlfriend and the brunette was his wife. He'd broken up with the blonde right before he met his wife-to-be, but, apparently, the ex had continued stalking him. After she left my office the day before, she'd gone to his office, thrown the photos on his desk and went berserk, screaming 'You left me for THAT?' Luckily, she stormed out, and his co-workers were sympathetic. Actually, he said they laughed their asses off after he explained. He took back his photos, left laughing, and told me I should check credentials more carefully before I took a job."

Emmalise was laughing too.

"I can't top that," she said, "but we have some crazy customers at the clinic. There's one lady who dresses her miniature poodle to match her outfits, as closely as possible. They both have curly black hair and wear the same color nail polish."

When Whit pulled onto her road, he said, "I'd love to ask you out for dinner tonight, but I have to work."

"Rain check, I hope," she answered, "I had a great time today."

He walked her to her door, leaned toward her, and said, "This is all I'll do in public."

He kissed her gently, and pulled her against him. She kissed him back, feeling it throughout her body. He let her go, still holding her hand, as he turned back to his car. Emmalise ran up the stairs to her apartment, collapsed on her couch, and told the cats it had been a good day.

Chapter 18

Emmalise received a text at work on Monday from Sheriff Dade, asking her to meet with him on Tuesday at 5:30 p.m., if she could. It was difficult to wait, but work was always distracting, and she had a long phone conversation with Whit on Monday evening. He asked if she could go out for dinner on Friday, which she accepted. Still she was excited when she parked down the block and walked into the Sheriff's office at 5:25 p.m. on Tuesday. The receptionist appeared to be gone for the day, but Deputy Kincaid waved her into the Sheriff's office from the doorway. He smiled as she walked in and sat in one of the wooden chairs facing the sheriff's desk.

"Hello, Emmalise," Sheriff Dade said. "Ready for an update?"

"Of course," she answered.

"I got lucky at the American Legion lunch yesterday," said Sheriff Dade. "The members at my table were talking about Printes's candidacy as a done deal. All I had to do was listen. Most of the men thought he would be a fine representative, a good conservative Republican. I noticed that Patrick Goins, the former fire chief, didn't say a word. I talked to him later after the meeting, and he said that he wasn't sure about Printes.

Pat had been in Science Club with Gideon. Thought he was quiet and stuck-up then, but hadn't kept in touch after high school. He said his grandfather had never liked the family, but he didn't know why. I asked if I could talk to his grandfather, and he said, sure, and gave me his number. The old guy is 92, but still with it, and lives in his own home. I also got a chance to talk with Art Bishop. He was in Debate Club with Gideon, and said Printes was not friendly to him. Art said he was good at debating, very well prepared, and could argue either side of a question well. Art thought it was very hard to tell what Gideon's own opinions were. Art also referred me to his grandfather. He said that his granddad had even worked at the Printes place a few times, and didn't think much of Oscar Printes. Art said I could talk to his grandfather, William Foster, his maternal grandfather, who lives in his own place, too, out in the country, with a second wife. Art's grandmother passed away from influenza twenty years ago. That made William 74, when he remarried a woman fifteen years younger. I can't wait to meet them."

"Those sound like they have potential," Emmalise was on the edge of her chair. "So who is going to talk to whom?"

"I'll want to talk with William Foster," said Sheriff Dade. "Sam, I'd like you to interview Peter Goins. If we have time, maybe we can both visit both men."

"What about the cook and the nanny?" asked Emmalise.

"I've been thinking about that." Sheriff Dade leaned forward over his desk, hands clasped. "I think it would be good if you went with Sam. I think you would make the ladies feel more comfortable. We need a cover story, obviously. I thought we could say we're thinking of forming a committee to help with Printes's campaign, but we want to know more about him before we give him our full support. Sam, you can tell them you're a deputy, but wear street clothes. We don't want to overwhelm them."

"Sounds good," said Sam.

Emmalise looked like her face was having trouble controlling itself. Finally she broke into a big grin. Sheriff Dade smiled at her, shaking his head slowly.

"Did you find out anything else from Miss Tippet?" he asked.

Emmalise went over Miss Tippet's character judgments of Printes's schoolmates, and that she'd suggested seeing Judge Turner again, and possibly Mary Leonard.

"OK. Let's do these other interviews first. Sam, you call and set up appointments at their convenience. You'll have to see Mrs. Washington and Mrs. Brooks sometime when Emmalise can join you. All right?"

"Yes, sir," said Sam and Emmalise, almost in unison.

"What's good for you?" Sam asked her.

"Weekdays from 5:00 p.m. on, and I have Thursday afternoons off. Sometimes I work Saturday mornings, but that varies."

"OK, I'll get back to you."

Sam had all of the appointments set by ten the next morning. He and Sheriff Dade headed to Belleriver after lunch to meet with Peter Goins. He lived in a small one-story brick duplex in a neighborhood of one-story homes. Some were well cared for with tiny lawns that could be mowed with a manual push mower, and colorful flower beds; while others were run-down with dirt and weed yards. At least the trees near the street were old and large, providing color and shade. Goins' house had a maple tree in the yard and spirea bushes surrounding the house. The grass was a little shaggy, but there were no bare spots and few weeds. As Sam and the sheriff walked up the sidewalk, a thin, elderly man opened the door.

"Good afternoon," Peter Goins called to them in a deep, firm voice.

"Hello, Mr. Goins," answered Sheriff Dade. "Thanks for seeing us."

"You're welcome, I think," he said without a smile. "I don't have a lot of company, so this could be a nice change of pace."

Goins was thin, straight-backed and walked with a very slight limp. He led them into his living room, which was filled with a couch, two armchairs, a television on one wall, a large window overlooking the front yard, and tables and shelves filled with taxidermy: squirrels, a fox, a skunk, a possum, two rabbits, a raccoon, an owl, a hawk and a variety of other birds.

"Don't mind my friends," chuckled Peter Goins, "They won't bite. Just have a seat and tell me why you're here."

"Some men at the Legion lunch were talking about Gideon Printes running for the state legislature," said Sheriff Dade, "even wanting to set up a committee to back him. Patrick seemed pretty lukewarm, but admitted he was basing his opinion on memories of Printes from back in high school. He said we should talk to you."

Goins had snorted softly at the mention of Printes running for office.

"I wouldn't trust him as far as I could throw him, assuming he's anything like his daddy," Peter Goins stated flatly. He sat on the edge of his chair, arms straight, hands on his knees. His white hair was wispy on his nearly bald head, but his dark eyes were clear.

"What can you tell us about Oscar Printes?"

"Rich, and I doubt he made it all legally. He not only didn't serve in the War, he actively tried to keep us out of it. An isolationist. And smarmy. People fell for it, especially other rich people. I just never liked him, never trusted him. There was something off about him."

"Did you know him personally, Mr. Goins?"

"We didn't run in the same circles, if that's what you mean. He wasn't from here originally. Ohio, I think. His wife Athena is a Belleriver girl. That big house they live in was her family's. They were well off from tobacco and farming, but not snooty. Mr. Walker built that house himself with some help from hired hands. They had no servants and only the one child, Athena. I went to school with Athena. Just a one-room schoolhouse back then. She was the most beautiful girl in the town. All the boys loved her, including me. She was friendly and kind to everyone, just like her mama, but she didn't date any of the local boys. She was only 16 when Oscar Printes showed up. He wanted to buy some of Mr. Walker's land, and he charmed Athena right off her feet. She was 17 when they got married. He was 30. Somehow Oscar ended up with all of Walker's land and the house. Mr. and Mrs. Walker lived with Oscar and Athena for a few months, then moved into town. They both died a few years later within weeks of each other. Everyone said of broken hearts."

"Why of broken hearts?" asked Sam. "Their daughter married a rich, charming man."

"They didn't talk about Printes or Athena's marriage, but their friends saw that the Walkers weren't happy. Why did they have to leave their own home? Plus, they weren't sure that Athena was happy. She had miscarriages and lost one infant at six months. That must've broken her heart and her parents' hearts, too. Meanwhile Oscar is buying up land all over the state, and when he's home, he wants parties. Big, fancy parties to which Athena's parents were not invited. Just rich people from Versailles and Frankfort. Anyway, the Walkers died and didn't get to see their grandchildren. Athena had Gideon when she was 29 and Faye two years later. Oscar had hired a black cook, and a gardener. He brought in other help for the parties. He hired a nanny for Gideon and Faye. Always black help. He acted like he was an old-time plantation owner, Southern royalty. I was a small farmer and volunteer fireman. Oscar wouldn't give me the time of day. The only time he spoke to me was to try and buy my land. I wouldn't sell. Then my wife became ill. Cancer of the womb. We were in our sixties, and I was still farming, but the bills were too much. That's when Printes got me. He took my land. Iva and I moved to town, to this house. This is where she died. Anyway, I've stayed away from the Printes family. Maybe Gideon and Faye grew up more like their mama than Oscar, but I don't know them. So, I guess I'm not much help."

"Sure you are, Mr. Goins," said Sheriff Dade. "Background is always helpful. Do you know anything else about Oscar that could cause problems for Gideon in the campaign?"

"No," Peter said slowly, dragging out the word, "not that I can remember."

"I have to ask," said Sam. "How did you get into taxidermy?"

"Ha!" chuckled Peter, "At auctions, if you'd believe it. After Iva died, I needed something to do, so I started going to auctions. You see all kinds of interesting stuff. Some of it historical. The first taxidermy critter I got was that little bluebird on the window sill, so it's very old. Iva loved birds and all wildlife. They remind me of her."

"I've never seen so many in one place," Sam smiled, "Some of them are very lifelike."

"I've got more," Peter grinned, "all over the house. Freaks out my son, but the grandkids like them."

"Thanks a lot for talking with us, Mr. Goins," said Sheriff Dade.

"Glad to, and call me Peter. I should've said that from the get-go."

Both officers shook hands with Peter Goins, and headed back to the sheriff's personal car, an older model dark blue Ford Edge. They hoped it would be less noticeable than the department vehicles.

"We're a little early for our appointment with William Foster," said Sam, "I'll call and make sure it's OK if we come now."

The sheriff drove out of Versailles, heading south, and easily found the Foster farm outside of Belleriver. A long gravel lane lead to a white two-story farmhouse with dark green shutters. Behind it was a newer looking white two-car garage, and a large, dilapidated barn, once red, but faded and weathered to nearly gray.

A light brown woman with white, curly hair and bright brown eyes answered Sam's knock. A golden retriever with a white face stood beside her, looking up at them.

"Come in, gentlemen. I'm Amelia Foster. This is Beth, our constant companion. Will is in the front room."

Sam and the sheriff followed Mrs. Foster into a small, pleasant living room. She wore a green shirtwaist dress with tiny yellow and blue flowers, and moved like a much younger woman. William Foster was sitting at a small table by one of the front windows, poring over a large puzzle. He looked up, as they came into the room. His brown eyes watched them intently out of a very wrinkled face. He was partially bald with a semicircle of white hair from ear to ear cut neatly over his dark skin.

"Sheriff Dade and Deputy Kincaid are here, Will," she said.

Foster nodded, and reached down to pet the retriever who had walked quietly to his chair. He motioned for them to sit down at the table in two wooden chairs that matched his own. Then he reached across the table to shake hands with both men.

"Feel free to help with the puzzle," commented William Foster in a gruff voice. The puzzle looked like a 1000 piece scene of racehorses and their jockeys headed for the finish line. The box lid with the complete picture was propped up against the window.

"Would you gentlemen like some tea or lemonade?" asked Amelia.

"Just water, please," said Sam and the sheriff, almost simultaneously.

William already had a glass of lemonade on the window sill.

"I believe you came to talk about Gideon Printes," said William.

"We're looking into his background, family, anything that could influence his possible election, for good or bad," said the sheriff. "Art said he thought you worked for the family for awhile."

"That was a long time ago," said William, moving a puzzle piece to its rightful place.

"Yes," said Dade, "but even long ago events can influence an election."

"Humph. True enough. Do you know Gideon Printes?"

"No, not personally."

"Then why do you care if he runs for election?"

The sheriff and Sam glanced at each other. Sam picked up a puzzle piece and placed it accurately.

"Good one, young man," said William.

"Call me Sam."

"Call me Will. Both of you."

"Parker," said the sheriff with a smile.

"Well, I don't know much about Gideon," Will said, his long fingers moving over the pieces like they had eyes in the tips. "I worked for Mr. Oscar pretty regular back in the day. Back when they had a big party every other weekend. I'd do repairs and upkeep two or three days a week, and butler the parties come Saturday. Saw a lotta fancy white folks at those parties."

Amelia returned with two glasses of ice water that she handed to Sam and the sheriff. A quick look passed between her and Will, and she pulled over a rose-colored arm chair and sat near her husband.

"When did you work there?" asked Sam.

Will stared out the window for a minute, then said, "Must've been in the late '50s and '60s. Art was a youngster, so Gideon was too. I was the night security at the Wild Turkey distillery then. Worked out well to have an extra job that way."

Sam and Parker looked at each other.

"What did you think of Oscar and Athena Printes?" asked Parker.

Will looked at him quizzically, then said, "They were good employers. Paid well."

"What were the parties like? Anything political?" said Sam.

"Fancy. Suits and dresses. Sometimes tuxedos and long dresses. Most of the parties were big crowds with drinks and finger food. Once in awhile they'd have dinner parties with not as many people. I suppose conversation could get political."

"Did Oscar want to run for office?" Sam tried again.

"Not that I noticed," said Will, his voice sounding hoarse. He took a long drink of lemonade.

"Did you know anyone else who worked for the Printes's?" asked the sheriff.

"Oh, sure. They had a full-time cook, Serafina Washington. When Gideon was born, they hired her niece Malayna to take care of the kids."

"Did they like working there?"

"Far as I know. Mrs. Washington was a fabulous cook, almost as good as my Amelia." Will reached over and squeezed her hand. She smiled at him.

"What about Malayna?"

"What about her?" Will shook his head. "I know you two are looking for something. Why don't you just be straight?"

Parker cleared his throat and said, "I don't want to support someone who has skeletons in his closet. No one knows a family like the people who work for them."

"Do you know Mr. Printes's politics?" asked Amelia.

"Conservative, but nothing specific," said Parker. "I think Arthur has reservations about him, but when I asked him, he said to talk to you."

"Well, he's too conservative for me, if he's a Republican," said Will. "I wasn't at their place that often. He just seemed like a rich person wanting to show off being rich. Now Mrs. Washington, Serafina, thought the world of Mrs. Printes, that I do know. You should talk to her and Malayna."

"We hope to," said Sam, "Do you know anyone else who worked there?"

"Samuel Porter was their gardener and handyman for many years, but he passed away in 1990," said Will. "He helped me get the part-time work there. Good man. Very hard working. He also thought highly of Mrs. Printes. He said Mr. Printes was exacting, but Samuel never gave him cause to complain. Anyway, he can't talk to you all now."

"Who did the gardening after Mr. Porter?" Sam asked.

Will took a long swallow of lemonade. He seemed a little tired, but answered clearly, "After Mr. Oscar died, and Mr. Gideon moved back, they had one migrant worker after another, mostly Mexican. They probably made better money following the crops, so they didn't last. They tried a couple of local boys, but they were too young, I guess. Or lazy. I know they had an older black man for awhile, not from around here. He seemed to be a hobo, just showed up one day. I think Mrs. Washington tried to shoo him away, but Mrs. Printes was there, and asked him if he wanted to work. I only met him once, and he was raking the yard. Saw him a few times after that, always working hard. He stayed all summer, into the fall, I believe. Then one day, he was just gone. Didn't see him no more. Eventually, someone started a yard work business, and the

Printeses used them."

"Do you remember the hobo's name?" said Parker.

"No, and why would you want to know, if he's gone?" Will snapped.

Amelia lay her hand gently on her husband's arm. He looked at her, and she smiled in the way of two people who know each other well. Will looked back at the puzzle and picked up another piece, fitting it in as part of a horse's nose.

"I appreciate your help and hospitality," said Parker, rising from his chair.

Sam quickly placed another puzzle piece, a jockey's hand. Will looked up at him and they nodded at each other.

"If you ever decide to tell me what's going on, you're welcome back," said Will, bending over his puzzle.

Chapter 19

When Sam called Emmalise with their Thursday 7:00 p.m. appointment to interview Serafina Washington and Malayna Brookes, he told her to wear a plain dress or skirt and blouse. She asked why.

"Those are Mrs. Brookes' instructions," answered Sam, "I'm supposed to wear a suit and tie, and carry a Bible. She said they have nosy neighbors, and we need to look like Jehovah Witnesses or some other missionaries."

"What did you tell her about why we're coming?" said Emmalise. "Doesn't that seem over the top?"

"I told her what Sheriff Dade said to say. That we want to discuss Gideon Printes as a possible candidate for the legislature. I also told her that I was with the Sheriff's Department, and she asked me not to wear my uniform. Then she went into more detail."

"Good grief, I may not have anything like that, but I can check with my mother," Emmalise laughed softly. "This is very interesting."

"Can you meet me at the office by 6:45 on Thursday?"

"Sure. Where do they live?"

"Here in Versailles. On the edge of town, but it's not far."

Sam watched Emmalise step out of her car on Wednesday, wearing a white blouse and a black skirt that covered her knees. Her hair was in a bun at the back of her neck.

"Nice touch with your hair," said Sam, smiling. He wore a navy blue suit, white shirt and a plain navy tie. He was carrying a Bible. Emmalise showed him a manila folder, stuffed fairly full.

"What's that?" Sam asked.

"Jehovah Witnesses always carry pamphlets, so I went to the Chamber of Commerce in Lexington and picked up some. They're not religious at all, so I hope no one asks for one."

"OK, good idea. Let's take my car. It's more innocuous."

"You know what else we haven't talked about?" Emmalise brought up. "Why am I involved? I'm not in the DAR or related to anyone in the American Legion, so why am I with you?"

"Glad you thought of that before we got there," Sam said. "I'm not in the Legion either. Any ideas?"

"We could both have a friend or relative in the Legion," said Emmalise.

"Or we don't have to mention the Legion. Just people interested in the election."

"I think I'll say I'm a Democrat looking into the opposition, which is true," decided Emmalise, "but why am I with you?"

"Friends. We're friends," said Sam. "We were out for dinner with several friends, Printes running came up, and we all decided to look into his past."

"How did we find these women?"

"I can tell the truth there. I'll mention that I met Judge Turner and he told me about them."

Emmalise sighed in relief. Their story was plausible. Sam handed her an envelope.

"What's this?"

"I typed out an update of our visits with Will Foster and Peter Goins."

Emmalise read the two pages quickly.

"The hobo-gardener sounds like the victim," she said hesitantly, "but you didn't learn anything about him."

"Mr. Foster was suspicious, and didn't seem to know the man, anyway. Maybe these ladies will know him. Mrs. Washington was certainly still working there."

They turned into a neighborhood of mostly brick one-story duplexes with small yards and not many trees or flowerbeds. Most had backyards fenced with chain link and one-car garages in back. They parked at the end of the block and walked past three houses to 207A. They climbed two steps to a narrow porch that extended the length of the house with the front doors to A and B side-by-side in the center. The house sat on cinder blocks that hid a crawl space. Small evergreen bushes set a few feet apart partially concealed the blocks. The front door and the window trim wore a fairly new coat of tan paint. Sam saw a curtain flick on the narrow windows on either side of the door when he rang the bell. A straight-backed, gray-haired African American woman opened the door and studied them.

"Good evening," said Sam. "Are you Mrs. Malayna Brookes?"

"Yes, I am. And I assume you are Mr. Sam Kincaid and Ms. Emmalise Pine. Please come in. Would you like to leave your belongings here on the hall table?"

They did as she suggested. The woman was as tall as Emmalise, and looked much younger than her 84 years. She gestured toward a room to their left where another elderly black woman sat on a worn gold-colored sofa. The white-haired woman looked up at them, as they entered.

"Auntie Serafina, these are the people I told you were coming, Mr. Kincaid and Ms. Pine," said Mrs. Brookes.

"How do you do?" said Sam formally, reaching toward Mrs. Washington's hand, which she raised to meet his. Hers was cool and light to the touch.

Emmalise shook both women's hands too. She sat in one of two arm chairs facing the sofa, and Sam took the other. Four cups and saucers, and a carafe of coffee, along with a plate of cookies, sat on a coffee table between the chairs and couch.

"Would you care for some coffee?" asked Mrs. Brookes, holding the pot over Emmalise's cup.

Both Sam and Emmalise accepted, and sipped the hot coffee. Emmalise took a cookie, nibbled a bite, and laid it on her saucer. She watched the two black women, amazed at their closeness in age, but differences in appearance. Malayna Brookes had gray hair, cut short, like a wavy cap on her head, but she didn't look close to 80. Her skin was mostly smooth, a light golden brown, with few wrinkles, except for deep smile lines on the sides of her mouth, laugh lines by her dark eyes, and frown lines between them. She didn't look like she wore any make-up, although her eyelashes were long and black. Serafina Washington looked closer to her age. She was plump and buxom, and her back was hunched from osteoporosis. Her hair was white and thin, but long enough to be pulled into a bun on top of her head with curly stray hairs surrounding her very wrinkled face.

"You said you wanted to talk about Gideon Printes," said Malayna Brookes.

"Yes," said Sam, "he is almost certainly running for the state legislature. Some of the men in Versailles are thinking about forming an election committee. I know most of them, and I wanted to learn as much as possible about him before I decide to support him."

"How did you find us?" asked Mrs. Brookes.

"Judge Turner told me that you both worked for the family and that you were their nanny, Mrs. Brookes," said Sam, as though he chatted with judges every day.

She nodded, and looked at Emmalise questioningly.

"And you, Ms. Pine?"

"Sam, his wife and I are friends," said Emmalise, looking at Sam with a smile. "I'm interested for a different reason. I'm a Democrat, so Mr. Printes would be the opposition. I don't mean to offend you, but that's the truth."

Mrs. Brookes blinked, and the corners of her mouth turned up slightly and briefly.

"I'm not offended, Ms. Pine. I just can't imagine what I can tell either of you."

"Well, I'm offended," interrupted Mrs. Washington, her voice strong and clear. "You don't even know that boy. He was the sweetest boy I ever knew!"

"That's why we're here," said Sam. "We want to get to know him."

Mrs. Washington still looked angrily at Emmalise, who tried to smile apologetically.

"Would you mind telling us how you came to work for the Printes family?" Sam tried to steer them back to smoother ground.

"I cooked for them from the time I was 21 years old, until I broke my hip when I was 71," stated Mrs. Washington proudly.

"And you were his nanny, Mrs. Brookes?" said Sam.

"Yes, Auntie recommended me. I was there shortly after Gideon was born until he was 12 years old. Faye was 10. I was only 14 myself when I started, but I had a lot of experience with babies. I finished high school and went to college part-time to get my teaching degree. One year after I graduated, in 1965, there was an opening at Belleriver Elementary, where I taught for two years. Then I moved to Simmons Elementary School and taught 5th grade until I retired. It was the same school I attended as a child, except it was segregated then. I guess I'm a little off point. Excuse me."

"Was there a special reason that the Printeses needed a nanny?" asked Emmalise.

"Not really. Mrs Printes was a little weak after Gideon's birth and couldn't produce enough milk. Breast feeding was not the norm back then in the upper classes, so he would've been on formula anyway. She recovered quickly and we shared caring for Gideon. It was Mr. Printes who felt the child should have a nanny. When he was around, he encouraged Mrs. Printes to be very social, both with ladies' organizations, and with parties that they both attended."

"You said 'when he was around'," repeated Sam. "What did you mean?"

"Mr. Printes was often gone on business," said Mrs. Brookes. "He owned land all over the state, so he had to keep an eye on his holdings."

"He was very proud of his children," broke in Mrs. Washington, "but Mrs. Printes adored them. She played with them and wanted to do everything Mr. Printes hired Malayna to do."

Emmalise looked at Mrs. Brookes, "Was Mrs. Printes jealous of you?"

Mrs. Brookes laughed, and shook her head, but before she could answer, Mrs. Washington said, "Oh my good heavens, no! I think she loved Malayna almost like a third child. She made sure my niece had time to do her lessons and graduate from high school. Then Malayna helped Gideon and Faye with their homework."

Mrs. Brookes looked skeptically at her aunt.

"Not quite like her own child, Auntie," she said, "but she was kind to me, and we had no problem sharing the care of the children."

"What was Gideon like?" asked Sam.

"Isn't this a bit intrusive for background on a candidate?" said Mrs. Brookes, frowning slightly at Sam.

"Force of habit," he answered. "Typical interview, actually. You never know what will connect, or point the way."

Mrs. Brookes didn't look convinced, but she answered, "Gideon was not a typical boy. He was very smart and curious, but not athletic. He liked science and books. Even in elementary school, he read science and history books. He didn't like fiction much. He had an insect collection at a young age. Also rocks. The most active thing he did was walk in the woods, and down by the stream, so he could forage for bugs and explore. He was very protective of Faye, and his mother, for that matter. Faye was the adventurous one, so when we did go for walks, we all kept an eye on her. Gideon preferred for his mother and Faye to stay home, so that he could focus on his 'work', as he called it. He was an excellent student, and did not get in trouble. If he had friends, he didn't bring them home. We had those birthday parties when you invite the whole class up until 4th grade, but he didn't seem to get along with anyone in particular. Auntie, did he bring friends home in high school?"

"Not that I remember," said Mrs. Washington. "It wasn't that he couldn't talk. He'd talk the ear off anyone who would listen about bugs, or rocks, or battles, or famous soldiers. I think he was too smart for those other kids."

"The talking your ear off is surely true," Mrs. Brookes said. "He talked to Faye, even though she didn't pay attention. He liked to talk to his mama and me, when he was young, but he also talked to some of the handymen who came and went, especially about history. Around age nine, he began to be interested in talking to men. He tried to talk to his father, but Mr. Printes would just pat his head and say how smart Gideon was, then go back to reading the newspaper."

"Do you remember any of the men who worked there?" Sam asked.

"What does that have to do with anything?" responded Mrs. Brookes dryly.

"Curiosity," said Sam, "and habit."

"The only men who worked for Mr. Printes with any regularity were Will Foster and Samuel Porter," said Mrs. Washington. "Mr. Porter was the gardener for years, and he's dead. After Samuel passed, we had lots of different men, mostly Mexicans. But they didn't last more than one spring through fall."

Mrs. Washington turned to her niece, "Malayna, I'm getting a little tired."

"Just one more question," said Sam. When the two women looked at him, he asked, "Have you seen much of Mr. Printes since you stopped working there?"

"He calls to see how we are," said Mrs. Washington.

"Actually, his mother calls," said Mrs. Brookes, "every week. She sends flowers or fruit baskets sometimes. Now I think we need to rest, if you'll excuse us."

Sam and Emmalise stood quickly, as did Mrs. Brookes.

"Thank you so much for your time," said Sam. He handed each woman a card with both his and Emmalise's phone numbers written on them.

"Have you made your mind up?" asked Mrs. Brookes, leading them to the entry way.

"Not yet," smiled Sam. "We have a lot to digest."

Mrs. Brookes handed Sam his Bible and Emmalise her packet. She closed the door firmly behind them. The porch light gave just enough light for them to see the walkway.

Sam noticed the picture window curtains in the house across the street move, letting out light from the room behind them. He waited until they were in the car to tell Emmalise.

She glanced at the neighbor's house, then back at Mrs. Washington's, and her mouth pinched ruefully.

"We didn't learn much," she sighed.

"Doesn't seem like it, but I think we need to let it simmer for awhile," said Sam. "We do have corroboration that multiple gardeners worked there over the years, and didn't last long."

"Have you ever worked a cold case before?"

"No, but Parker has. Even a regular case can be frustrating. People lie or forget or just don't realize what's important. Besides eye-witness testimony is not that trustworthy," Sam suddenly realized what he'd said. "Not you. I didn't mean you. You're unusual."

Emmalise laughed.

"It's OK. I know what you mean. It's just discouraging. It's like that puzzle you said Mr. Foster was doing, 1,000 pieces. They all have to fit to see the whole picture."

"Don't worry. I think we only need to find about 800 more to have a good idea of what happened."

Chapter 20

Emmalise looked across the table at Whit, liking what she saw, his blond hair combed back, and gray eyes that looked straight at her. They were sharing a garlic and mozzarella pizza with artichokes and bacon at Pies and Pints in Lexington. It wasn't quiet, but they could talk, and had been for over an hour. At 9:00 o'clock, the families with small children were mostly gone, which helped reduce the noise level. They were both still nibbling the pizza, and sipping draft beers.

"Did you grow up here?" Whit asked.

"Not far. Down in Belleriver."

"I've never been there."

"It's a pretty little town. Not much going on. It still has its own elementary school and a library."

"What about your family? Are they still down there?"

"My mother is. And my sister Tara is living with her at the moment."

"Your dad?"

"No, he died a long time ago."

Whit cocked his head, frowning slightly, and asked, "Don't you want to tell me about your family?"

"Sure. Why not?"

"Well, you're giving pretty short answers. I don't mean to grill you."

"Oh, you're not," Emmalise smiled at him. "I'm just not a big talker. I'll give you the whole rundown, but then it's your turn."

He nodded and smiled back.

"My brother Dillon is the oldest. He's 38, married with three kids, and lives in Louisville. He's a plumber. Then Franklin, or Frank, 36, divorced, no kids; he's a mechanic in Evansville, Indiana. I'm next—ta-da! Jana is a year younger than me, so 32. She's married with two kids, and is a bookkeeper for the Ford dealer in Frankfort. Griswold is 30 and in the Army."

"Griswold?" interrupted Whit with a grin.

"Yeah. I think you can tell my mother liked unusual names. He goes by Gris. He's a Sergeant, and will probably be for life. Next is Tara, who lives with Mom, and works at the feed store in Belleriver. She's 28. And last is Ezekiel, or Zeke, who is 26, and wandering. He's a great carpenter and electrician. He never has trouble getting a job. He's in Montana now, but rarely stays anywhere more than a year or two."

"Wow! Seven of you!"

"Yes, and my mother did most of the childrearing. My dad was an alcoholic and died in a car accident, when Mom was pregnant with Zeke. Mom always said it was a blessing he didn't take anyone else with him. Any of us or some other driver. Dillon was 12, the oldest, and I was 7. Dad had been a construction worker, and left Mom the house, and an insurance policy. With seven kids that wasn't going to last long. She was a waitress, and went back to work a month after Zeke was born. We all learned to help around the house and take care of each other. After Zeke was in school, Mom started making quilts by hand for our beds. Each of ours had a personal picture in the quilt, usually an animal we liked, or something she thought suited us. A friend of Mom's saw one of the quilts while Mom was working on it, and told her it was good enough to sell, and where to sell it. She felt they were too personal, but eventually her friend convinced her to try the local general store. She made one with a red barn and some horses in a field, and it sold within three days. Mom doesn't even waitress anymore. She sells them in Versailles and Frankfort, as well as Belleriver. No two are alike."

"She sounds like an amazing woman," said Whit.

"She is."

"What was your quilt? The picture on it? Cats, I'll bet."

Emmalise smiled, "She did make me one with cats a few years ago, but the first one was a dragon."

Whit's eyes widened, and he laughed out loud. Still chuckling, he said, "She knew you were dangerous."

"Hmmm, maybe," Emmalise cocked her head, and grinned. "Actually, I just really liked dragons as a kid, and I wanted to fly. I don't think I cared about the fire-breathing part."

"I'd like to see it."

"I'll show it to you sometime. Now it's your turn."

"OK. I've mentioned Claire, the oldest. She's 36, married, with three kids under five. Her husband's an attorney, and she's a court reporter. Well, she was. She probably won't go back to work, until all of the kids are in school. Then Marie, who is 33, also married, one little girl, Tessa, three years old. Marie is a dentist, and went back to work after six weeks. Her husband is a freelance writer, works from home, and his mother comes most afternoons to help."

Suddenly Whit stopped. He was looking out the window, seeing only their reflections and the vague shapes and lights inside of the restaurant. Emmalise waited, immediately sensing his change of mood. He sighed, rubbed his forehead, as if it hurt, and looked at her again.

"My youngest sister Sylvia disappeared when she was sixteen, and we haven't found her," his voice was quiet, but rough, and his gray eyes were immeasurably sad.

"Oh, Whit, I'm sorry." Emmalise reached across the table and touched his hand. He gently covered her hand with his. She thought this might have had something to do with his choice of work, but she didn't say so.

"My parents did everything they could. Police. Private detectives. Everything. No sign of her. She was at play practice, supposed to ride home with two friends. They went to their lockers separately and were supposed to meet by the doors to the parking lot. Sylvie never showed. The girls went back to the auditorium, but everyone had gone. They came to our house to see if she'd gotten home some other way. Marie and I were in Louisville, at college. Claire had her own apartment, was already working. Mom called her and she came over. She said Mom and Dad were remarkably calm. They reported her missing, and began searching the area between the high school and home. They called all of her friends. The police came right away, even though they suspected that she'd run away. Sylvie would never have run away. Even the police finally admitted there was no evidence of that—no problems at home or at school. Anyway, Marie and I came home the next day. We searched again, put up posters, talked to her friends again. Mom and Dad made Marie go back to school the next week, but I stayed. They never broke down in front of us. They've never given up. After a few weeks, they both went back to work. Dad's a dentist and Mom's a Chemistry professor at U of K. I went back to school the next semester and finished my Justice degree, and became a private investigator. It's been fourteen years since Sylvie disappeared, and I haven't found a lead. You wouldn't believe a person could disappear without a trace, but that's what happened to my little sister."

Emmalise felt his terrible sadness, and she couldn't think of one word of comfort.

She left her hand in his, and watched his face. Finally she said, "How is your family after all this time?"

"My sisters are OK. They have their families. I'd say they're overprotective with their kids, which is understandable. I don't think they believe Sylvie will ever be found. My parents still work, and are happy to see us, and their grandkids, but they'll never give up.

They even have a Facebook page called "Find Sylvie" with pictures, asking for people to contact them if they've seen her. That had thousands of hits, but nothing real. They want her to come home, one way or another."

"What about you?"

"I guess I want to know what happened. I wish I could think of a different way to search, something we haven't tried, but I don't know what it is."

Emmalise decided not to question specifically what had been tried. It sounded overwhelming. She could imagine losing one of her sisters or brothers in that way, and feeling so helpless. No wonder Whit hadn't wanted to talk about his work the other day.

"I've never told any of my dates about this before," he said quietly.

He reached across the table with his other hand, and she gave him hers. Warmth flooded through her, turning her cheeks red.

"Let's try something," suggested Whit. "I'll name an activity, and you say whether you've done it, and if you liked it or would like to try it. Then you can ask me."

"OK."

"Skiing."

"Water or snow?"

"Both."

"I tried water skiing and tubing in high school a few times. Enjoyed both. Would do again. Never tried snow skiing. But I like sledding."

"Laser tag."

"Uh, no. I guess I'd try it."

"Miniature golf."

"A couple of dates, and I didn't have fun, but that was the dates, not the golf."

"Horseback riding."

"Ha!" Emmalise laughed. "Once when I was eight or so, Jana and I got into a neighbor's horse pasture, and tried to ride their ponies without permission. They ran away with us, and bucked us off. We got back on a few times, but eventually they ran back toward the barn, and we didn't want to get caught. So I've been on a horse, but not for long. I would love to do it again!"

Whit smiled back at her, and said, "Your turn."

"Roller skating."

"No. I'd try it."

"Canoeing or kayaking."

"Yes, and yes."

"Sky diving."

"No. Only if absolutely necessary."

"Bungee jumping."

"Same as sky diving."

"Roller coaster riding."

"Not since I was a kid. I could live without ever doing it again."

"What a wimp!"

"OK, what about you? Want to sky dive?"

"No, thank you."

"Bungee jump?"

"No."

"Roller coasters?"

"Absolutely. Haven't gone since an eighth grade trip, but I loved it. I'd go again!"

"So, sort of a wild woman."

"Yep. Sort of."

"What do you do for fun after work?"

"Not anything we've been talking about," admitted Emmalise. "I play with the cats, read, run, watch movies."

"What about weekends or vacations?"

"The same. I don't take vacations. I spend time with my family. Although I do have this new activity I like."

"Which is?"

"Karaoke."

"Hey! Me too!" They grinned at each other.

"What else do you do in your free time?"

"Pretty similar, except no cats. I used to hang out with Jake, but he's been busy lately.

I go out for drinks with the people you met the other night sometimes. I cook."

"You mean regular I-need-to-eat cooking or gourmet cooking?"

"I like to eat good food, lots of different kinds, so I try to make it myself, rather than just going to restaurants."

"That's fantastic! I can cook, but we grew up on dishes that could go a long way, and now I just cook for myself usually. I haven't experimented very much."

"Next time, I'll cook for you. How's that?"

"Sounds great!"

They left the restaurant hand-in-hand. Whit drove her home, and jumped out of the car to walk her to her door. As he began to pull her close, Emmalise said softly, "Would you like to come up?" Whit barely nodded, or maybe she just felt his answer. Her hand reached back to his, and he took it, as they climbed the stairs.

About three hours later, Emmalise rolled out of bed, and opened the door for the two cats waiting outside. Looking back over her bare shoulder, she said, "I can make scrambled eggs and toast in the morning. Want to stay?"

Chapter 21

We have to get a couch," said Mac. "This is ridiculous.

Sam and Mac were lying on a blanket and pillows in front of their living room fireplace. They had finished dinner, and the dishes, and thought about lighting a fire, but ended up on the blanket. Mac was on her side, looking at Sam, who was on his back, eyes closed, arms behind his head. He opened his eyes, and looked back at her.

"I don't know. This is pretty comfortable."

Mac flopped back on her pillow.

"Tomorrow, Sam. We go to Lexington, if necessary, and make a decision."

"No problem," he said, closing his eyes again.

Then his cell phone rang. He looked at it with irritation, and then surprise. It was Malayna Brookes.

"Hello, Mrs. Brookes."

"Hello, Detective Kincaid. This is Malayna Brookes. Oh, well, you know that. I'm sorry to bother you in the evening. I was wondering if we could get together again to discuss a few things pertaining to, um, our last conversation."

"Of course," said Sam. "What time would be good for you?"

"Well, I'd like to meet you somewhere else. Would you have time to have breakfast Monday or Tuesday morning?"

"Monday's good. Where and what time?"

"How about 7:30 at Melissa's?"

"OK. Do you need a ride?"

"No, thank you. I'll see you then."

Sam turned onto his side and looked at Mac.

"Well?" She said.

"That's weird. Malayna Brookes wants to talk to me again. Away from home. At Melissa's Cafe for breakfast. On Monday."

"I guess you'll just have to go and find out. At least you'll have a good breakfast."

"Are you implying that I don't make a good breakfast?"

"No, but you can prove it tomorrow morning."

"I'd be happy to."

Sam leaned over and kissed her, which lead to more kissing.

On Monday, Sam was at the restaurant early, but Mrs. Brookes was already waiting at a table in the back, sipping coffee. He shook her hand and said 'good morning', as he pulled out a chair. A middle-aged, harried waitress hurried over, took their orders for bacon, scrambled eggs and toast, and poured coffee for Sam, too.

"I hope it's all right that I wore my uniform today," said Sam, when the waitress left.

"I thought about that," Mrs. Brookes answered. "It might look more odd for you to be in civilian clothes. I doubt anyone will notice, but if someone asks, we can say we're discussing some vandalism in my neighborhood."

"Is there any vandalism?"

"There was a little, but we figured out who it was, and why, and put a stop to it."

"Doing my job for me?" Sam smiled.

"Just good old neighbors talking to neighbors, and the right person talking to a certain young man. We gave him some cleaning up to do, and told him he could get paid for odd jobs, instead of destruction."

The waitress brought their orders, and asked if they needed anything else.

"Why, no, Doris," smiled Mrs. Brookes. "Thank you for such fast service."

Doris flushed and walked away looking happier.

"Let's eat, while it's hot," suggested Mrs. Brookes, "then we can talk."

Sam wolfed his food down quickly, then drank coffee, while he waited for his companion to finish. He studied her calm, smooth face, and decided she must have been a lovely young woman. He wondered if she'd always worn her hair so short, like a black cap (now gray) on her pretty head, sitting lightly on her long neck and slender shoulders. Today she wore a simple brown and white dotted shirtwaist dress and a black cardigan. Her hands were smooth, too, with long, graceful fingers. She seemed almost untouched by age. She caught him staring.

"Take a picture," she said archly.

"I'm sorry," said Sam. "You just look so young, and I know Gideon Printes is in his '60s."

"Good genes, a kind husband, and no children, I suppose," she replied. "I was only 14 when I became a nanny, and Aunt Serafina was only 24."

"What did you want to talk to me about, Mrs. Brookes?"

"You might as well call me Malayna," she said, and sighed. "I'll be telling you some personal information."

She looked down at her half-empty plate, and put down her fork. She looked back at Sam and began speaking softly, but clearly.

"As I said, I was only 14 when I came to work for the Printeses. When Mr. Printes was home, he wanted me to put Gideon to bed, and he expected Mrs. Printes to join him for dinner. While they ate, I gave Gideon his bottle and rocked him to sleep. When he was in bed, I would go to an adjoining room to do homework, and sleep. Usually Mrs. Printes would look in on Gideon and also on me. To see if I needed help with homework, or anything before bed. I slept there in case the baby woke in the night. Mr. Printes thought his wife needed to sleep without being disturbed, which was true right after his birth. Mr. Printes was home for a month after Gideon was born, and one night, he came into the room to look in on his son. Then he came into my room and stood in the doorway, looking at me. I was startled. I jumped out of the chair where I'd been reading, and curtsied to him, as Auntie had taught me. He walked over to me, and tipped my head up with two fingers under my chin. I was terrified. All I had on was my long white nightgown, but it covered me from my neck to the floor. His fingers ran down my neck to the collar of the nightgown and touched the top button. 'What a pretty little thing you are,' he said. He paused there, but then he turned back into Gideon's room. Mrs. Printes was just coming into the room. I'm not sure if she saw him in my room. I just stood there, frozen. First, she went to Gideon's bed and stood next to her husband, looking down at their baby. Mr. Printes took her arm and led her out of the room. Except a minute later, she came back, hurried to me, and hugged me tightly. She whispered, 'Thank you for taking care of Gideon, and I'll take care of you.' I barely slept that night. The next night, when I went to bed, there was a sliding lock on the inside of my door. Mrs. Printes told me I could keep the door locked any night I wanted to, but to keep the transom open, so I would hear Gideon if he cried."

Malayna had been staring into her coffee cup for much of her recital, but now she looked at Sam again, tears trembling at the edges of her brown eyes.

"I know it doesn't seem like much, Sam, but I knew. I'd heard stories of white men and black girls. And when I began my womanhood just a few months before I became a nanny, my Mama told me then to watch out for men, especially white men. I don't think she was worried about Mr. Printes, because Aunt Serafina set such store by both the Printeses. I was thin then, and tall, but I looked younger than my age. Still I knew what he wanted that night. And I kept my door locked from then on, every time Mr. Printes was home. He never came to my room again, or looked at me that way again. In fact, he didn't look at me at all, even if he gave me an order."

Sam sighed deeply.

"I'm so sorry, Malayna," he finally said. "What about your aunt?"

"Oh, I did not tell her. Not to this day. She loves that family, and if she'd known that, she wouldn't have been able to stay there, or let me stay there. I knew she needed that job, and I needed mine. I trusted Mrs. Printes, so I didn't say a word, and I stayed."

"Did you hear anything else about Oscar Printes?"asked Sam. "Men like that, it's not usually a one time thing."

"There were rumors, but nothing I witnessed," Malayna responded.

"What were the rumors?"

"It was bad. I didn't want to believe it."

Sam waited.

"Once in awhile, people who worked at his other farms would come through here, visiting family, or passing through town. They said he liked little black children. One woman left his employment and took her two children up North. He had taken them into a barn to show them a litter of puppies. But he showed them a lot more and touched them. A six-year-old boy and an eight-year-old girl. They were terrified, but told their mama. She wanted to kill him, but settled for moving to Indianapolis, where she had cousins. I heard that story when I was about eighteen. I'll admit I was a coward, but I didn't know who to tell. You know how it was. And is. Who would believe a poor black teen-age girl over a rich white man?"

She looked at Sam defiantly, but her eyes were full of tears.

"It's not your fault, Malayna."

She nodded and brushed the tears away quickly.

"Tell me about leaving, and teaching," Sam encouraged her.

"Somehow Mrs. Printes got me school books and she helped me get a high school diploma. When Gideon and Faye were both in school full-time, she paid for me to take classes at Kentucky State in Frankfort. Only one or two at a time, but still, it was a start.

She even drove me over, or had the gardener drive me, if Mr. Printes was home. In 1965, I left their employ to go to school full-time. Mrs. Printes said she could easily take care of her children and insisted I go to college. I had saved enough for tuition and Mrs. Printes found me a place I could stay in return for cleaning and preparing dinner for an elderly white lady in Frankfort. I finished my teaching degree in two and a half years and began teaching third grade at Simmons Elementary in Versailles in the fall of 1968. It had been an all-black school, but was integrated by then."

"You loved teaching, didn't you?" Sam asked her.

"Yes, I did. My husband and I were never blessed with children, but I had my school children for more than thirty years. I got to teach different grades over the years, ending with sixth graders, so I got to watch them grow up."

"How did you meet your husband?"

"He taught math at Woodford County High School. He was one of the few black instructors. We met at church; Aunt Serafina and I still went to church together. He'd come to Versailles from Ohio, so he was visiting churches to find one he liked. He said I was the reason he stayed at Macedonia Baptist Church. I have to admit I did notice him right away."

Malayna was smiling to herself, and Sam was glad he'd asked about her husband.

"We married in 1970. I was 31, and Andrew was 34. We were very happy for twenty-two years. He died much too young from lung cancer, and he had never smoked. I cannot pretend to understand the Lord's ways, but we were blessed to have each other for as long as we did. I continued to teach. Aunt Serafina retired from the Printes household a few years later. She was having a lot of leg and back pain. Mrs. Printes gave her a retirement package, just like Social Security, maybe better. It included the little house you saw for no rent. I'm not sure Mr. Printes would have approved, but he was dead ten years or more. I sold my house, and bought Auntie's from Mrs. Printes, and moved in with her."

Malayna's face was more and more expressive, as she talked. Sam marveled at the difference between her now and the stiff, serious woman he'd met last week.

"Did your aunt ever talk to you about any men who worked for the Printeses after you were teaching?"

"Just Will Foster and Samuel Porter. Aunt Serafina mentioned them the other night."

"What about after they left? Say around 1992 or '93?"

"My husband died in the fall of 1992. I was focused on him and school, nothing else. I don't remember Auntie talking about work. I'll have to think about later," she gave Sam what he thought of as the school teacher look. "I know there is something you're not telling me. Maybe if you did, I could give you a better answer."

"Maybe later," Sam answered. "By the way, why were you so concerned about us coming to your home in costume, so to speak?"

Malayna shook her head.

"Maybe it's my imagination, but we seem to have an overly nosy neighbor."

"And?"

"There's always at least one nosy old biddy in every neighborhood. Some just like to hear gossip, or keep tabs on everyone. Some are like the neighborhood watch. Can't sleep. Look out their window for entertainment. Maybe that's all this is, but Mary Sue Tomlinson across the street is like that, only worse. And she's younger than we are, in her '60s, I think."

"How is she worse?"

"She comes over almost every day. If one of us is outside for any reason, there she is. Asking questions. If we don't come outside, she comes to the door. Borrowing sugar or flour or bug spray. More questions. It our pastor stops by, or a friend, or a package arrives, she wants to know who, what, where and why? At first, we'd chat, even invite her in, but it was so hard to get rid of her, I've started being downright rude!"

"Do you think she's lonely?"

"Well, probably. But she started asking a lot about Mrs. Printes, and what it was like working there. She even asked if we thought we'd be in Mrs. Printes's will!"

"That's pretty forward," said Sam, beginning to understand Malayna's concern.

"Well, then you wanted to come over, and talk about Gideon running for office," Malayna paused, looking at him pointedly.

Sam frowned. Then he got it.

"You thought we were in cahoots?" He grinned at her.

"Only briefly, but it got me thinking about Mr. Gideon. Maybe he's worried about his inheritance. Or perhaps he thinks we might gossip about working there, spoiling his campaign. I really don't know, but I began thinking he might be behind Mary Sue and her questions!"

Chapter 22

Emmalise's cell phone rang as she pulled into Wags and Purrs' parking lot at 7:25 Monday morning. She parked before looking at the screen. It was an unfamiliar number, but local, so she answered.

"Hello."

"Ms. Pine, this is Serafina Washington."

"Well, hello, Mrs. Washington," Emmalise tried to keep the surprise out of her voice.

"I was wondering if you would like to chat some more. You seemed interested in what it was like back in the old days."

"Yes, I am."

"Would you be able to come over some evening after work? What time do you get off?"

"I'm off at 4:30, and could probably be there by 5:00, or I could come after dinner."

"Would tomorrow evening be too soon? Say 7:00 o'clock?"

"No, that would be fine. I'll see you then."

Emmalise was baffled by the invitation, but hoped to learn more about life at the Printes's, especially any missing yardmen.

Miss Tippet called her at lunch, asking her if she was free Thursday afternoon to meet Judge Turner. Emmalise eagerly accepted, thinking her research was certainly looking up this week.

When she had any free moments, she thought about Whit. They had ended up spending the weekend together, mostly at her place. They had gone out to a matinee movie and to the grocery, so that Whit could cook. His chicken enchiladas with beans and rice were delicious. They made love in different parts of the apartment, usually having to move the offended cats to another room to stop themselves from laughing. They slept late on Sunday, and he made omelets for Sunday brunch. They played with the cats, watched the Hitchcock movie Rear Window, and made love on the couch. It all seemed easy and natural. He told her that he didn't always have weekends free; his job required odd hours, and he asked her if she minded. She said 'no', thinking that as long as he kept cooking, and touching her like he had, she'd see him anytime.

He left early Monday morning. He said he had a busy week, but that he would call her.

She thought about him as much as she did the case during the day. She still felt warm and relaxed and excited. He called that evening and they talked for about an hour. He asked her if she'd like to join their friends at karaoke that Friday and she said 'yes.'

As she drove to Mrs. Washington's on Tuesday evening, she was thinking about Whit.

She really liked him, and the sex was incredible, but she thought of herself as a realist. It would last for however long it would last, and she would enjoy it for that time. Then she laughed out loud. Who was she kidding? This silly, goofy happiness was something she had never felt before. She was falling in love. At the very least, infatuated. Which was scary. Was this something she even wanted? Well, too bad. It was happening. She couldn't let herself think ahead, plan, imagine. She just had to let it happen and try not expect anything.

She was still smiling and shaking her head at herself, when she pulled up in front of the house she had visited just a few days ago. She saw a curtain move, and Mrs. Washington opened the door, as Emmalise walked up the concrete steps.

"Good evening, dear," beamed the elderly woman. "How are you tonight?"

"I'm fine, thank you. How are you, Mrs. Washington?"

"I am feeling well. And, please, call me Serafina."

She shuffled aside to let Emmalise into the small entryway.

"Please call me Emmalise."

"Come in and sit down, Emmalise. You look much more comfortable tonight."

Emmalise smiled and said, "I am. I guess I was trying to look more businesslike."

She was wearing her usual jeans and a long-sleeved tee; she'd actually forgotten about the previous subterfuge. Mrs. Washington had eased herself into the same armchair, and was smiling gently at her.

"Is Mrs. Brookes home tonight?" asked Emmalise.

"This is her card playing night. She has a lot of activities, but I'm slowing down."

"Why did you want to see me?" Emmalise hoped she wasn't being too direct.

"Well, for one, I wanted to encourage you to support Mr. Gideon. He's a very smart, and fine man."

Emmalise waited.

"And I enjoy talking about the old days, but Malayna has heard all of my stories. You seemed interested," she trailed off, looking at Emmalise expectantly.

"I am interested. I grew up around here, but I think the Printeses lived a very different life than I did. Or anyone I knew."

"Well, they certainly lived a different life than me and mine. Malayna and I were just in the background."

"You must be a very fine cook for them to have kept you for so long."

Mrs. Washington beamed, then suddenly looked flustered, and started to get out of her chair.

"Excuse my manners. I have coffee and cookies in the kitchen that I meant to bring in here."

She was struggling to get up. Emmalise bent across the coffee table and touched her arm.

"You stay there. I'll go and get it."

"Why, thank you, dear, if you don't mind," Mrs. Washington settled back into her chair.

Emmalise quickly returned with a large tray that held a coffee urn, two cups and saucers, cream and sugar, and a plate of oatmeal raisin cookies. She placed it on the table, and poured Mrs. Washington a cup of coffee.

"I'll take it with cream, please," said Serafina, "and a cookie on the side."

Emmalise filled the request, fixed her own black coffee and a cookie, and sat down. She sipped the coffee and took a bite of cookie.

"Oh my gosh, that is the best oatmeal raisin cookie I ever tasted!"

Mrs. Washington smiled, took a bite of her cookie, then quickly finished it.

"This is delicious coffee too," added Emmalise, "I'll have to stick to one cup, or I won't sleep tonight." She reached for another cookie, closing her eyes as she bit into it.

"Was there anything in particular you wanted to know about the Printeses?"

Emmalise wanted to ask about the hobo yardman, but knew that was too direct.

"I heard they had big parties, when Mr. Printes, Oscar Printes, was alive. Did you cook for all of those people?"

"Of course I did, and it was a lot of cooking, even when it wasn't a sit-down dinner."

"Who came?"

"I didn't come out of the kitchen, but William Foster, or whoever was butlering, would tell me about the parties. There were politicians, doctors, lawyers, judges, businessmen, anyone who was anyone in Versailles and Woodford County. Sometimes state Senators and Congressmen would come. And they all brought their wives. Mr. Oscar liked it fancy, so the men wore tuxes, and the women wore gowns. William said it was a beautiful sight, but not always beautiful conversation or behavior, if you know what I mean."

"Not really. Like what?"

"People will be people," Mrs. Washington hid behind her coffee cup, and raised her eyebrows.

Emmalise laughed.

"Oh, come on, Mrs. Washington, uh, Serafina. What did you hear?"

"Just because people are dressed up doesn't mean they can hide their true selves. A few would get drunk, and not just the men. Flirting, more than flirting," here she wiggled her eyebrows over wide-open eyes, "swearing, arguing. I felt sorry for William sometimes. He had to stand out there, and listen to them talking about niggers and the good old days in the South. That wouldn't last long, if Mrs. Printes heard it. She would not abide racist talk in her house."

"What did she do?"

"Well, usually Mr. Printes would try to quiet the person down, or get him out of Miss Athena's earshot. Once, though, a local lumber mill owner said something about niggers shouldn't be allowed to vote, and Miss Athena heard him. He was fairly drunk and loud, hard not to hear him. She walked over to him, and put her hand on his arm, sweet as you please. Then she began talking to him very softly about a new gazebo she wanted, and that she'd just then decided to use trees from their own land, and hire her own workers to build it. He stared at her with his mouth hanging open. She just smiled and walked away. She took him off the guest list, too, and anyone else who she knew was racist."

"What about Mr. Printes?"

"He was a businessman, and wanted to impress folks. He wanted to be like the lord of a Southern mansion, only not with slaves. He paid good wages, and was friendly, unless you didn't do your work. He was quick to fire a lazy person, but he usually did what Miss Athena said, too. Of course, he was gone a lot, and she ran the house, that's for sure."

"So, do you think Gideon Printes takes after his mother or father?"

"Oh, he's his own person," smiled Serafina. "Very smart, like Malayna and I told you. He adores his mother. I don't think he ever had much in common with his father. Not interested in tobacco or big business. I'd see him watch Mr. Oscar sometimes, who was charming and liked to tell stories, talk a lot to company. Mr. Gideon was shy and quiet with other people. I think he knew he couldn't be like his father, and it bothered him for awhile. Miss Athena encouraged Gideon to go his own way. I do think he went to law school to help his parents take care of their land and all, but he didn't want to run the business."

"Where was Gideon during these parties?"

"With Malayna in his room, then in the nursery after Faye came along. When they got past the toddler stage, they'd have supper in the kitchen. Malayna, too, of course, since I was kind of busy. If it was a dinner party, they stayed upstairs. If it was a party with drinks and finger food, they'd come visit me before bed. When Mr. Gideon was in high school, or home from college, Mr. Oscar would bring him out to be introduced to the guests. Mr. Gideon would only stay for an hour or so. He hated that, the small talk and all. Sometime during his college, the parties just stopped."

"Why was that?"

"I'm not sure. Mr. Oscar was in his sixties, not that old, but he seemed to be slowing down."

"What was Faye like? You said the other night that she was an adventurous child."

"Oh, yes. She was a funny little thing, loved to climb, and play in the dirt or mud on the edge of the river. She took to swimming very young. Like a little duck. She wasn't any more social than Mr. Gideon, though. She liked to be alone, except for family, well, her mama, and Malayna, and Gideon."

"How did she meet her husband? I heard he runs an antique store in Versailles."

"Mmmm, I don't know. She went to college, then worked as a secretary in Frankfort at a law firm. She eventually became the Office Manager. She married in her late 30's. I only knew him as Mr. Luther Wynn from Ohio, but she knew him from Frankfort somehow. He was a CPA. I always thought him to be a bit showy. They moved in with Miss Athena about five or six years ago, when they both retired, and he started the antique store two years ago."

"Since they all seem to be such private people, why do you think Mr. Printes wants to run for Congress?"

"You know," Serafina paused with her teacup in the air, "that did surprise me. It does seem out of character. But he's been a lawyer for a long time, and has probably met all kinds of people. Maybe somebody talked him into it."

Emmalise put her cup and saucer down on the coffee table. She was frustrated, but couldn't think of a way to steer the conversation to the missing gardener.

"It's been lovely chatting with you, but I don't want to wear out my welcome," she said.

"You're sweet to say so," Serafina looked at her anxiously, "but you don't have to go yet. Can you stay a little longer?"

The elderly woman lifted the plate of cookies up toward Emmalise, who took it from her trembling hand, and smiled.

"Oh, you are tempting me! Of course I can stay."

"Would you like to hear more about the guests at the parties?" asked Serafina.

Emmalise nodded and listened to the former cook's memories of the high and mighty of Woodford County. Serafina knew quite a bit beyond what she heard about at the parties. Many of her family, friends and neighbors worked for those people and shared their experiences in the community. She was a good storyteller, too, and had Emmalise laughing for the next hour.

"You could write a book, Miss Serafina!"

"Not unless I outlive a few more people!"

"Did you have a favorite guest at the Printeses?"

"Oh, my, yes. Judge Wainwright Turner was very kind to Miss Athena, and to me. He even came into the kitchen to compliment my cooking!"

"What about other staff?"

"We just helped each other out. Most of us came home to the same neighborhood. Samuel Porter was a neighbor and friend. He was the Printes's gardener for many years. They had a time finding good help after he passed."

"Were there any mysteries over the years? Trouble? Any ghosts?"

"Ghosts! He-he-he!" Serafina laughed with delight. "No ghosts. Mr. Oscar didn't die there. So no ghosts."

She giggled softly, breathy, and sighed, wiping the corners of her eyes. Emmalise smiled at the older woman and waited.

"We did have a gardener who disappeared," Serafina looked past Emmalise's shoulder, as though she were looking back in time. "He stopped at the back door, like they used to years ago, looking for work. The Mexican man we had left to work crops, like they usually did, so the timing was good. Miss Athena took him on, and he did good work, took care of the yard and small repairs. He was there the whole summer; then one day he just disappeared. Left in the afternoon and never came back."

"Did you know his name? Or where he stayed after work?"

"He just said to call him James, and he'd answer. When Miss Athena asked him his last name, he chuckled and said to call him James, first or last, made no never mind. So we all called him James. We asked him if he needed a place to stay in Belleriver, but he said he'd be fine. I fed him lunch, and dinner if he stayed late. He'd eat on the back stoop. I don't know how he did it, but he seemed clean, no stink, and his work clothes looked freshly washed of a Monday."

"So you had no idea where to look for him? No contacts?"

"Not that I remember. Miss Athena was puzzled; she thought he liked working there. I thought so too. But he was a hobo, just needed to move on. Mr. Gideon said he'd find a lawn care service, and he did."

"Well, I really must go now," said Emmalise. "Let me take the tray back to the kitchen for you."

"Thank you, child."

When she returned to the parlor, Emmalise took Serafina's nearest hand in both of hers and said, "I have enjoyed myself so much. I hope I can come again. Maybe I can get that cookie recipe out of you."

"I would love for you to visit again," smiled Serafina. "I'll be sure to write down the recipe."

Emmalise felt excited on her drive home. She knew it was just a small clue, but maybe James James could take them somewhere.

Chapter 23

Emmalise had a difficult time focusing at work the next day. She didn't get a break to call Sheriff Dade until lunch, and both he and Deputy Kincaid were out. Her work day ended later than usual as well, and both men had already left the office when she called again. As she drove home, she heard her phone ping twice with text messages. As soon as she found an easy spot to pull over, she did, and pulled her phone out of her purse.

The first text was from Whit: "Miss you. Work tonight, but will call soon. Get ready to sing!" She smiled and texted back a goofy face and a microphone.

The second text was from Sam: "Can you meet Thursday afternoon at 4:00 p.m. at the office? From your messages, you have news. I have some too." She and Miss Tippet were seeing Judge Turner at 1:30 on Thursday; surely they would be finished in time for her to meet Sam and the Sheriff by 4:00. She quickly texted back: "See you then." She didn't want to wait that long to talk to them, but knew they had other work and she had to be patient.

Continuing her drive home, she thought of Whit, wishing she could tell him the whole story. Her instincts were to trust him, but it was just too soon. She wondered if Sheriff Dade and Sam knew him. Should she ask them about Whit? Would they want to bring him into the investigation? Did she want him involved?

She pulled into her drive and parked. She heard a soft "woof," as she climbed the back stairs.

"I'll be down in a bit, Archer," she said with a smile.

She opened a can of wet food for Lance and Guin, then changed into her sweats and tennis shoes. She wore a ponytail at work most days, but redid it quickly. She gave each cat a quick pet, and headed back downstairs to get the dogs. Mugsie and Archer sat without a command, and waited for her to attach their leashes.

"Kellon should be a dog trainer," Emmalise thought.

She left the house with a dog on each side. It had been a cloudy day, and was getting dark quickly. The dogs' leashes and collars were reflective, and she had on gold sweatpants, and a black and gold Hornets' sweatshirt. She didn't like running in the dark, but it couldn't be helped in the fall and winter. The side road she took didn't have much traffic, and she often ran down the middle of the road. She let the dogs relieve themselves beside the road, scooped it up in the plastic bags Kellon provided, and threw them in the lidded waste can in his mudroom.

Emmalise transitioned from a walk to a jog to a run, and the dogs matched her pace. At the end of a mile, they slowed, turned, and she switched Mugsie to her left side with Archer. They could have all run further, but she decided to jog the second mile home. Sometimes they would do the whole section, but that included some walking. Emmalise carried her cell phone, but rarely listened to music. She preferred letting songs or thoughts run through her head as she ran. When she got a good rhythm, she could zone out and think of nothing, the closest she figured she ever got to meditation.

She barely noticed the tire noise of a car behind them. She felt a hard bump, then she was in the air. She heard a dog squeal. For an instant, she saw red lights; then she landed hard on her side in the grassy ditch. She felt no pain, but something was pulling at her wrist, and she could hear growling.

"Archer," she called, but it came out as a hoarse whisper. Immediately the big dog was licking her face, and whimpering. She pushed herself up on her right elbow, then her knees. A few feet away, she could see the brown and white form of Mugsie, lying still.

"No, no, no," she cried, crawling to the dog, Archer beside her. She stroked Mugsie's head, and his brown eyes opened. Archer was nudging him, and whining. Emmalise kept petting his head.

"Oh, thank God! You'll be all right, boy. It's OK."

Suddenly she thought of the car. It didn't stop. It was nowhere in sight. Emmalise was furious at first. Then she thought, "What if he comes back now?"

She slid her arms under Mugsie gently and tried to lift him. She was feeling pain now, in her right shoulder and both hips. She could slide him across the ground, so she did, pulling herself and the dog into the brown cornstalks in the field beyond the ditch. Archer picked up the leash and pulled too. Mugsie had yipped when she first moved him, but was quiet as they jerked along the ground. Once they were between two rows of corn, she tried to push up the stalks they'd knocked down, and hoped they would be well enough hidden. They remained noticeable bent, but it couldn't be helped. She found her cell phone in her warm-ups pocket, luckily undamaged. She tried calling Kellon first, but he didn't answer. Remembering that he was at work, she knew he might not even have his phone with him. She thought of Whit, also working. She had no idea what he was doing, but a ringing phone could cause him problems. There was always 911, but she knew the Sheriff and a Deputy, and they knew her. None of them had expected this kind of trouble, when they exchanged phone numbers, but Emmalise was so glad to have them now. She called Sam's cell. Relief flooded her, when he answered.

"Sam, I need help. I was running with the dogs and someone hit us. Mugsie is hurt. I can't carry him," she felt herself choking up, and tried not to cry.

"Where are you?" Sam asked.

She explained how to get to the road, and that they were hiding in the corn field.

"I'm coming from home, so it will be awhile, forty minutes or so." She heard him talking to someone else, then a door closed.

"Are you sure you don't want to call an ambulance?" He continued. She could faintly hear footsteps on gravel, a car door opening and closing, the car starting.

"No, Sam, I'm OK. I don't think they want to come for a dog, sadly."

"All right. I'll keep my phone on. Don't hang up."

Emmalise put the phone down, and snuggled up against Mugsie, who seemed sleepy. Archer lay down on his other side, licked Mugsie's face, and rested his big gray head on his paws. She listened carefully for car noises on the road, but no one drove by them. The shoulder and hip she had landed on ached, as did her other hip and thigh. It hurt to move, so she lay still, petting the two dogs alternately. She heard sirens twice, but the sound didn't reach her street. Still, it was only twenty-five minutes, until she heard a car on the road pull over, a door slam, and Sam's voice calling her name.

"We're here," she yelled, pocketing her phone, slowly getting to her feet, and pushing her way out of the corn. Archer was up, too, barking fiercely.

"It's OK, Archer," she said, pulling up on his leash, which was still around her wrist.

Sam had a flashlight, jumped the ditch, and hurried over to her. A slender, long-haired woman was right behind him.

"My wife, Mackenzie," he said, "You need to go to a hospital."

"No, I really don't. It's just bruises. But we need to take Mugsie to my vet."

Emmalise pushed her way back into the corn field to where Mugsie still lay. Sam scooped the dog up and carried him to the Jeep Cherokee parked on the road. He laid Mugsie gently on the back seat, and Emmalise climbed in next to the dog. Archer jumped in with them. He sat on the floor with his head next to Mugsie's on the seat. Mac was driving, so Emmalise gave her directions to Wags and Purrs. She called Dr. Dunnigan on her cell, and asked her to meet them at the clinic.

"What happened?" Sam asked.

"We were running. Coming back toward home. I barely heard the car before it hit me. It must've hit Mugsie too, even though he was on my right side. I heard it drive away. I didn't see anything. I was trying to get to Mugsie."

"You're going to the hospital, as soon as we get the dog checked," Sam said firmly. "Are they your dogs?"

"No, my neighbor's. I've got to call him."

Emmalise dialed the number of the ambulance service, and explained why she needed to talk to Kellon. The dispatcher was immediately sympathetic. She said Kellon was on a run, but she would tell him to call as soon as he returned.

A few minutes later, they pulled into the vet clinic's parking lot. Emmalise was relieved to see Dr. Dunnigan's car parked near the door and lights on in the building.

She let Sam carry Mugsie, while she got the door. The vet was waiting and led them back to an examining room.

"What happened?" asked Dr. Dunnigan.

"He was running with me and got hit by a car," explained Emmalise, choking up for the first time. "He's my friend's dog. I haven't been able to reach him yet."

The veterinarian looked Emmalise over quickly, apparently deciding she was not in immediate danger, and began examining Mugsie. The dog lay still under her gentle touch. When Dr. Dunnigan palpated his left hip, Mugsie whined and tried to sit up.

"We'll do X-rays, Emmalise, if you'll help me."

Sam carried Mugsie into the radiology room, then waited outside. In a few minutes, they were all looking at the X-rays on the vet's computer.

"I don't see any broken bones, or damage to organs," Dr. Dunnigan smiled at Emmalise, Sam and Mac. "This is one very lucky dog. He'll be sore for a day or two, but should be fine."

Emmalise hugged the doctor joyfully.

"I didn't do anything, Emmalise. But I will give him a shot for pain, and give you some meds for his owner to give him tomorrow."

Emmalise introduced Mac and Sam. Dr. Dunnigan shook hands with them, and petted Archer's gray head.

"Thank you so much for coming in at night, Doc," said Emmalise.

"Part of the job," Dr. Dunnigan answered. "If you're too sore tomorrow, just stay home."

"I'll see you tomorrow," Emmalise responded.

Sam carried Mugsie to the car, and they headed back the way they'd come.

"Sam, do you think this could have anything to do with our investigations?"

"Do you think you were hit on purpose?"

"Yes. I was off the road. He had to swerve to hit me. Then he just left. I was knocked into the ditch. Mugsie was on the other side of the ditch. I was afraid he might come back to make sure I was dead, so I crawled into the cornfield."

"Did you see anyone? Why do you think it was a man?"

"No, I didn't see the driver. Just an assumption. I didn't get the plate number either. I just saw red taillights going away."

"Could you recognize the taillights? They can be distinctive to a make of car."

Emmalise closed her eyes, picturing the image.

"I'm not sure. Maybe if I saw them at night again. In my memory, they're blurred."

"Well, that's understandable," said Mac.

"What about the kind of car? A sedan? An SUV?" Sam pushed.

"It was a big sedan, like a Cadillac or a Lincoln. Just a big, dark shape," said Emmalise.

"So you think Printes found out somehow?" Sam was turned in the passenger seat to look back at her.

"We've talked to a lot of people. We saw Mrs. Washington and Mrs. Brookes last week, and I talked to Mrs. Washington again yesterday evening. That's what I was going to tell you and the sheriff."

"Malayna Brookes called me and we talked yesterday too. At Melissa's Cafe for breakfast. She thinks one of their neighbors is a little too nosy."

Emmalise heard her cell phone's distinctive banjos ringtone. It was Kellon. She explained what had happened, and he said he was leaving for home and would meet her there. When she hung up, Sam reminded her about going to the emergency room.

"We need to take Mugsie and Archer home," she said firmly. "I promise I'll see a doctor tomorrow. It will be less expensive, and I'd rather see my own doctor, anyway."

Kellon was standing in the drive, when they pulled in. He rushed over to the car and pulled open the back door. Archer leaped out, and Mugsie sat up, licking Kellon's face in delight.

"She seems fine," he said, rubbing her all over, while Archer waited beside him.

"Doc gave her pain meds. She sent some home for you to give her, since she might be sore for a day or two. I'm so sorry, Kellon," said Emmalise.

"What the hell happened?" he asked. "Are you all right?"

"I'm OK. I'll be sore too." Then she explained about the run and the hit-and-run driver, leaving out her suspicions. She was too tired to tell the whole story, and wasn't sure that she should yet.

"That son of a bitch!" He lifted Mugsie in his arms, "Thank you for taking her to the vet. Send me the bill."

Emmalise smiled, and shook her head. She introduced Sam and Mac, and he thanked them, as well. They all headed toward the house, Sam and Mac walking Emmalise to her door.

"I don't like this," said Sam. "I'm not sure you should be staying here alone."

"I'll be all right. Archer is a guard dog, and will alert us to anyone prowling around. Besides, that coward took off so fast, I think it will take him awhile to try anything else. He's probably hoping to hear of my death in the papers tomorrow."

Sam frowned, but nodded slightly.

"Go take a hot bath," said Mac, "and some ibuprofen."

"That's my plan. Thank you for helping me tonight."

"No problem," said Mac.

"See you tomorrow," added Sam.

As she climbed the stairway, Emmalise could hear Lance and Guin crying behind the door.

"I'm coming, babies," she said, stepping inside. "Want to watch me take a bubble bath, and hear about my day?"

She fixed herself a peanut butter sandwich and a glass of milk. Her entire body ached. While the ate, she glanced at the kitchen clock and was surprised to see that it was almost 10:00 o'clock. She felt like it should be 2:00 or 3:00 in the morning. She headed into the bathroom, undressing slowly on the way. She turned on the tub faucets, adjusting the water to very hot, but was too tired to add bubbles. The cats had followed her, and watched as she sank carefully into the hot water. It burned where her skin was scraped, but still felt good overall. She had brought her cell phone out of habit, laying on the bathmat. It began ringing, just as she settled back. She smiled a little when she saw it was Whit.

"Hey, gorgeous! I'm sorry it's late, but would you like some company?"

"You have no idea!"

Chapter 24

Athena heard Gideon's footsteps on the backstairs that lead to his third floor rooms. The sounds were different, slow and heavy, not his usual quick, light tread. She knew something was wrong, but wasn't sure she should approach him.

When he was young, he shared everything with her, Malayna, or Serafina, whoever was available, and willing to listen. Actually, all three women were usually interested in his observations, and exclaimed over the rocks, insects and frogs he brought home, even though the living finds were quickly put in glass jars, and eventually released. They would listen, while continuing to work, and stop now and then to look at his serious face, nod, ask a question, pay attention, listen. His father Oscar rarely paid attention, or even pretended to listen; Gideon could have been talking to a wall. Sometimes Oscar would leave the room in the middle of Gideon's recitation, leaving behind a confused, hurt little boy. The only time Oscar expressed pride in his son was over his report cards, and that was usually a curt "Good job, Gideon" at the dinner table. Athena knew that sons rarely stop trying to impress their fathers, but Gideon did stop trying to talk with Oscar.

In Gideon's junior high years, Athena wondered if Oscar would have been interested in a more athletic son. The boy just didn't show any curiosity about organized sports. Physical activity was only important in the pursuit of scientific exploration, such as hiking, climbing and swimming. Because they lived near the river, Athena did teach her children and Malayna to swim, which became a favorite activity in the hot summers. They could each row a boat as well, but Oscar never wanted to accompany them. Athena wondered what happened to the man she thought she had married, who liked to go for long walks with her, or boat rides, or even horseback riding. Somehow during the years of infant deaths, they had lost touch; maybe they'd never shared enough. When Gideon and Faye survived, she was so desperately happy to have children, but Oscar only seemed to see them as his responsibilities. He focused on the tobacco business, and business contacts, expecting big parties when he was at home. He also liked poker, although he was not a particularly adept player. Athena thought he might teach Gideon, when the boy reached high school, but Oscar shook off that idea. "Not a good habit to get into," he told his wife. "One gambler in the family is enough."

Oscar showed a brief interest in Gideon being in Debate Club. "Wonderful training for public life!" he said, when he heard that Gideon had joined. "Good for politics, or the law!" While his quiet son was excellent at preparing arguments for a debate, Gideon was too shy for effective speaking, and did not do well in debate competitions, so Oscar dropped that subject. The one mention of law was enough for the boy to follow that path in college, and he did succeed as a law student, and then as a lawyer—in any legal work that didn't involve trials: estates, taxes and wills. By then, Athena knew more about Oscar, and didn't care if her husband and son had a relationship.

Athena was in bed, when she heard Gideon come home. She could hear him pacing through the rooms above her, his sitting room, bedroom and bathroom in a line like hers.

She heard him walking and walking, which he only did when in deep distress. She hadn't heard him walk like that in years. She lay still, thinking about going up to see him, confront him, try to find out what was upsetting him so. Maybe he would finally confide in her again. Suddenly he stopped walking. She heard the soft thump and creak of his body collapsing in the stuffed chair in his bedroom. Then she heard faintly the sounds she remembered hearing from her young son, when he was in bed and the lights were out, and he didn't know anyone heard him crying. These were worse. She heard the deep and agonized sobs of a man in despair. Athena was frozen. She couldn't go to him. Her body began to tremble as if from cold, and tears slid down her cheeks. She didn't know what had happened to Gideon that night, but she was afraid that she knew the root of his pain.

Athena stayed awake, even after she couldn't hear his anguished weeping anymore. She heard him walk around the room, probably undressing. She heard him splash water on his face in the bathroom. She heard him walk back into his bedroom about the distance to his bed, and imagined him lying down, and pulling up the covers. She wondered if he would sleep at all that night. She did not.

Chapter 25

Whit stayed overnight, but slept on the couch. He insisted that Emmalise needed her bed to herself to be comfortable. She was too tired to tell him anything but the abbreviated (no background) hit-and-run story. He accepted her reason for not calling him, but insisted that she should have. He also seemed to understand why she called her 'friend' Sam instead of 911, and looked relieved that Sam had Mac attached to him.

In the morning, he made her scrambled eggs, cinnamon toast, orange juice and hot tea.

He called her doctor, and managed to get a before-hours appointment, then he left a message at Wags and Purrs explaining that she would be a little late.

"I wish you'd just come back home after the doctor's, and go to bed," he said.

"I'll see how I feel," she hedged. "I think it will be better if I keep moving."

She had to insist on driving herself, and telling him to go to work. She didn't want to miss any of her appointments that day, or have to explain them.

Doctor Martha Addison examined Emmalise thoroughly, and agreed with her self-assessment that she would be bruised and sore for a few days. The doctor also told her to go home, take some ibuprofen, and take it easy for one day. Emmalise's hips and right shoulder ached so much that she reluctantly agreed. She called work from the clinic parking lot; then she called Miss Tippet to postpone their meeting with the judge. She texted Whit that she was taking his and the doctor's advice. His reply text simply said 'good.' Driving home, she decided not to skip her appointment with the sheriff and Sam.

They really needed to compare notes.

After sleeping the rest of the morning, and having a late lunch, Emmalise soaked in a hot bubble bath for thirty minutes. She added hot water periodically to keep the tub steaming. It felt heavenly. While drying off, she checked herself in the mirror. Her right side from neck to knee was varying shades of reddish purple, while her left hip and thigh were nearly black. A long, scabbed scrape glared angrily from the middle of that bruise. She dabbed gently with the towel. No blood. She dressed carefully in the softest black leggings she owned, and a long sweatshirt. Lance and Guin watched.

"I'll be OK, guys." Their green eyes expressed doubt.

She arrived about five minutes early at the Sheriff's office, but didn't have to wait. Sheriff Dade stood in his doorway, and motioned her inside.

"How are you feeling?" he asked, looking worried.

"I'm fine," she smiled at him reassuringly.

"I'm concerned that we've poked a hornets' nest."

"It just confirms what I thought all along."

Deputy Kincaid tapped on the door, and joined them, also asking how Emmalise felt.

She said, "Good." He handed her a bottle of water, and sat down.

"We need to catch up, and look at what we have," said Sheriff Dade. "Sam, why don't you start with your meeting with Malayna Brookes?"

Emmalise was surprised, and listened in amazement to Sam's account.

"So Oscar Printes was a predator!" she exclaimed. "That's motive! Gideon wouldn't want that getting out."

"No," said the sheriff, "but did Gideon even know? And how would the victim know anything to threaten Gideon with? What evidence could he have had?"

"I might know his name, the victim's name," announced Emmalise, and she told them about her meeting with Serafina Washington.

"So you think his name was James James?" asked Sam.

"I don't know if she ever knew for sure, but that's what it sounded like."

"It is so weird that those two women each called one of us, and didn't tell the other one." Sam was shaking his head in disbelief.

"You know what else is weird," said Sheriff Dade. "Malayna Brookes is worried about her nosy neighbor, then someone runs down Emmalise. It's not a coincidence."

"I also checked Printes's car registration," said Sam. "He drives a black Lincoln MKS. They have triangular taillights."

"I don't know," said Emmalise, shrugging, "I'd have to see them in the dark, I think."

"I'll see if I can get a video," Sam suggested, "but that's not much of an identification."

"What do we do next?" she continued. "Can we do anything official yet?"

The sheriff shook his head, "Not yet, but let's look at everything we have. Sam, could you go get that white board in the squad room?"

While Sam was gone, the sheriff cleared his desk. Sam came back with a white board about twenty by thirty inches, which they lay on the desk. Across the top in erasable marker, he wrote the names of the people they had talked with, and below their names, he listed the information received. Emmalise and Sam joined him behind the desk, watching, and making suggestions. Sheriff Dade used arrows to connect people with other people and information. Judge Turner lead to Serafina Washington who linked with Malayna Brookes and James James. Peter Goins lead to Athena Printes and Oscar Printes, who linked with Gideon and Faye Printes. Under each name he wrote a concise identification and information related to the investigation.

"We might need a larger board," commented Sam.

"We could tape envelopes under each name, and put the complete information on notecards in the envelopes," Emmalise suggested.

"OK," said Sheriff Dade, "let's each write up the cards for the people we interviewed, and we'll add those next time. Sam, I think you and Emmalise should talk to Judge Turner again. Tell him what we're doing. Find out if he heard any of those rumors about Oscar Printes. I'm going to talk to William Foster again, level with him too."

"I want to talk to Mrs. Brookes again," said Sam, "Maybe she can help us find the mother who moved to Indiana with her kids. And what about the nosy neighbor, uh, Thomas, or Thomlinson? Should we find out if she's in touch with Gideon Printes?"

"Not directly. Not yet. She would alert him for sure," said the sheriff.

"If Printes is the driver who hit Emmalise, he's been alerted," said Sam.

"I'd like to get some evidence, before we talk to Printes, or anyone in his family," Sheriff Dade said firmly. "Or the nosy neighbor. Do either of you have anything else?"

"Well, this isn't related to the case, but I'd like to ask you both something," Emmalise said, her cheeks flushing.

"Sure," said the sheriff and Sam simultaneously.

"I've been seeing someone, and I wonder if you know him. Whitman Pierce."

"The PI?" asked Sheriff Dade, then he frowned, "You didn't go to him...."

"No, no," interrupted Emmalise, "I met him through my neighbor and his friends. We've been dating for two weeks or so—hmmm. That's not very long. Anyway, I haven't told him anything about this. I just wondered if you knew him."

"Sure," the sheriff responded. "I don't know him well. He has a reputation as an excellent private investigator. Sam?"

"I've heard the same things about him. Jeff Parker worked with him on something and thought he was a good guy," Sam looked at Emmalise, "Jeff is with the Versailles police.

In general, law enforcement doesn't work with PI's, but it happens."

"Do you want to bring him in on this?" asked Sheriff Dade.

"I'd like to tell him about it," she answered. "I want him to know what we suspect about the accident. Being an investigator, maybe he could help."

"I think he could," said Parker Dade. "Talk to him, and bring him to our next meeting. Let's try for next Tuesday about 5:00 p.m. Call me, if you finish your interviews sooner. Emmalise, don't run for a few days, please. Try to be with people as much as possible."

She gave him a nod and a grim smile. As she and Sam walked out of the office, she asked him if Miss Tippet could set up the interview with Judge Turner and join them. Sam agreed, and said he could do Friday evening or Saturday morning, if she could, and the judge was agreeable. Emmalise thought of the planned karaoke night, and sighed. She would hate to miss that, but then she wouldn't have to face questions from Kellon and Jake's friends. As soon as she got in her car, she called Miss Tippet, who said how disappointed the judge had been, and she would get back to Emmalise.

Meanwhile, Sam was sitting in his car, calling Malayna Brookes. He asked if they could meet again the next morning, explaining that he had news and more questions. Malayna said 'fine', 'where and when?.' Sam suggested the pavilion in Big Springs Park around 8:00 a.m., and he would bring doughnuts. Mrs. Brookes agreed. Sam started his car, and headed home to an evening with Mac and shopping for furniture and rugs online.

Emmalise had texted Whit, asking him if he could come over. 'Planned on it', he texted back, then 'how's carryout?'. 'Excellent!' she typed, 'see ya soon.' She drove home, wondering how he would react to her investigation into a cold case murder.

Whit brought Italian beef, and made salads from lettuce and carrots that Emmalise had on hand. Emmalise was surprised at how hungry she was, and she realized that she felt better overall.

"Are you sore?" asked Whit.

"Not right now, just sitting here," she smiled, "and I didn't take my pain med since this morning."

"That's good. I just don't understand how someone hit you, and then left. Was he drunk? I'd like to find that guy."

"I might be able to help with that," Emmalise said. "It's kind of a long story."

Whit looked stunned, and confused, but he soon settled into his calm, listening mode.

So she told him, beginning with her ten-year-old self visiting kittens in an old barn. Only his eyes widened at certain parts of the story; otherwise, his face registered no emotions.

When she finished, he sat very still, looking down at the table. Finally he reached for her hand, and said, "I gather you're not looking for a crazy, vengeful boyfriend to kill this guy, although part of me feels like that would be worthwhile."

"No," she smiled, "but you believe me? Does it make any kind of sense?"

"Of course I do. But you've got a lot of hearsay and gossip, not evidence. It does seem likely that Printes came after you with that car. I'd like to prove that."

"Would you like to help? Sheriff Dade and Sam would like you to. I would like you to. I know you have your job. We're all doing this on the side."

"As long as that's not why you're dating me…." He gently pulled her over onto his lap. She wrapped her arms around his neck, and kissed him lightly, tenderly. He moved his lips down her neck to her collarbone, and slid his hand under her sweatshirt.

"Bedroom," she whispered.

They walked awkwardly, still kissing, pressed against each other. Luckily, it wasn't far. Emmalise lay back on the bed and Whit started pulling down her leggings, panties too. Then he stopped.

"Oh my God, Emmalise," he said. It wasn't passion. It was pain. He was looking at her bruised and scraped body.

"It's all right, really, Whit. It looks worse than it feels."

He sat next to her on the bed, while she finished removing her leggings, and pulled her sweatshirt over her head.

"Your turn," she said, unbuckling his belt. He undressed with her help and crawled under the covers next to her. She snuggled against him, and he wrapped his arms around her. They lay that way for awhile, warm, breathing together, and Emmalise wondered if he'd fallen asleep. Then he kissed her again, and kept kissing her, every bruised inch of skin, until they finished what they'd started.

Chapter 26

Sam and Malayna Brookes sat across from each other at a pavilion picnic table on Friday morning. They each had a glazed doughnut, and a paper cup of coffee. A box with more doughnuts sat on the table between them.

"I have a story to tell you," began Sam, "and it needs to stay between us for now."

"All right," Malayna said calmly, sipping her coffee.

"Twenty-three years ago, a little girl witnessed a murder. She was hiding in a barn loft, playing with kittens, and two men came into the barn, a white man and a black man. The black man was in work clothes, and said he had something for the white man. The white man asked the black man where he found it. The black man told him 'in a toolbox in an old shed.' He handed the white man a small red box. The white man took it, and said, 'you shouldn't have been nosing around,' and shot the black man. The girl could see parts of the men, and the box, and she saw some of the dead body. Based on what she could see and hear, the white man took the body out of there in a wheel barrow, maybe to his car, then he threw water on the blood on the floor and covered it with hay. He left. The little girl stayed hidden for hours, but eventually went home, and the next day told her teacher and a local deputy. They believed her, found the washed-out blood stain, but no body. They never found the body. Twenty-three years pass, and one day, the girl, now a woman, hears a voice on the television news. She knows that voice. She has an eidetic memory, and is sure the voice is the same one she heard in that barn. So she comes to see the deputy, who is now the sheriff, and she tells him who she thinks murdered that black man."

Malayna was gripping her hands together fiercely. She closed her eyes and shook her head slowly back and forth. Finally, she looked at Sam, and whispered, "Gideon Printes."

"There's more," Sam said.

He went on to tell her about the investigation so far, and, finally, about Emmalise's hit-and-run accident.

"Oh, no!" Malayna cried, "Is she all right? That poor girl!"

"Yes, she's fine. So is the dog. They're both tough," Sam reassured her. "I know it's a lot to take in, but you can see we still don't have hard evidence. I was wondering if your neighbor asked about us after Emmalise and I came over."

"She did. That's also how I found out that your friend came over again, when I was out. Serafina invited her. She just wanted some new company, I guess. So Mary Sue did come over after you both came, and again after Emmalise came. Luckily, I answered the door both times. I thought about saying you were Jehovah Witnesses, like we planned, but I said you were here about the campaign, in case she talked to my aunt some other time. When she came back about Emmalise, I said that she and Serafina hit it off and were just visiting, which is the truth."

Sam shook his head.

"She sounds like a pain," he said.

"She is," agreed Malayna, "and now I think, more than ever, that she is passing this on to Mr. Printes."

"The timing is suspicious. Emmalise came over Tuesday night, and was hit the next evening. It is enough time for Ms. Thomlinson to report to Printes, and for him to find out where Emmalise lives. He could've known about her since the murder. He had to have followed the investigation, and heard about the little girl. When they didn't find a body, he probably felt safe. I'm not sure why he has your neighbor spying on you."

"He may not have liked that his mother gave Serafina the house. Jealousy or wanting the money. He would know that servants see and hear a lot. Getting his own information was some kind of insurance."

"What do you think of Serafina remembering the black handyman who disappeared?

Emmalise thinks what he said about his name means it's James James. It sounds like he disappeared around the time of the murder, so he could be our victim."

"I agree, but I wasn't at the house then. I don't remember Auntie mentioning that name, but she did talk about his disappearance. I have no idea how to find out about him."

"Malayna, I want to ask you a favor, but don't feel obligated. I don't know how risky it is."

"What is it?"

"Is there any way you could find out about the woman who moved her family to Indianapolis? If we could talk to her and her children, it might help. We need more than rumors to use Oscar Printes as a motive."

"I'll see what I can find out," she answered thoughtfully. "I'll have to think about who else lived in the old neighborhood back then. I don't like this, Deputy, not one bit. I'll give you a call."

Sam thanked her, and they finished their doughnuts and coffee. Sam offered to give her a ride home, but Malayna thought a taxi was a better idea.

"Good heavens! Can you imagine what Mary Sue would pass on, if you brought me home!"

Sam laughed, and nodded. He offered her the extra doughnuts to give Serafina a treat, and she accepted.

Emmalise went back to work on Friday, feeling just a little stiff and sore. She thanked Dr. Dunnigan again for her help, and offered to pay her.

"No, no," said the vet, "I'm just glad the dog is OK. And you too!"

During her lunch break, Emmalise checked her messages and saw that Miss Tippet had left a voicemail and a text, rescheduling their visit with Judge Turner for Saturday morning. Emmalise texted Sam, got his OK, and texted Miss Tippet that Saturday morning would be fine.

Around 9:00 a.m. Saturday, Sam picked up Miss Tippet in Belleriver, and drove up to Versailles to meet Emmalise in front of the Sheriff's office. He was driving his wife's Jeep Cherokee, which had a little more backseat room, and he offered to drive to the Judge's place in Frankfort. They arrived promptly at 10:00, and the judge ushered them into the kitchen with an oval table for four in a nook with a curved wall of windows, looking out on his still-green backyard that was enclosed with a brick wall. A simple fountain splashed over rocks into a small pool. Bushes and flower beds fronted the wall, chrysanthemums and other fall flowers still blooming.

"I didn't know you were a gardener," said Miss Tippet to the judge.

"I can't take the credit," he smiled at her. "My wife did all the gardening, and now my son and daughter take care of it. I help, but only under their strict direction."

"It looks so peaceful," said Emmalise.

"That was the idea," Judge Turner gestured toward the table set for four with a plate of muffins and sweet rolls in the middle.

"Does anyone want anything besides coffee to drink?" he asked.

They all accepted coffee, which he poured into four different mugs.

"I'm going to come clean with you this time, Judge," began Sam.

"No book?" Judge Turner looked at him over his glasses.

"No book," acknowledged Sam. "Emmalise, why don't you start?"

Emmalise retold the story of the murder, involving Miss Tippet and then-Deputy Parker Dade, and recognizing the murderer's voice over twenty years later. She and Sam described the investigation to that point, answering the judge and Miss Tippet's questions as needed. When they finished, Judge Turner leaned back in his chair, and sighed.

"I think the old word 'flabbergasted' describes how I feel," he said.

Miss Tippet nodded.

"Your telling us about Serafina Washington and Malayna Brookes really got us started," Sam said. "We're just wondering if you can think of anyone else who could help. Were there any rumors about Oscar Printes back then?"

"Among his peers? I don't think so. He would've been ostracized, if anyone thought he was a child molester. Affairs could be tolerated, but not child abuse. I wonder if Athena knew. If it's even true. I cannot imagine her staying with him."

"Now, Wainwright, you are not that naive," Miss Tippet spoke. "White people, especially rich white people, have always been very good at hiding their sins. The worse they are, the deeper they hide them. And with the slightest hint, rumors flourish. No one said anything to you, because you were the law, and not a gossip."

Judge Turner sighed, and shook his head, "I suppose I'm attributing my own feelings to everyone else. If it became public, people would be suitably horrified, but if it was unspoken.... You are quite right, Lorraine."

"I don't know Mrs. Printes," added Miss Tippet, "but a mother will bear anything for her children. If she knew, I'm sure she would not have wanted them to know."

"Gideon Printes had to know. Why else commit murder?" said Emmalise. "There had to be something he didn't want the handyman to reveal. I wish we knew what was in that red book."

"Could it have been a diary, or a small photo album?" asked Miss Tippet.

"Either one," said Emmalise, "but surely he destroyed it."

"Judge, can you think of anyone else we can interview?" said Sam. "I just don't think we have enough to talk to the family, let alone confront Printes."

Judge Turner leaned on the arm of his chair, rubbing his forehead between his eyebrows.

“This is the difficulty with a cold case,” he said. “You don’t have a body. Our witness was a child at the time. There was no DNA testing, or much in the way of forensics. Did Parker save a sample of the blood?”

“Yes, he did,” answered Sam, “but we don’t have a body for comparison.”

“You said Samuel Porter is deceased, but did he have any children or friends who are still alive, besides Mrs. Washington? I think the black community at the time knew everything that was going on in the white homes where they worked. I’m sure they would not have talked to Sheriff Dade back then, and most of them are dead now. That is the thread to follow, if you can find anyone.”

Sam explained that they were going to talk to William Foster again, and Malayna Brookes was looking into the family that moved to Indianapolis.

“You know,” said Miss Tippet, “it seems that Serafina Washington would have more information, if she knew the whole story.”

“According to Malayna and Serafina’s own words, she idolizes the family, particularly Mrs. Printes, and Gideon,” Emmalise said.

“Perhaps I could talk to her,” suggested Judge Turner.

“We’d have to arrange that without her neighbor knowing,” said Sam.

“It might break her heart,” said Emmalise. “I hate to do that to an elderly woman.”

“We can think about it, and talk to Malayna first,” said Sam.

“The truth is best, especially for the old,” said Miss Tippet quietly.

Chapter 27

Saturday evening brought much needed relaxation to everyone involved in the Printes investigation. Sheriff Dade and his wife Clare watched Shane on television. Judge Turner took Miss Tippet out for a lovely dinner; they shared stories of teaching and trials, and no talk about the case. They both knew they needed to be circumspect in public. Sam and Mac discussed baby names, while arranging their new living room furniture. Malayna and Serafina's niece/great-niece and her husband came for a visit and played Hearts until 10:00 p.m. Emmalise and Whit went out for karaoke and dancing with their friends from the night they met. None of them talked about the case, but it crept into all of their minds before they fell asleep.

Sheriff Dade decided to set up another visit with Will Foster. Judge Turner searched his mind for someone else who might have known the missing gardener. Sam Kincaid and Whit Pierce both planned to search online for James James. Malayna made up her mind to talk with Serafina on Sunday, and tell her the truth about Oscar Printes. Emmalise wondered if she could finish what she had started.

Chapter 28

Malayna's talk with Serafina on Sunday after church had been as difficult as she expected. Serafina did not want to believe a word of it, but Malayna's own experience had convinced her aunt that Mr. Oscar had not been a good man. Her denial changed to anger, then tears for Miss Athena, Gideon and Faye. She felt terrible not knowing what Malayna had gone through.

"It was just that one time, Auntie," said Malayna, "and he scared me more than anything. He never did anything else. I didn't hear about the other children until years after that."

"Now I know why Miss Athena changed, and seemed so sad," sighed Serafina.

Next Malayna told her the story of the gardener, possibly killed by Gideon Printes, according to Emmalise Pine's eidetic memory. Serafina was upset all over again. She couldn't believe that Mr. Gideon would shoot anyone. What could the hobo-gardener have shown Gideon, anyway, to cause such a reaction? How could a little child remember something so clearly that she would recognize a voice over twenty years later? Then she began thinking of all the scenes she remembered from her childhood, and young adulthood, and she didn't have that special photographic memory.

The older woman spent most of the afternoon and evening reading her Bible, and staring out the window, seeing the past. She and Malayna had a quiet dinner, and Serafina went to bed early, feeling wrung out. Malayna worried that she'd pushed her aunt too far.

When Serafina came downstairs Monday morning, her walk was slow, but as steady as usual. She found Malayna making oatmeal and coffee in the kitchen.

"I remembered some things, Malayna," Serafina announced. "That young woman who moved away with her children was June Franklin. Her mama lived in the old Belleriver neighborhood. Helen Dorsey. I believe she has passed, but her brother Hank may know where June is. Also, that James James gave a local reference. Said the pastor could vouch for him. Do you remember Pastor Rose? He was a traveling preacher, up here, down in Belleriver and a few other small towns. I don't know why I didn't think of him when I was talking to Miss Emmalise. Actually I don't know whether Miss Athena ever talked to Pastor about James. I saw James at church a few times, when Pastor Rose came to town. I imagine you can find him, if he's still alive."

Malayna stared at her aunt, dumbfounded. When she could speak, she asked, "Did you sleep at all last night?"

Serafina sat down at the kitchen table.

"I did, and when I woke up, those names just popped into my head. I prayed for the Lord to help me do the right thing, so He must want me to help you and the sheriff."

Malayna poured her aunt a cup of coffee and added a little milk. Then she dished up a bowl of oatmeal and put it down in front of Serafina, and pushed the sugar closer to her.

"Thank you, Auntie," said Malayna. "I do think we need to help get to the bottom of this. It breaks my heart that Gideon might have killed someone, but I believe Emmalise. I think I'll talk with Hank Miller and try to find Pastor Rose before I call Deputy Kincaid. People are more likely to talk with me than the sheriff."

Sheriff Dade nearly bumped into Sam coming in the office door, as the sheriff was walking out.

"Did you deliver that subpoena?" Parker Dade asked his deputy.

"Yes, no problem," answered Sam.

"I'm heading out to talk to Will Foster again," stated the sheriff. "Want to come?"

"I would, but I have to look into what I can find on James James," said Sam.

"Good luck, Sam," said the sheriff.

He climbed into one of the Woodford County sedans, and headed south to Belleriver.

This time when he pulled up in front of the white farmhouse, William Foster was sitting on the front porch, rocking slowly in a wooden rocker with a cane seat and back. The sun was warm, when Sheriff Dade pulled himself out of the car. As he approached the porch, Amelia Foster stepped through the screen door, watching him.

"Good morning, Mr. and Mrs. Foster," said the sheriff.

"Call me Will, Sheriff," said Will Foster, "and you can call my wife Mrs. Foster."

He added the last part with a grin.

"I'm Parker," said the sheriff, smiling back, and extending his hand, first to Will, then to Mrs. Foster.

"Would you like something to drink?" asked Amelia.

"No, thank you, ma'am. I'd just like to have a chat with your husband. You're welcome to join us."

"You two go ahead," she answered with a smile, and slipped back into the house.

"What's up this time?" Will looked at the sheriff skeptically.

"I have a story to tell you, Will. After I do, I hope you won't repeat it to anyone except Mrs. Foster. And I hope you'll be able to help me."

"Sounds fair, Parker. Speak up."

Sheriff Dade explained the whole case to Will Foster, beginning with Emmalise Pine's witnessing a murder, the recent hit and run, and their dead end with James James. Will listened quietly, nodding now and then, and glaring angrily at the attack on Emmalise.

"I appreciate your being straightforward with me, Parker. How did you get the name James James?"

"Serafina Washington thought of it, just reminiscing. I don't know whether Malayna or Emmalise has confided the whole story with her yet. Do you remember anything about him?"

"I remember Serafina calling him James, but not his last name. She hadn't wanted to let him talk to Mrs. Printes at first, but she admitted he was a hard worker, once he was taken on. I saw him at our church several times, talking with the minister after the service."

"Do you know anyone who might have known him?"

"He didn't hang around and chat. Maybe Pastor Rose knew him. They seemed friendly."

"Do you know where I can find Pastor Rose, or his first name?"

"He was Ezekial Rose, and I heard he was in an old folks' home in Lexington, but I don't know which one."

"Thank you, Will," said the sheriff. "This could be a big help."

"I hope so. I can tell you a little more about Oscar Printes, too."

Parker nodded, so Will continued.

"When I worked at the Printeses, my first wife and I were living in the colored neighborhood of Belleriver. Just two blocks with black folks on both sides of the street, on the east side of town. About fifteen or sixteen families. One couple was Fred and

Helen Dorsey, who had four children, grown and scattered around the state. Their daughter June had the misfortune to marry Harry Franklin, a farm worker who traveled the state working the harvest on tobacco farms. I say misfortune, because that was a tough life. She went with him, and they had two kids, a boy and a girl. They thought they got lucky when Harry got some manager's job on one of Oscar Printes's farms, and June was hired to help cook for the workers."

Will paused, reaching down slowly to pick up a glass of water on the porch next to his rocker, and took a long drink. He bent over again, putting it back down carefully. Then he continued.

"One summer, June suddenly came home with the two kids. She was about twenty-seven or twenty-eight, and her little girl was eight, the boy five or six. They didn't stay long. After they left, her parents said she moved up north to get a better job. Said they had family in Indianapolis for her to stay with for awhile. Eventually, though, word got around that Oscar Printes had messed with those little kids. Every now and then, another abuse story would come up, but you know how it was back then. Still is, most of the time."

"I hope not," said Parker, "at least not with us, and not everywhere. Do you remember when this was, when June left to go to Indianapolis?"

"Early '70s. Probably '72 or '73. I remember, because the parties ended then. I didn't butler anymore. Just repair work once in awhile."

"Can you think of anyway I could get in touch with June Franklin?"

Will looked down at his wrinkled hands, resting on his thighs. His forehead furrowed in concentration.

"Not so many folk from that old neighborhood still alive," he muttered. Then he looked up at Parker.

"Let me think on it. If I think of someone, I'll give you a call."

Parker nodded, and thought for a minute, as well. Eventually, he asked, "Will, do you know why the parties stopped?"

"No, sir, but I was glad. After hearing about those children, I didn't like seeing Mr. Oscar having fun and playing lord of the manor. I didn't see him much after the parties ended, but he didn't seem to be as energetic. He stayed home more. He started selling his properties."

Will looked tired all of a sudden, staring off into the distance. He drank the rest of his water.

"It's hard living as long as I have, and not being able to right some of the wrongs of this world," Will said quietly.

"I think you're helping right one now," said Parker.

Judge Wainwright Turner stood in the doorway of his closet, staring at his suits, and trying to decide which one to wear on his visit to Lorraine Tippet's the following afternoon. They had enjoyed their dinner conversation so much (at least he had), that they decided to get together again. Lorraine had invited him for Tuesday tea. She suggested they each bring a book to exchange, read, and discuss later. Wainwright was delighted. He was a widower of many years, but had fancied Miss Tippet for a long time. He was frankly curious about her. It was so unusual for a beautiful, intelligent woman to remain unmarried. Not that he had any matrimonial inclinations at his advanced age, but he thought it would be fun to get to know her. He pulled out a dark gray suit with a navy pinstripe running through it, and nodded.

"That's an oldie, but a goodie," he said to himself. He continued staring at it, and suddenly smacked himself in the forehead with his hand.

"Rudy! Rudolphus Bingham!" he cried out loud.

The judge hung his suit back in the closet, and dialed Lorraine Tippet's number on his cell phone. She answered after two rings.

"Lorraine," said Judge Turner, "I've thought of someone. Do you remember Rudolphus Bingham, the tailor?"

"Well, yes," she answered, "I do. All the well-off men in the county had at least a few of their suits made or altered by him."

"And I was among them," said the judge triumphantly. "Don't you think he might know something about Oscar Printes?"

"He might," Lorraine said. "He's between us in age, I think, older than I, and younger than you. He retired about eight or ten years ago. I haven't run into him in ages."

"I'll find him! When I do, would you like to visit him with me?"

"Of course, but it will depend on the circumstances. He might speak more openly to just you."

"All right. I'll start looking and get back to you!"

"That would be fine, Wainwright."

After he hung up, he realized he wasn't sure how to look for his former tailor. Then he thought of Ada Hope, his last and youngest secretary. If anyone knew how to find someone, it would be Ada. She was still working at the courthouse, but he called her anyway. She laughed, when he told her what he wanted.

"Just google him," she said.

"What?" asked the judge.

"You do have a computer at home, don't you? Just type his name into Google search. That should give you plenty to work with. You can also look in the White Pages online. It's the new phone book."

So, Judge Turner googled Rudolphus Bingham, Versailles, KY. He got lots of repeat information on Bingham's Tailor Shop, closed four years earlier. Eventually he found Rudy's phone number and a Versailles address in the White Pages, just like Ada had said. He called the number, only to hear the "no longer in service" message. Momentarily stumped, he thought for a few minutes, and decided. He opened the door to his garage, stepped out, and locked the door behind him. He hit the garage door opener. He unlocked the door to his two-toned cream and green 1953 Chevrolet BelAir, and settled into the comfortable seat. He had restored the engine himself twenty-five years before, and found the best body shop to do the paint job, and the interior work. After he retired, he decided to take the car out of retirement and use it, instead of saving it for occasional jaunts. Lorraine had loved it!

Now he patted the dash, fastened his (not-original) seat belt, and put the three-speed on the column in reverse. Wainwright had never cured himself of talking to his car, at least when they were alone.

"Well, old girl, are you up for a trip to town? Should be a nice spin!"

Sam was hunched over his keyboard, when Sheriff Dade walked into the squad room.

Sam looked up at his boss, and nodded "hello". Only one other deputy sat at the far corner desk, peering at his computer screen and typing laboriously.

"Any luck?" Parker asked Sam.

"Some," said Sam. "There are a lot of James Jameses with middle initials just in Kentucky. Over 3,000. But only one with no middle initial, so I've been following him. What about you?"

"More computer work for you," the sheriff pulled up a nearby chair and sat down. He filled Sam in on Will Foster's information. Sam took notes.

"So we need to look for June Franklin, possibly in Indianapolis, originally June Dorsey from Belleriver. She can verify the possible motive for the murder. And can you search for Ezekiel Rose, a minister in the area, who is now supposed to be in a nursing home in Lexington? Maybe he can tell us more about our victim," Sheriff Dade concluded. "What did you find on James James, no middle initial?"

"This James James was born in Morehead, KY in 1955, which makes him just two years younger than Gideon Printes. His father went to prison for theft, and died there. His mother was a seamstress, who managed to raise four children. The daughter stayed in Morehead with her mother, married, divorced, and worked as a secretary. The three boys were all drafted and served in Vietnam. One was killed over there. One came back and became a mechanic. He's in Lexington. James served and returned, but wandered away, apparently. He had a driver's license in 1975 after he came back from Nam, but it expired, and wasn't renewed. No tax returns after 1983, either. No criminal record. No address. No phone. No medical records after the Army."

"Well, it fits," said the sheriff. "He could be our victim."

"And I can probably talk to the brother and sister for verification," added Sam.

Just then, Ida Masters stuck her head around the corner, and said, "Excuse me, Sheriff."

Sam and the sheriff looked at her expectantly.

"Emmalise Pine and a young man are here to see you. Without an appointment," Ida said pointedly. She also nodded at the wall clock, eyebrows raised. It was 4:55 p.m.

"That's fine, Ida," answered Parker. "Sam, let's meet with them in my office."

Emmalise and Whit stood outside the sheriff's office, waiting, as Parker and Sam walked around the corner. Emmalise introduced Whit Pierce after they were all inside, and the men shook hands.

Emmalise said, "He'd like to help." Whit said, "I'd like to help" simultaneously.

"We can use it," responded Sheriff Dade. "We have a lot of searches to do."

He explained about June Franklin and Reverend Ezekial Rose's involvement in the case. Sam repeated what he had found on James James, and the need to get more information on James's brother and sister.

"I found the same information on James James as you did, Sam. I agree that the other men with that name aren't viable candidates. I can do searches on June Franklin, the minister, and James's brother and sister tonight," said Whit. "I'll let you know what I find tomorrow."

"That would be great," said the sheriff. "My office will repay you for the searches."

"Not necessary," said Whit. "Also, I checked out Printes's car at his office. There's a small dent and paint scraped off on the right front panel by the headlight. It's obviously been washed thoroughly, so I doubt there's anything for evidence. Not repaired yet, but easily explained. I took photos anyway."

"That's good. Thanks, Whit," said the sheriff.

Sam and Parker watched Emmalise and Whit leave. Whit held the door for her, and she smiled at him as he did.

"I checked him out," said Sheriff Dade. "He's very good at his job. Respected by law enforcement and attorneys, which is unusual!"

"Good to know," said Sam, thinking with a slight grin. "He's a goner now!"

Chapter 29

On Tuesday morning, Whit was back at the Sheriff's office when it opened. As he approached the door, he met an older couple coming in, a short, gray-haired man in a fedora, and a younger-looking woman. Whit held the door for them, and the old man stepped aside to let the woman enter first. She smiled at Whit, thanking him, and the man looked at him over his dark-framed glassed and nodded. Inside, Penny Hitt, the office's second part-time receptionist, didn't seem at all surprised by the early visitors. Penny was black and much younger than Ida with a calm expression that always put people at ease. She wore a black pencil skirt, a tailored white blouse, and black slip-on flats. Her hair was black, shining, and very short, and she wore gold hoop earrings in her small ears. She was looking at them expectantly, with a slight smile on her intelligent face.

"Please tell Sheriff Dade that Wainwright Turner and Lorraine Tippet would like to speak with him, if possible," said the old man after removing his hat.

"Yes, Judge," said Penny, and looking at Whit, she added, "I'll be right with you, sir."

They could see the sheriff seated at his desk through the glass windows, but he was already rising, as Penny tapped on his door.

"Thank you, Penny," said Sheriff Dade. "Why don't you all come in? I have the feeling you're here about the same thing. Penny, could you see if Deputy Kincaid is here, and have him join us?"

Penny disappeared around the corner, while the sheriff introduced Whit to Miss Tippet and Judge Turner, and explained that everyone was helping with the same cold case. He closed the blinds covering his office windows.

"I'm happy to see you're finally waking up the office," said Judge Turner, removing his glasses, and wiping the lenses with a handkerchief.

Sheriff Dade returned the judge's gaze. Whit was puzzled by the remark, but Miss

Tippet seemed to understand.

"We had to wait for Mrs. Beaumont to retire," the sheriff responded. "The timing was perfect, since Penny's son just started first grade. We've had a black deputy for a few years, and just hired a Hispanic female deputy."

"Hmmm…all kinds of diversity!" The judge nodded in approval. "Took long enough."

"I taught Penny," added Miss Tippet. "She's organized, and a strong person."

"And very good at this job," said Sheriff Dade. "We're lucky to have her."

Just then Sam appeared, carrying a pitcher of ice water and some paper cups. Penny was right behind him with carafe of what was undoubtedly coffee. Penny moved stacks of papers on a small table to make room for the drinks, and left the office, closing the door.

The sheriff had motioned Miss Tippet and the judge to take the two chairs in front of his desk, while he sat behind it. Whit and Sam stood.

"I wasn't expecting you, Judge, so why don't you start?" said Sheriff Dade.

Judge Turner explained about remembering his old tailor, who would have known Oscar Printes, and trying to find him.

"Rudolphus Bingham was one of the few black businessmen in this town when I was on the bench," said the judge, "He was an excellent tailor, and anyone with money went to him for suits. He worked well past retirement age, but closed his shop four years ago at age seventy-three. I found his home address online, tried to call him, but his phone was out of service. I invited Miss Tippet to accompany me, and we went to the address listed. Not there, but thanks to Lorraine, the current owners felt comfortable telling me that he is living at that nice retirement village outside of town."

Miss Tippet quietly stepped over to the table of drinks, poured the judge and herself cups of water, and brought them back. The judge sipped his, giving her a smile. She looked at Sam and Whit, who both shook their heads 'no.'

"I called first, then went out to see him," continued the judge, "I took Lorraine home first; she insisted that Rudy would be more forthcoming with me alone, and I believe she was correct. He has his own apartment, and seemed happy for the company. We reminisced about many of his former customers, especially the deceased ones, before I brought up Oscar Printes. At first he would only speak in general, and respectfully. It's difficult for a black man of his age to criticize a white man, especially to another white man. I did not tell him about this case, but I did say that Gideon might run for the legislature, skeletons in the closet, etc. I told him a couple of stories about the parties

Oscar used to have, the apparent bigotry of some of the attendees, how different from each other Oscar and Athena were. Finally I asked him how Oscar treated him when he ordered suits, or came for fittings. Rudy said Oscar was like most rich white men, talked big and friendly, like a master talking to an old slave. Then he mentioned an odd incident. Oscar came for a fitting, and when he took off his suit coat and handed it to Rudy, a small photo album fell out of the pocket. It fell open to a picture of a young black girl in a white dress or slip. Rudy and Oscar both reached for it. Oscar snatched it up, closed it and turned bright red. He put it back in the coat pocket, and said something about his cook's grandchild or niece, that she had shown him the pictures and he needed to give them back. Rudy didn't know the child, but he said the picture was an old Polaroid and the photo album cover was dark red."

They all looked at each other, stunned.

"Well, I think we know what James James was trying to give Gideon Printes," said Sheriff Dade.

"And why Gideon shot him," said Lorraine quietly.

"Did you talk to Mr. Bingham about the rumors about Oscar Printes?" asked Sam.

"He just said that until he saw that photo album, he'd hoped they were just rumors. Afterward, he believed they were true," answered the judge. "He said he'd only told his wife about the album, and now, me. When Oscar died, Rudy hoped he'd gotten his just reward, and that hell couldn't burn hot enough for a sin like that."

"Oscar was foolish enough to keep the photo album, and, somehow, James James came across it," said the sheriff. "I wonder if James was just returning it, or looking to blackmail Gideon."

"We know that Gideon has seen it, based on Emmalise's eyewitness account," Miss Tippet said.

"Surely he wouldn't keep it," Sam's voice was incredulous. "That would be dangerous."

"He was willing to kill to keep James silent," said Judge Turner. "It would've been easier to just destroy the album."

Sheriff Dane looked at Whit, and asked, "Did you have any luck, Whit?"

Whit nodded, and spoke from memory.

"Pastor Rose is at Sunset Village just outside Lexington, so he'll be easy to see. James's mother and sister are still in Morehead. His brother Roy is in Lexington. June Franklin is in Indianapolis; her children are grown, and live up there as well. I have phone numbers and addresses for everyone, even June's children. I assume we won't talk to them without her knowledge, even though they're grown."

"Good work, Whit," said the sheriff. "We'll approach James's family and the pastor first. I'll go see Pastor Rose. If I have time, I'll look up Roy James, as well. Sam, I'd like you to interview Mrs. James and her daughter in Morehead, so call and make an appointment. You can't make a next-of-kin notification, since we don't have a body. And you can't tell her about this case or Gideon Printes. Just see what you can find out about James, and whether she knew anything about his life down here."

"Yes, sir," Sam answered.

"If it helps, I could drive up to Indianapolis and interview June Franklin," said Whit.

"Maybe Emmalise could go, and help put June at ease."

"That's a good idea, Whit," said Sheriff Dade. "I'll get back to you. I appreciate the help."

"Any chance that Lorraine and I could join you, Sheriff?" asked Judge Turner.

"If the nursing home will allow three visitors, I don't see why not," said the sheriff.

Chapter 30

Sam held his identification up to the storm door, so that Mary Louise James could see it clearly. The short, plump, elderly black woman held her bright blue glasses by the frame as she peered closely at the card. A middle-aged, but very similar-looking Lena James looked over her mother's shoulder, reading the card as well. Lena had red glasses, and wore jeans and a red flowered print shirt that seemed oddly coordinated with Mary Louise's blue flowered print dress. Sam stood on the small concrete porch of the two story brick home. Two white wicker chairs and a small, round wicker table were to his left. Looking to his right, he could see the smaller house next door that belonged to Lena, a one-story with yellow siding. They were in a well-kept neighborhood of homes built just after World War II, a few brick, but mostly wood, updated with siding. The front yards were simple and neat; almost all of them had one old oak or maple or sycamore tree, as well as bushes or flower beds fringing the houses.

"Come in, please, Deputy Kincaid," Mary Louise James made up her mind about him, and Lena opened the door further, while her mother turned back into the house, walking with a cane. She lowered herself carefully into a stuffed armchair. The room was small, neat and uncluttered, with just two soft-looking chairs, a small lamp table between the chairs, and a couch facing them. There were only a few photographs on the walls, portraits, and unidentifiable scenes from a distance. Lena sat in the other chair, and motioned for Sam to sit on the couch.

"How can we help you, Deputy?" asked Mary Louise. Her voice was quiet and steady, and her face was not very lined for someone who had to be at least in her late '80s.

"We're looking into an old case from down around Belleriver," replied Sam, "and the name James James came up. He worked odd jobs down there, and went to a church, too, with a traveling minister. We're trying to find out more about him. Do you have a son named James?"

"Yes," said Mary Louise. "What kind of case are you talking about?"

"I'm sorry, but I can't tell you about the case," Sam answered, "not yet, anyway. Do you know where your son was in the early 1990's?"

"He was here in 1980, Mama," said Lena.

"Yes, he was. After that he wandered, but he always called, or came home for Christmas. That is until 1993. We have not heard from him since then." Mary Louise was looking at one of the photographs on the wall, "Lena, could you get that picture down for the deputy?"

Lena walked to the wall, and gently lifted a framed eight by ten inch photograph off of its nail. She handed it to Sam, and pointed to each person, naming them.

"That's James in his uniform, age 18, then Roy, 19, and Lester, 20. Lester was killed in Vietnam. James and Roy came home."

"Those are handsome young men, Mrs. James," Sam handed back the photo. "I'm sorry your son was killed."

Lena laid the photo on the table, and sat down again.

"It was a terrible war," said Mary Louise James. "It took my Lester's life, Jimmy's mind, and Roy's spirit."

"Do you mind talking to me about the boys?" asked Sam. "Especially James."

"I thought I was so lucky with those boys," Mary Louise sighed,."They took their father's being in prison as a warning, and tried to stay away from trouble. They were all good at sports, especially baseball, so that helped. Still, after high school, they each had bad numbers in the draft, and one by one, they enlisted. Lester re-enlisted, hoping he could keep his brothers safe over there. Instead, he was killed, shortly after Roy arrived. Six months later, they sent James home, honorably discharged, with what they called 'battle fatigue,' and six months after that, they sent Roy home, as well. Roy was wounded in his left leg, and received a Purple Heart medal, but it took him a long time to heal."

"Patty saved him," inserted Lena. "He'll tell you that. At least he was smart enough to marry her!"

"True," her mother agreed with a smile, "but the deputy wants to hear about James."

"Tell me whatever you want," said Sam, thinking how terrible it would be to lose someone in a war, or to fight in one.

"James didn't seem different at first, when he came home," continued Mary Louise. "He'd always been quiet, but now he was sad underneath. Anxious, nervous."

"Depressed," said Lena.

"He couldn't hold a job for long. Mostly he worked construction, but couldn't handle long stretches. He'd just walk away from the job site. He talked to a doctor at the VA Hospital, who put him on some medicine, but that didn't seem to help. He kept trying to work: warehouse labor, bartending, even washing dishes at a restaurant. He didn't drink, thank the Lord. Just never took to it. People were mostly kind, and he was a good worker for as long as he could handle it. Then something would come over him and he'd leave. I think he got embarrassed about living at home, and he finally took off. He'd disappear for months, but always come home for Christmas. He'd stay for two or three days, and leave again. He told us about some of the towns he went to, and odd jobs he had. He must've walked hundreds of miles. He said he tried to hitchhike at first, but didn't like it. Maybe something happened, or maybe people don't like to pick up strange men anymore. Can't blame 'em."

"Did he ever mention Belleriver, Kentucky?" Sam asked.

"Yes," answered Mary Louise, "that's where he said he'd been before the Christmas of 1992, and that he thought he'd go back there for awhile. Said he found a preacher who he liked, and some work doing repairs around town. He mentioned Nicholasville and Keene, too. He did better moving from job to job, doing things he could finish in a few days."

Sam could feel his cell phone vibrating in his pocket. He ignored it, and it went to voicemail. Mary Louise began describing the handmade gifts that James had brought them that last Christmas, when Sam's phone started vibrating again. He apologized, and pulled it out of his pocket to see who was calling. It was Mac. She rarely called him during work hours; she would text, and let him call her back, if necessary. He excused himself, and answered.

"Sam, come to Baptist Health Hospital as soon as you can. It's Sarah…the baby," Mac was trying not to cry. "Dr. Matthews is with her."

"I'll be right there," said Sam.

He apologized to the ladies, who just hurried him out the door, urging him to get to his wife, thinking she was having pregnancy problems from Sam's garbled explanation. Using lights and siren once he was on the highway, Sam was at the hospital in forty-five minutes. The woman at the information desk didn't know that Sarah Quinn was even in the hospital, let alone where, but Mac appeared at his side and pulled him away.

"She's still in emergency," said Mac, reaching for his hand, as they hurried down the hallway. "Dr. Matthews was with her when I came to meet you. No news yet."

As they walked into the waiting room, Dr. Matthews was talking to Connor. They stood in a small group of Mac's dad Gabe, and Aunt Tina. When Mac and Sam reached them, Dr. Matthews smiled briefly at Mac, and continued her explanation.

"Just a cervical polyp, nothing to worry about. She should go home and resume all normal activities. Sarah is upset and worried, so she needs for all of you to be encouraging and hopeful, as I am."

"Does this make her more at risk of losing the baby?" asked Connor, his voice trembling, and his face pale.

"No, no," said Dr. Matthews, "many women have spotting from polyps or other causes in pregnancy, and it is not a sign of future problems. We're going to keep a close eye on her, but she is having a normal pregnancy. I'm more concerned about Sarah's mental state, so we all need to reassure her. She has low blood pressure normally, and I don't want that to change."

"Should she continue teaching?" Connor still sounded anxious.

"Absolutely," Dr. Matthews smiled just a little. "Mr. Quinn, let's sit down. Could someone get him a cup of water?"

Aunt Tina hurried to a water dispenser with small cups, filled one, and handed it to Connor, who had managed to find a chair. He tossed back the water like a shot of whiskey. Dr. Matthews pulled a chair up directly in front of Connor, and everyone else found chairs around him. The doctor looked calm and patient. Mac thought she probably had patients waiting at her office, but her focus was clearly on Connor now.

"May I call you Connor?" When he nodded, she continued. "You've been through one miscarriage, Connor, and that is a terrible loss. But now you have a new baby on the way. Take a deep breath for me."

Connor did, a shaky one. His eyes filled with tears. He looked skyward, then brushed his eyes with his hands, and took another deep breath.

"I'm OK now," he said, looking at the doctor, then at his family.

"Good," said Dr. Matthews. "Sarah is fine. The baby is great. I know this will be rough, until he or she arrives, but try to relax and enjoy the experience. Sarah and the baby need for you not to worry. You should be able to feel the baby move in about three weeks or so. You can talk or sing to the baby now."

"Oh, my gosh, don't sing!" laughed Mac.

Connor smiled at her, and shook his head.

"And don't talk about cows all the time," said Gabe.

Connor laughed at that, and thanked Dr. Matthews, who said, "Go on back and see Sarah. She'll have to go to the door in a wheel chair, but that's just rules."

Mac clung to Sam's hand, until Sarah appeared a few minutes later in a wheelchair, as required. She smiled at everyone, her face flushed.

"Sorry for the scare," she said. "The baby and I are fine. Let's go home!"

Connor walked next to her, holding her hand. He bent over and kissed her head, saying, "I'll go get the truck."

"Would you like us to pick up a pizza or something?" asked Sam.

Sarah looked at Gabe and Aunt Tina, and shook her head.

"No, thanks, Sam. If you all don't mind, I think I'll just go home and collapse. I have to call the school and tell my principal that I will be in tomorrow."

"It's only 4:00 o'clock now," said Gabe, "Connor and I can whip up some supper."

After Connor held the truck door for Sarah, Aunt Tina waved and headed toward her car. Gabe walked with her.

"I'll check with work, but I can probably come home now," Sam said to Mac.

"Meet you there," Mac smiled.

Chapter 31

Sheriff Dade rode with Judge Turner and Lorraine Tippet to Sunset Village on Wednesday afternoon at 2:00 p.m. He had changed into casual khaki pants and a pale blue shirt, so he wouldn't be eye-catching as law enforcement. He had called ahead to make sure they wouldn't be interrupting anything Pastor Ezekiel Rose might have had planned. The staff person he talked with said the pastor would be delighted to have company.

They walked through double glass doors to a curved wooden information desk that was in front of a large, open, nicely furnished reception area. A pleasant-faced woman with white hair, and a smiling, gray-haired man sat at the information desk. Both looked up, and said, "May we help you?" simultaneously, then grinned at each other.

"We have an appointment with Pastor Ezekiel Rose," said Sheriff Dade, introducing himself and his companions.

He noticed that many people of varying ages were using the big, reception room to visit, play cards, or walk through. A low hum of conversation provided a comfortable background, instead of the usual innocuous music.

The gentleman greeter stood, came around to the front of the desk, and said, "Pastor Rose's rooms are right this way, if you'll follow me. By the way, I'm Roger Higgins, one of our many welcomers, if you have any questions."

They followed him down a long hallway. He stopped at an open door near the end, and knocked.

"Ezekial, it's Roger. Your guests are here."

"Come in. Come in!" called a strong voice from the room.

The sheriff, Miss Tippet, and the judge each shook hands with Roger, as they passed him, and entered the room. It turned out to be a small, but open suite. Facing them, Pastor Rose sat in a stuffed armchair rocker with a couch to its right and a television on a bookcase to the left of the door. Further left was a kitchen separated by a half-wall with a round table and four chairs under a window. To their right behind the couch was another half-wall with railings through which they could see a bedroom, and a door that presumably led to a bathroom. The parlor area walls were painted a bright royal blue and the woodwork was white. The kitchen was yellow, as was the bedroom. Above the television, a simple wooden cross was hung, but the rest to the walls were covered with fairly large photographs of Kentucky plants and trees, all close-ups showing great detail and both bright and muted colors.

"Please take a seat," said Pastor Rose. "Someone will need to pull in a chair from the kitchen. Forgive me for not getting up. My back is giving me fits today."

They each shook hands and introduced themselves to the small black man with the deep voice, and sat down, Miss Tippet and the judge on the couch, Sheriff Dade bringing in one of the wooden chairs from the kitchen.

"Your photographs are just beautiful," said Miss Tippet, "Striking. Are they yours?"

"A member of my congregation took them many years ago. She gave me that red tulip the first year I came to Belleriver to preach. I was so taken with it, that she gave me one every Christmas after that for almost twenty years. It's wonderful to have them here, now that I'm not out and about as much as I was."

"She had a good eye," said Judge Turner, "very gifted. Did she sell her work anywhere?"

"I doubt it," sighed Pastor Rose. "A black woman photographer would not have been welcomed in any galleries back then. I don't even know how she came to have a camera, or how she paid to have them enlarged and framed. It was very generous of her."

"We would like to ask you about another member of your congregation, if you don't mind," began Sheriff Dade. "Do you remember a James James? An itinerant worker or handyman around Belleriver area in 1991 or '92?"

"May I ask why you want to know about him?" Pastor Rose looked down at his hands folded in his lap, then up at his questioner.

"It's part of a very old case," answered the sheriff. "His name came up, but we can't find him. He isn't in any trouble."

"I don't know where he is, either," said the pastor. "I remember him, though. For about a year or so, we would talk after services. I was a traveling minister, going to the small towns around Lexington mainly. I didn't have a particular parish. I preached how to live God's word, and most of my congregation were black workers, especially poor, itinerant workers. I spoke in old, abandoned churches or other buildings. I stayed where I was invited, mainly by people who came to hear me. Sometimes other ministers would offer their homes and churches. I was a traveling fixture around here for close to twenty years. Anyway, after one service in the winter of '91 or '92, a youngish black man came up to me and asked if I believed that killing in war was murder, since the Lord commands 'Thou shalt not kill.' After that, we would talk at least once a month, when he found where I was preaching."

"What did you tell him?" asked Judge Turner.

"Oh, we talked about all kinds of things, not only God."

"I meant, how did you answer his question about killing in war?"

"Mmmm," the preacher nodded. "Well, I mentioned 'Give unto Caesar…,' as most people do, but I told him that I truly didn't know. I said it seems to me that the commandment is clear, that killing is wrong. Still I didn't see how killing in self-defense or to protect someone else is murder. Can we stretch it to defending our country? I don't know. I do firmly believe that God forgives us, and loves us. He seemed to find some comfort in that."

"What can you tell us about James James? Do you know any place that he lived or worked?" asked the sheriff.

"He was a traveling man, like me," said Pastor Rose. "He said that he was originally from Morehead, and had family there, whom he visited about once a year. He told me that he served in Vietnam, and had a brother die there. He said he liked physical labor, but just couldn't stay in one place for more than a few months. I'm sure he had what they now call PTSD. I'd ask him where he was staying, and he'd just say he was fine. Sometimes he'd tell me what kind of work he was doing. He'd wash dishes at a restaurant, or pick up downed tree limbs, pile 'em up and burn 'em, or chop 'em up for kindling. He liked to do handyman work: repairs, yard work. Sometimes he worked in the fields with the Mexicans; he said they didn't bother him with questions. I think that was a hint for me to back off!"

Pastor Rose chuckled, shaking his head.

"He was a good man, a thoughtful man, and going by his muscles, a hard-working man. We had some good discussions—some about guilt, or why people hurt each other, or why God allows bad things to happen. I don't think we found any definite answers, but we helped each other find a little peace."

"Did he mention any particular homes where he worked?" Sheriff Dade tried again.

"I'm not sure. I'll have to think about that," said Pastor Rose. "If he worked at someone's home, they would've been white folks, and I didn't always know them."

"Do you remember when he stopped coming to your services?" asked the sheriff.

The elderly minister's face scrunched and his mouth pursed in concentration, then suddenly relaxed in a smile.

"I do remember the year he came! It was the winter of 1992, because that year a new member of my congregation said we could use an old barn for our services. His boss Mr. John Blake volunteered the place. He's a horse trainer near Belleriver. He had some old tractors in there, but there was plenty of space to set up wooden folding chairs, which he also donated. James showed up that January. I think he did some work for Mr. Blake sometimes. That's the only person I can think of right now. We used that barn until I retired in 2010."

"When did you last see James?"

"It was fall, so it would've been the fall of 1993," answered Pastor Rose. "He just stopped coming. Disappeared. No one knew where he went. I surely did miss him."

"Did he act any different in the weeks before he left?"

"Not that I recall. I'll think on it. My memory isn't what it was," the minister smiled a little wistfully.

"Do you mind telling us why you retired?" Miss Tippet leaned forward and touched the arm of Pastor Rose, "Your mind seems quite strong to me."

He looked at her, and smiled happily this time, "Thank you. That's kind of you to say. I had throat cancer, and, obviously, couldn't preach. Then I developed intestinal cancer, which weakened me quite a bit. I managed to beat them both, thank the Lord, but it was a long haul. During that time, I got old, and just couldn't handle the traveling. I settled here, again thanks to Mr. Blake's generosity. I have Bible study once a week, and sometimes I counsel other residents. I had a good life, and still do."

Sheriff Dade thanked the minister for his time and information.

"I hope I was helpful," said Ezekiel Rose. "If you can ever fill me in on the whole story, I'd like that."

"Yes, you were, and I hope we can," said the sheriff, shaking his thin hand. Pastor Ezekiel still had a firm grip.

"Could the judge and I come back for a visit?" asked Miss Tippet, holding the minister's hand in both of hers.

"Certainly!" beamed Pastor Rose. "Anytime!"

As they walked to the judge's Bel Air, the sheriff said, "Maybe he'll remember more visiting with just you two."

"Maybe," said Miss Tippet, "but I found him fascinating. I'd like to hear more about his life."

Judge Turner opened the car door for her, saying, "I liked him too. I'm glad you included me in your request. I think he'll have plenty of stories."

As he settled in the driver's seat, Wainwright thought, "It's also another good excuse to spend time with you, Lorraine."

Chapter 32

Whit and Emmalise had spent most of the three hour drive to Indianapolis talking about where they had and hadn't been. Whit had traveled extensively in the south and Midwestern United States, primarily for work, while Emmalise hadn't left Kentucky.

"This is my first time out of state!" Emmalise smiled. "Indiana is pretty. I love the trees, the fall colors."

"Where would you like to go most of all?" Whit asked her.

"The national parks out west," she answered immediately. "Yosemite, Yellowstone, Grand Canyon, Redwood National Park. I'd like to hike in them, camp out, not just do some bus tour."

"Yep, me too," said Whit. "Do you camp often?"

"No," she laughed, "I never have. I don't like bugs, or peeing outside, but I'd still like to try camping. It would be the only way I could afford any of those trips. Have you gone camping?"

"Sure, with Jake and some other friends, when we were kids. Most of the time we didn't even have tents, just sleeping bags. I haven't gone as an adult. We can give it a try sometime, if you want."

"OK. Better practice before we try Yellowstone!"

They drove into Indianapolis on I65, not talking as much. They were using the GPS on Whit's phone to find North New Jersey Street in Fall Creek Place. After they pulled off the interstate, the homes were small, mostly one-story, with leaf-filled yards and colorful trees. In the third block, Whit pulled the Camaro over in front of a partly sided, partly brick house with an enclosed front porch. A white-sided garage sat at the end of a paved drive, behind the house, with an older dark blue Chevy sedan in the driveway.

Whit started to get out, but Emmalise touched his arm to stop him.

"You're the professional, so I'll let you do the talking," she said.

"Thanks," Whit smiled back, "but when you think I'm finished, if you have any questions, ask away. This is your case."

Whit rang the doorbell, and a thin, fiftyish black woman answered within moments.

"Hello, Mrs. Franklin, I'm Whitman Pierce. This is Emmalise Pine. Thank you for seeing us."

June Franklin stepped back, holding the door open.

"Please come in," she said, with a polite smile. She was dressed in black slacks, a white blouse, and low black heels, with her hair pulled back in tiny braids leading to a small bun. She led them into the Scandinavian-style living room and motioned them to a tan fabric couch. The room was very neat, with sleek padded chairs, and decorated in warm accents, like the orange throw pillows. High contrast, brightly colored weavings were widely spaced on the walls. It wasn't what Emmalise had expected, but the pitcher of iced tea and three glasses that sat on a glass-topped coffee table was. Southern hospitality was part of life, no matter the life style. June sat opposite them in one of the simple chairs.

"As I told you on the phone, we're investigating a cold case from twenty-three years ago in Woodford County," explained Whit. "I'm sorry I can't give you details, but I hope to eventually. Your reasons for leaving Kentucky are related to the case. I'm sorry to ask you about painful memories, Mrs. Franklin, but your answers may help us."

"It's too late to bring the man responsible to justice," June Franklin answered. "Perhaps he is being punished in the afterlife, if you believe in that. I hope he is. I want some good to come of my children's frightening experiences at Oscar Printes's hands, so I'll tell you what they told me. I'd prefer that you not talk to them about this, but we can do that, if necessary."

"Could you tell us their story, please?" Whit asked.

"My husband was a foreman at one of Printes's tobacco farms. I was the housekeeper and cook in the house where his manager lived. I had to arrange the meals for the transient workers, as well. Our kids went to a so-called school on the farm for all of the workers' children. It was difficult for me to have eyes on them with my work. Printes stayed at the house, when he visited. He had his own separate apartment. Louisa was eight years old that summer, and Paul was five. I did finally notice that they were more quiet than usual. Louisa usually loved to tell me about school, what she learned. She would read books to Paul in the evenings. Paul liked to play with his daddy, too, if Harry was home. They became more quiet, but irritable too. They weren't eating as much. I assumed they were getting sick."

June paused. Emmalise and Whit could see her struggle. June's lips trembled, and compressed; her mouth turned down at the corners. Her eyes shone with tears. She closed them, and took a deep breath. Emmalise wanted to touch June's hand, but decided that would be too much.

"Finally one evening Louisa wouldn't eat at all, and when I asked her if she felt sick, she ran from the table crying. I followed her to her bedroom, and she held on to me for dear life, sobbing. When she could talk, she told me that Mr. Oscar had been taking her and Paul to the barn to look at animals after school. There were just a few animals, like chickens, and a milk cow, and a barn cat. The cat had had kittens, so the kids were thrilled to see them. She said Mr. Oscar took pictures of them holding kittens. Then he told them how cats made kittens, and showed them where the kittens came out of the mama cat when they were born."

June stopped again, choking with tears and anger this time.

"He said people had babies the same way, and that he could show them their baby-making parts. Then he did. Dear God. He touched my babies."

June covered her face with her hands, and bent over, shuddering, for a minute or more. Then she straightened, pulled her hands down in her lap, took a deep breath, and then another.

"I'm sorry. I thought I could get through this. I haven't talked about it in so long," June's voice was very soft and trembled in her throat.

Emmalise and Whit's hearts broke for her and her children. They couldn't speak. June breathed deeply again, and she looked at them.

"Louisa said she felt frozen. She looked at Paul once, and said he looked frozen too. Then she couldn't look at him anymore, or at Mr. Printes. She stared at the wooden barn wall and thought of nothing. She said she made herself be a block of ice that couldn't feel anything. He let them go. Of course, he said not to tell anyone. This was their own private school, and he was their teacher. 'That's all for today,' he said, just like a teacher.

It's really a miracle she told me. You have to understand that black children learn to obey whites from an early age. Self-protection. We were very lucky in one way. Mr. Oscar had to leave the farm the day after he abused my children. Louisa told me about it a week later. I took them and left the day after she told me. We caught a bus back to Belleriver, and then here to Indianapolis. I didn't even tell their daddy at first. I don't know if I was more afraid that he would kill Mr. Printes, or that he wouldn't."

June wiped under her eyes with her fingers.

"I'm very sorry for what happened to you and your children," said Whit. "Do you know if that experience has affected Louisa or Paul since then?"

"They both finished high school, are working, and happily married," June answered, "so I don't think the effects were lasting. It helped that their daddy followed us here within a few weeks. He was angry and confused with me at first. When I told him what Printes had done, he nearly left to find and kill him. I convinced him to stay and help me talk to Louisa and Paul. That was very hard for all of us. We must've said something right, because they seemed better afterward. I don't think they've forgotten, though. I know I haven't."

"Would we be able to speak to your husband? I'd like to ask him if he noticed anything with Oscar Printes on the farm, if he paid attention to other children," Whit said.

"No, he died five years ago. Heart failure," June replied. "I did ask him that. He didn't know of anything. Mama told me she heard rumors, especially after what happened to her grandchildren."

"I'm sorry about your husband," said Emmalise, then asked, "Do you have pictures of your children?"

June rose, went down the hallway, and returned with some framed photographs. She showed them a small double frame first of a young boy and girl.

"These are their first school pictures after we came here," she said.

The girl was large-eyed and pretty, with curly pigtails, but serious. The little boy also had big eyes and thick lashes, and smiled mischievously.

"Oh, they're so cute," smiled Emmalise. Whit nodded and smiled too.

They exchanged photos with June, who handed them 8 x10 inch frames of two families. Louisa was beautiful, and unmistakable as the same person, sitting next to a tall, handsome black man, with a boy of about ten in front of the man, and a baby boy on her lap. Paul had on a baseball jersey and his arm was around a young white woman holding a baby with a baby-sized ball cap on his little head. Both photos were candid, and everyone was smiling 'fit to bust,' Emmalise thought.

"Paul plays for the Indianapolis Indians," said June proudly, "Third base."

"The Triple A team," Whit said, "I thought I recognized the jersey. That's great!"

"You have a lovely home," said Emmalise, "Did you raise them here?"

"Not at first, but John, my husband, got a good-paying construction job, and I took a court reporter course. That's what I still do. So we moved here two years after we arrived."

They talked a little longer, then Whit thanked June Franklin for her help.

"You're welcome," she said. "I hope you can tell me what this is about someday."

"I think we will," answered Whit, shaking her hand.

Emmalise shook hands with June as well. Then she and Whit drove south. They were silent for a long time. After about an hour, Emmalise spoke.

"That made me sick to my stomach. So terrible for that family."

"Yes," Whit answered, reaching across to take her hand, "and I don't think Gideon Printes would want the world to know what his father did."

CHAPTER 33

On Friday evening, Sam arrived home carrying three large pizzas. Mac met him at the door and he pulled her into a hug with his left arm, balancing the pizzas on his right. Mac reached over to hold the boxes, too, kissing him quickly.

"Kitchen table," she said."That's a lot of pizza."

"I'm hungry, even if no one else is," Sam grinned at her.

"And I'm eating for two. I love that excuse."

Mac already had a big bowl of salad on the table and seven places set. Paper plates, cups, two liters of soda, pitchers of tea, and ice water were on the counter.

"Parker should be right behind me. I told everyone 6:00 o'clock," said Sam.

Sheriff Dade was the next to arrive, followed by Judge Turner and Miss Tippet, then Emmalise and Whit within five minutes of each other. Everyone complimented their new home-in-the-hill, which looked more inhabited with an extra-long sectional, a Southwest patterned rug, and the rolltop desk in the living room. Sam watched Mac greet Emmalise, knowing his wife was curious about the woman who started it all. He had cleared including Mac in the meeting with his boss, and Emmalise, who both thought it was fine.

"She's been through her own mystery," the Sheriff had said. "I imagine she'll be able to contribute."

Emmalise, like anyone who read the local papers, knew about Mac's involvement in the murder/kidnapping case almost two years before. She admired Mac's art, which she had looked at online. She wondered if they would have a connection from their contact with murderers, even though the stories were different.

Mac pointed everyone toward the kitchen, and urged them to help themselves.

"We have plain cheese, meat lovers', and a supreme with lots of everything," she said.

"There's plenty, so don't be shy."

"I'm not shy about eating," said Miss Tippet, leading the way. Her tiny frame seemed to contradict that, but she put one piece from each pizza on her plate.

Soon they were all seated around the long kitchen table, munching with gusto, and without a lot of conversation. Whit did ask why they decided to build their home into a hill.

Mac laughed, "Well, the hill was here, so…."

"We were going to build on top of the hill at first," Sam smiled with her, and continued, "but decided to go energy efficient. There are three recessed skylights in the top of the hill, plus solar panels. We have a mild climate here, but it's still nice to eliminate electric bills. We did a lot of research, and found some homes that we liked, then did our own design. That was mostly Mac."

"I imagine there's plenty of natural light from those front windows and skylights," said Emmalise. "I like it."

"It certainly becomes part of the landscape," Lorraine observed."The logs are a natural touch."

They ate, until all of the salad and most of the pizza were gone.

"That was great!" said Judge Turner, pushing back a little from the table. "I forgot how much I love pizza!"

"Homemade brownies," announced Sam, placing a plate in the center of the table. "Would anyone like coffee?"

Sheriff Dade, the judge, and Whit acquiesced, so Sam and Mac brought them steaming mugs. The plate of brownies was passed around, and everyone took one.

"Does anyone object to using first names?" began the sheriff. "I'm Parker. I don't think we need to be formal at this point."

"Sounds good to me," responded Miss Tippet. "Lorraine."

They continued around the table: Wainwright, Sam, Mac, Emmalise and Whit.

"We can each tell about our interviews this week," said Parker, "then we'll decide what to do next. Sam, why don't you start?"

Sam repeated what Mary Louise and Lena James had told him about Lester, who was killed in Vietnam; Roy who was wounded, but came home to work and marry; and James, who undoubtedly had PTSD, but worked intermittently and wandered. His last visit was Christmas, 1992, and he mentioned Belleriver, and a preacher he liked.

"That was Pastor Ezekiel Rose," said Parker. "He knew and liked James James. He definitely places him in this area. They had church meetings in one of Robert Blake's old barns."

Mac and Sam looked at each other. It was Blake's champion stallion that was wounded by the sniper, when Mac was sketching the horse. Parker nodded at them, knowing what they were remembering.

"Pastor Rose also said that James worked for some private families around here," added Lorraine. "He couldn't remember any names, but said he would call us if he did."

"Serafina and William Foster put James at the Printes's place," said Emmalise.

"Yes," agreed Parker, "and it's the year he disappeared. Emmalise, I think everyone needs to hear what June Franklin told you and Whit about Oscar Printes."

Emmalise repeated what Mrs. Franklin had said about she and her husband working for Mr. Printes at another farm in western Kentucky, and how Oscar had abused her children. She went into as much detail as Mrs. Franklin had given them.

"She asked that we not talk to the children, unless it was necessary," said Emmalise, "but I think they would agree to an interview, if it would establish a motive for Gideon."

"The little girl was eight years old when it happened," added Whit. "I think she would remember more than her brother. Mrs. Franklin said they did not seem to have suffered any permanent damage, and they haven't had therapy, but both parents talked with them, and tried to reassure them that it wasn't their fault."

"It's sickening," murmured Lorraine.

"I wish I could've sentenced him to life," stated Wainwright.

"At least they told their mother, and she got them away," said Sam. "It could have been so much worse."

"It probably was for some of the other workers' children," Whit's voice was low and rough, "the ones who didn't tell anyone, and weren't taken away."

"Sheriff, should we be talking to the District Attorney?" asked Emmalise. "Do we have enough for him to press charges?"

Parker Dade looked around the table at each person, his expression grim.

"Possibly," he said at last, "but first, I'd like to talk with the Printes family, especially Athena. I don't know when that will be. It's probably just going to be Sam and me from now on. I know you're anxious, Emmalise. I'll keep you posted."

Emmalise sighed in frustration. Whit took her hand under the table, and squeezed it. She gripped his tightly in return.

Chapter 34

Mac and Sam spent most of Saturday painting the baby's room bright blue. They didn't know the sex of the baby, but Mac said she needed a base of sky blue for her mural.

"Plus, I really hate that blue is for boys and pink for girls nonsense," she added.

"What's the mural going to be?" asked Sam.

"You need to help me decide. I'll use this wall opposite where the crib will be. Maybe just above the chair rail. Or the whole wall? Clouds going up into the ceiling. Or stars and a moon on the ceiling?"

"Let's get the main theme first," Sam suggested. "Will you be willing to paint over it as he or she ages?"

"Oh crap! What if we have a mini-Goth who wants it all black in high school?" laughed Mac.

"That's a definite no!" said Sam.

They worked in silence for awhile, then Sam asked, "What's the latest from Sarah and Connor?"

"Sarah feels good. Having that scare turn out OK seems to have helped her. Connor is overprotective, and trying not to be. You remember we're going over there for dinner tonight?"

"Yes," said Sam, "we still can't tell them, can we?"

"No, I don't think so. When Sarah goes another two or three weeks, I'll be three months. She'll be well past the times she miscarried before, so maybe that will be a good time to let everyone in the family know."

"I just hope you and Sarah both do well, and we have two healthy baby cousins," Sam said seriously.

Mac put her roller in the paint pan, walked over to Sam, and hugged him, resting her cheek against his chest.

"It is kind of hard not to get all silly and excited about this with them," she said.

Sam hugged her back with one arm, letting the one holding the paint roller hang by his side.

"Well, we can get silly about this room, right?" Mac looked up into his blue eyes, and said. "What about a bunch of animals doing crazy things?'

"Like what?"

"Like dancing? Having a party?" Mac grinned. "Something completely different than what I usually paint!"

"Playing in a band!" suggested Sam, getting into the idea. " A conga line!"

They went back to painting, now and then one of them tossing out an idea. Then Mac changed the subject.

"Looks like it's all back in the Sheriff's hands now," she said, "and yours."

"Yep. Probably a good thing. Makes me nervous having civilians involved," answered Sam.

"It will probably be frustrating for Emmalise, especially if it drags on, or the DA won't charge Printes," Mac said, thinking she knew very well how Emmalise would feel.

"It would help if we had a body," Sam said. "Without one, the judge will definitely allow bail, so Printes will be free, and that seems dangerous. I don't know if we can prove he hit Emmalise with his car. I'm sure he's cleaned it by now."

"He had a lot of land to bury a body, even after his father sold their farmland," mused Mac. "Have you ever been out to the Printes place?"

"No, have you?"

"As kids, we would ride our bikes out that far sometimes. It's on the other side of Belleriver, closer to Aunt Tina's than to home," said Mac. "We were just curious about the big, old house, the closest thing to a mansion around here. Once in high school, a bunch of us took boats and canoes on Turtle Creek, and went right by it. Big, sprawling place, with a porch all around, up on a small hill above the creek."

"I'd heard that people boat on Turtle Creek once in awhile," said Sam. "We've never had any accidents or problems out there."

"It gets pretty deep in the spring, and stays deep enough for boats and swimming through the summer," Mac continued. "It doesn't run very fast, but there can be a big difference in depth depending on rain. Kids told stories about drownings, but I have no idea if they were real. We should ask Aunt Tina tonight."

A few hours later, Mac and Sam were seated around the big kitchen table with Gabe, Sarah and Connor, and Aunt Tina. Dinner conversation had been about Sarah's week back at school (parent-teacher conferences coming up), ranch work (sold a horse), Tina's neighbors (grandkids visiting) and card-playing friends (competitive) and Mac and Sam's decorating (getting there). Sam rarely talked about work, and he and Mac had not shared the work on the Printes cold case. They didn't that evening either, but Mac wanted to find out what Aunt Tina knew about Turtle Creek's history.

As they ate oatmeal raisin cookies, and sipped coffee, Mac said. "I was telling Sam about a bunch of us boating on Turtle Creek in high school. Did anyone ever drown out there, Aunt Tina? Dad?"

Gabe and Tina looked at each other, frowning slightly.

"Lefty Gilbert used to say that his brother Alfred tried to drown him, but didn't succeed," Gabe said with a grin. "Neither one could swim when they were young, but I don't think the water was above their waists."

"Kids always told lots of stories," said Tina. "I think grown-ups were trying to scare them away from the creek, or get them to learn to swim. There was one sad story about a toddler wandering away from a family picnic, and drowning. Many variations: church picnic, black family, white family, Fourth of July celebration, little boy, little girl, but always a toddler who wasn't watched carefully. I have no idea if it's true. Why do you ask?"

Sam answered, "Mac was telling me about boating on the creek, and asked me if the Sheriff's office had ever had any trouble out there. I just said not since I'd been working here, thankfully."

"It's usually too shallow for boating," said Gabe. "At least that makes it easy to cross on horseback. I've taken horses there to train them to cross water, if they have trouble with the puddles we get here."

That launched Connor and Gabe into funny horse training stories. Sarah and Mac slipped away to the kitchen.

"Since Connor likes to cook, I've always felt I should do the dishes," said Sarah.

"That's the way we always did it," Mac smiled at her friend. "Plus, we can talk in private."

They worked quietly for awhile, Mac washing, and Sarah drying and putting the dishes away. The Quinns had a dishwasher, but only used it about half the time. Mac hummed softly, while she worked. When Sarah recognized Walking in Memphis, she started singing, and Mac did too. Finishing in harmony, they grinned at each other. Sarah kept staring at her friend, a quizzical smile on her lips.

"Mac, is there something you want to tell me?" she finally asked.

"Uh, no. Can't think of anything."

"Yes, there is! I know you. You are particularly happy about something," Sarah pressed. Then she gasped, "You're pregnant!"

Mac stared back at Sarah, stunned, "How did you come up with that?"

Sarah grabbed her and hugged her!

"You are! You are! Congratulations! Why haven't you told anyone?" As soon as she said it, she knew why. "Oh. Mac, it's OK. It's wonderful!"

Sarah hugged her again. Mac hugged her friend hard, then they pulled back, and looked at each other.

"Listen," said Sarah, "I'm still a little scared, but I think everything will be fine this time. I've been thinking about it all week, and I just feel so much better. How far along are you? Can we tell the others?"

"About eleven weeks. And Sam knows!" she laughed. "Let me warn him before we tell everyone. We just decided to wait a little longer."

"We're going to have babies together!" Sarah's face beamed. "Our kids will grow up together!"

"I know!" Mac grinned. "Let me call Sam."

"Call me what?" Sam asked, walking into the kitchen with three empty coffee mugs.

Sarah spun away from the sink, and hugged him around the middle, while he lifted the mugs out of the way.

"You told her," he said with fake irritation, looking at Mac over Sarah's head.

"No, she just knew. Don't ask me how," said Mac. "So let's go tell everyone else."

Chapter 35

Do you mind staying in tonight?" Emmalise asked Whit, when he called.

"That would be fine. How about I cook dinner?" he answered, hearing the tiredness in her voice.

"Really? We could do takeout. I have to be here at least until five to run Kellon's dogs."

It was 3:00 p.m. Whit was sitting in his Camaro outside his office, getting ready to drive to his apartment or to Emmalise's place, where he'd been spending a lot of time.

"I can pick up some groceries, and be there by four or so. We can run the dogs, and then I'll cook. I'll rent a movie too. What do you feel like?"

"A comedy. Old or new, just something funny."

He almost asked her if she really wanted him to come, but he didn't like the idea of her staying alone. He at least liked to know that Kellon would be there.

"See you soon," he said instead.

She smiled when she met him at the downstairs door, and gave him a quick kiss. She was dressed in sweats and a long-sleeved tee, ready for their run. They put groceries away quickly, and he left a bottle of red wine on the counter for the cats to inspect.

"What movie did you get?" Emmalise asked.

"*Let It Ride*," he said. "Ever seen it?"

"Never heard of it. Who's in it?"

"Richard Dreyfuss. It's an oldie, but hilarious. Guaranteed to lift your spirits."

"Am I that easy to read?" She was leaning against the counter, absently stroking Guinevere, who was rubbing the wine bottle with her cheeks, then Emmalise's arm.

Whit stepped over to her, and wrapped his arms around her, rubbing Guinnie's head with one hand, before pulling Emmalise close.

"You're just a little quiet," he said. "Preoccupied. Besides, you're usually a lot happier to see me!"

Emmalise chuckled, pressing her face into his chest, and squeezing him back.

"Poor man," she said. "Don't worry. I'm happy to see you. It's the case, you know. I'm sorry not to be part of it anymore."

"Oh, you're part of it," Whit said. "You started it, and you'll be there for the finish, probably in court. You know that part will be rough. His defense attorneys will try to make you look bad."

"Yeah. I can't even imagine. Have you testified before?"

"Sure, but never for anything like this. It was pretty cut and dried, not an attack on me personally or professionally."

"I would sure like to be there when the sheriff talks to his mother, and confronts him,"

Emmalise said with a little more fire. "I'd like to see his face!"

Whit took hold of her shoulders, pulling her back to face him.

"I don't want you anywhere near Printes," he said, his voice low and firm. "I mean it, Emmalise. He hit you with his car! He could have killed you!"

"I know," she said, looking away.

He tried to pull her back into him, but her body had stiffened. He softened his grip, but only let go with one hand. He lifted her chin to look into her eyes again.

"Tell me you haven't been trying to figure out a way to be there, to get Sheriff Dade to take you with him."

She lowered her eyelids and admitted, "Well, yes, but not seriously. Just thinking."

Whit pulled her close again, and kissed the top of her head.

"Please tell me you won't go to see him, or his mother."

"I won't," she answered, "It would be foolish. That hit and run was close enough."

"OK, let's go run the dogs. Then I'll cook, and we can watch the movie."

"Sounds good. Are you going to run in jeans? You left some sweatpants here, which I washed for you."

"Thanks. I'll change."

He stepped into her bedroom, pulled off his jeans, and slipped on the sweatpants. Emmalise leaned against the doorjamb, eyeing him with just the corners of her lips turned up.

"I don't think I'll break much of a sweat in two miles," he said.

"That's too bad," she said, glancing at him sideways, "I was hoping you'd join me in the shower, but if you can't even work up a sweat...."

"I'll run backwards," he laughed, as they hurried down the stairs.

A few hours later, after their run, a long shower, dinner and the movie, Emmalise lay snuggled next to Whit on the couch.

"Oh my God, that movie was hilarious!" she said, grinning, "I loved it!"

"I thought you would," said Whit.

"I know your favorite part," she continued, "Jennifer Tilly in that dress!"

"I'd rather see you in that dress!" Whit joked, "No, wait. Without the dress!"

"That's good, because I would never wear a dress like that. I hardly wear dresses at all. I think there are two in my closet."

"Whatever you wear or don't wear is fine with me," Whit kissed the side of her head, and squeezed her more tightly in his arms, "This is kind of off the subject, but you know what I'd really like?"

She looked at him with a wicked grin, and he smiled, but said, "No, not that. Not yet, anyway. I'd like to start meeting your family."

Emmalise stared at him. "Really?" she said.

"I want you to meet mine too, but yours is closer, and I already know my sisters will like you," he trailed off.

"Mom is having a family dinner tomorrow," said Emmalise, "Not everyone will be there, but you can meet some of them."

"OK, good. Good," Whit looked up at the ceiling, his expression thoughtful.

"Change your mind?"

"No," he smiled at her, "I wasn't sure you'd go along with it. What should I wear?"

"Jeans are fine. Casual, always casual with my family," said Emmalise.

Whit held her close with one arm, while his other hand slid down her back, over her bottom, and up to the button of her jeans, which he deftly unfastened. Their eyes were open, locked on each other. She reached up to touch his cheek, and then moved her hand down to the button of his jeans, opening it slowly.

"Not always casual, Emmalise," he whispered, "Not with you."

She kissed him hard; he kissed her back, and their eyes closed.

Chapter 36

Serafina Washington and Malayna Brookes had decided to beard the lion, not exactly in his den, but in theirs. They had invited their neighbor Mary Sue Tomlinson over for an evening of dessert and visiting. They had decided on that course of action on Friday evening. Serafina was worried about Gideon's intentions, and Malayna wanted to know for sure that he was behind Mary Sue's nosiness. Malayna had seen Mary Sue out sweeping her walk on Saturday morning, crossed the street, and said 'it had been just too long since they had a nice visit with Mary Sue, so could she come over that evening?' Mary Sue had looked disconcerted, and a little alarmed at Malayna's approach, and was distinctly relieved by her friendly manner and the invitation. She said she would be happy to join them.

At 6:52 p.m., their doorbell rang. Their visitor was just a little bit early, probably excited about any forthcoming news. Malayna opened the door, and welcomed Mary Sue, ushering her into the parlor. Serafina was seated in her comfortable armchair. She smiled at their guest.

"Good evening, Mary Sue," she said, "Sit down, and have a piece of cake. Do you like coffee? This is decaf, if you don't mind."

Three pieces of lemon cake sat on three china plates on the coffee table next to three empty cups on saucers, and a silver coffee pot.

"Oh, this is just lovely!" gushed Mary Sue, "I would love some coffee, thank you, Malayna. I drink decaf myself in the evenings or herbal tea."

Malayna was pouring coffee into each cup.

"Do you take sugar or cream?" she asked.

"Both, please," said Mary Sue, "Two spoonfuls of sugar. I do have a sweet tooth!"

"Then you will just love Aunt Serafina's lemon cake," Malayna smiled, pouring just a few drops of cream in her aunt's coffee.

Mary Sue Thomlinson was a light skinned black woman, about 65 years old, skinny, with a thin face and features, and very black hair, possibly dyed, definitely straightened, and cut in a pageboy that curled against her cheeks. It was stiffly sprayed so that it moved as one piece, like a helmet. She had dressed up, wearing a knee-length rust skirt with a matching jacket and an ivory blouse. She held her plate of cake up close to her chin, and ate it quickly, as though she was starving. When she finished, she lay the plate gently on the table, sighing almost with regret.

"Well, that was delicious!" she said, and sipped her coffee.

"Would you like another piece?" asked Serafina.

"Oh, my, no, I couldn't!" Mary Sue answered.

"We'll give you some to take home," said Serafina, "That's too much cake for the two of us!"

"Just one piece would be nice. There's only me. Speaking of which," Mary Sue slid into her questioning mode, "You never did tell me who that young man and woman were who visited you awhile back."

Malayna and Serafina had to avoid looking at each other to keep from smiling at the odd transition. They took bites of cake, and chewed slowly, their eyes closed in blissful enjoyment.

"They were political canvassers," Malayna finally said.

"What did they want?" asked Mary Sue, secretly wishing she'd accepted that second piece of cake.

"Just to ask us some questions," said Serafina, popping another bite of cake into her mouth.

"Why didn't they come see me?" Mary Sue said, "Or anyone else on the block?"

"That's a good question," said Malayna.

She and Serafina continued to eat their cake, and drink their coffee.

"Well?" Mary Sue said in frustration.

"Mary Sue," began Serafina, "You know that Malayna and I used to work for the Printes family, correct?"

"Um, yes, I believe you told me that," Mary Sue looked down into her coffee cup.

"Have you heard that Mr. Gideon Printes is thinking about running for a judgeship?" asked Malayna, looking directly at Mary Sue, who glanced up, and then back down.

"I saw that clip on the news awhile back, but that's all," Mary Sue answered, "Has he decided to run?"

"Not that we've heard," said Serafina, "but that's why those people stopped by. They were asking us questions about him and his family."

"Really? Like what?" Mary Sue leaned forward eagerly.

"Like 'were there any family secrets that could hurt his election?'" said Malayna.

"Are there?" Mary Sue asked excitedly.

"No!" Serafina cried indignantly, "and if there were, we certainly wouldn't repeat them! We worked for that family for years and years. Malayna helped raise those children. Good heavens! Miz Athena still calls us, and sends flowers or gifts sometimes. Goodness! We sent them on their way! Nosy parkers!"

"I'm sorry," said Mary Sue meekly, leaning back on the loveseat. Then she remembered something, "But I saw the young woman come back a few days later."

"She came to apologize," said Serafina, "and she wanted to do some Bible reading together. So we did."

Malayna placed her empty plate on the table, and picked up her cup and saucer.

"You know, Mary Sue, we don't know much about you," she said, "We always seem to be talking about us, and our visitors. How is your family?"

"There's not much to tell," Mary Sue said, looking uncomfortable.

"Are your parents still with us?" asked Malayna.

"No. No, they've passed on," said Mary Sue.

"God rest their souls," Serafina said softly, "Where are you from? Do you have any brothers or sisters?"

"I was raised in Birmingham," answered Mary Sue. "I have a brother and sister. We've kind of lost touch."

"That's very sad," said Serafina gently. "How did that happen? I always think it's so sad when families drift apart."

"My brother is in prison," Mary Sue sat up straight, looking at something in between her inquisitors. "He got in with gangs, and sold drugs. He got caught."

"I'm so sorry," Serafina said. "That must've been terribly hard."

"Did that bring you and your sister closer together?" asked Malayna.

"No. Not so much," Mary Sue's lips trembled, and her eyes filled with tears. "She was too busy stealing my fiancé from me!"

Malayna and Serafina glanced at each other. What had been a ploy to distract Mary Sue from asking questions had become a real conversation.

"That's terrible! What did you do?" Malayna asked.

"I moved away. I moved to Louisville, then Lexington, and now here." Tears dribbled from Mary Sue's eyes, as she sobbed and made gasping sounds, when she tried to talk. Malayna handed her a box of tissues.

"That was a long time ago, Mary Sue," said Serafina. "Why are you still so upset?"

Mary Sue held a wad of tissues to her eyes, and nose, and partly over her mouth. She finally managed to choke out, "I've never done anything I really wanted. I never married, or had children. I don't have any friends!"

Mary Sue was crying even harder. Aunt and niece waited in silence, not sure of what to say. Gradually Mary Sue's sobs quieted, and she blew her nose a few times.

"Do you attend church?" asked Serafina. "It can be such a comfort."

"Yes, most Sundays I go to Immanuel Baptist in Lexington," sighed Mary Sue, wiping her eyes, "but I haven't felt terribly welcomed. I am so sorry. I don't know what came over me tonight. I never cry in front of other people!"

"It's alright," said Serafina, comfortingly. "We all need to cry sometimes. Maybe you should try coming to our church this Sunday."

Malayna stared at her aunt, trying to disguise the horror she felt at that suggestion.

"What do you do for a living?" Malayna said, changing the subject.

"I'm a secretary, uh, uh, a legal secretary," Mary Sue made an effort to control her crying. She wiped under her eyes, trying not to smear her makeup, but that was pretty much a lost cause.

"For whom do you work?" asked Malayna .

To her surprise, Mary Sue said, "Clifford Sims, in Lexington."

Malayna looked quickly at Serafina; they had been expecting Mary Sue to mention Kirkendall, Printes and Bibb, Gideon's firm.

"Does he have his own firm?" asked Malayna. "Do you work alone?"

"He's partners with John Lefford, who has his own secretary, Martha Gullion," said Mary Sue, sniffing, but calmer.

"What's your workday like?" Malayna continued to draw out Mary Sue.

"Oh, it's interesting work. A lot of typing, but the different cases are always interesting. We have an office in Lexington, and a small one down here in Versailles, so sometimes I get to stay here in town. It just depends on what Mr. Sims has scheduled."

"Do you get along with everyone at work?" said Serafina.

"Well, yes. Mr. Sims is very considerate and respectful. He wanted an experienced secretary, he said when he hired me. He and Mr. Lefford are young, just starting out three years ago. Martha is young too, very pretty. She's pleasant to me, but we don't have much in common."

"Are either of the gentlemen married?" Serafina mentioned.

"No, not yet. I think Martha would like to make that happen," Mary Sue added with a sly smile.

Serafina and Malaya chuckled.

"Do you ever see other attorneys at the office?" asked Malayna.

"A few times. When they're meeting for lunch or something." Mary Sue seemed to think this was a boring topic.

"Have you ever seen Mr. Printes there?"

Mary Sue's face changed instantly, flushed and wary. She put down her cup and saucer, and brushed unseen crumbs from her lap.

"No. Never," then she got back on firmer ground. "Only black lawyers have ever come to the office."

Serafina turned to her niece and said, "Malayna, why don't you put a piece of that cake in Tupperware for Mary Sue to take home?"

"Of course," said Malayna, leaving the room.

"Thank you so much," said Mary Sue, picking up her purse from the floor, and standing. "I really should be going. It's been so nice visiting with you."

Serafina pushed herself to a standing position, walked slowly around the table to Mary Sue, and put her arms around the other woman. That's how Malayna found them, Mary Sue's face wet with new tears, staring at Serafina gratefully.

"I was just telling Mary Sue that she really needs to try the Macedonia Missionary Church," explained Serafina. "She will find welcome there from the Lord and parishioners too. We have a friend who gives us a ride most Sundays. Be ready by 8:30 tomorrow morning, and ride with us."

"Thank you. I will," said Mary Sue. She accepted the container of cake, and thanked them both again.

After the door closed behind their neighbor, Malayna whispered to Serafina, "Why on earth did you do that? Now we'll see her more than ever!"

"She needs friends," said Serafina, walking back to her chair. "Maybe if we are her friends, she'll think twice about spying for Mr. Gideon. Maybe she will even confess what she's been doing."

"I did feel sorry for her," admitted Malayna. "I guess we'll see. The Lord does work in mysterious ways."

"Amen," said Serafina.

Chapter 37

Athena Printes sat in a white wooden rocker on the verandah that bounded two sides of her home. It was early afternoon on Sunday, still warm for October, a sunny day with just a few leaves beginning to turn. She appeared to be watching Faye and Luther playing a fairly energetic game of croquet. Faye had found the old set in the garage, and they'd played most Sundays all summer. Athena usually loved watching her slim, athletic daughter move around the yard, hitting the ball, running to follow it. Faye and Luther touched each other frequently, sweetly, unconsciously, and Athena was happy to see their love for each other so evident. She had recognized in herself early that her love for her children came first. Once she no longer loved Oscar, her children and their happiness engulfed her. How differently their lives had turned out than she hoped or expected, and now it seemed that only Faye had found the joy in life.

Athena remembered a conversation she'd had with Faye soon after she and Luther had moved into the family home. They had discussed that decision at length, because Athena didn't want Faye to feel tied down. That day the two of them had been unpacking boxes in the room that would be the Wynn's sitting room, and Faye suddenly turned to her mother.

"Mama, I hope you won't mind not being a grandmother," she said. "We found out that we can't have children. I can't."

Athena started toward her daughter to hug her, but something in Faye's body language stopped her.

"It's all right, Mama, really. I'm not sure I wanted children anyway."

"Sweetheart, I don't mind. I just want you to be happy."

"I am happy. I think Luther is too. We talked about whether we wanted kids before we married. He said he'd never imagined it, but that he would love anything we did together. I don't think I ever had a "mothering" instinct... maybe toward animals, but I didn't play with the dolls you gave me."

"I know," Athena smiled. "You liked the cats and dogs we had over the years, but you didn't dress them, or play house. You liked taking them on "explorations" with you, if they would go."

"Remember Jasper, the swimming cat?" asked Faye. "I had to keep a leash on him, so that I could get him back in the boat."

"You liked wild animals, too, but you never tried to keep them as pets."

"I knew they were meant to be free. Even if Mother Nature was harsh, the animals were wild, and meant to live that way. I don't know if I read that somewhere, or just felt that way. Or maybe Malayna taught that to me."

"Your brother told you that if you touched a wild baby, its parents would reject it."

"That's true. And Gideon didn't have a nurturing bone in his body!" Faye laughed.

Athena smiled, and agreed, "He liked to watch and learn about nature, but not try to change it."

"He won't give you any grandchildren either," Faye looked at her mother with concern.

"No, he won't," said Athena. "I doubt he'll ever marry. It would take quite a woman to carry that off! He's just different, but he seems content. That's not a bad thing, being content. I am. I'm happy to have my children near me, as long as you like it that way."

Then Faye quickly crossed the distance between them to wrap her arms around her mother. Athena hugged her back, and felt reassurance in Faye's honest openness to life.

Now Athena worried. How was she going to keep Gideon's problems from touching Faye and Luther's lives? She didn't know for sure what was bothering Gideon, but something was, and deeply. He was gone from the house more than ever, often missing the usual family meals, and grimly silent when he was present. If she asked him if anything was wrong, he tried to brush it off as extra work. At first he appeared to make light of her questions, but soon he grew irritable and snapped his answers, so she stopped asking. When he went to his rooms, he said he had to work, but she could hear him pacing back and forth, sometimes late at night, or early in the morning. On weekends, if he didn't disappear in his car, he walked for hours on the fifty acres they still owned. Most of it was farmed by a neighbor, but timber lined parts of the creek, and still had trails for hiking or horseback riding from long ago. The trees had been cut back more and more along the creek, but a few areas were half a mile wide, and you could feel like you were lost in an old forest. Gideon had once said he wanted to leave some nature on the place, not have all of it invaded by people.

Athena was afraid that Oscar's past, and hers, had caught up with Gideon. She hoped not, and couldn't imagine how, but her fears were growing. That Sunday afternoon, she had finally decided that she needed to search Gideon's rooms. She was trying to figure out when. A weekday when everyone was at work would be best, but she didn't want to have to explain herself to her caregivers either. One of the ladies was usually with her. Maybe she could pretend to nap, while they were preparing supper. She could request a time-consuming meal with a pie, so she would have enough time. She couldn't imagine what clue he might leave, but she didn't want to confront him without having some idea what was torturing him. He'd kept notebooks and sketchbooks as a child of his scientific explorations of plants, rock, insects, and animals. Maybe he kept some kind of journal now.

Just then, Faye walked up the steps, and flopped down in one of the other wicker armchairs near Athena's rocker. She was just a little out of breath, and smiled at her mother. Luther was out in the yard, collecting the mallets, wickets, and balls.

"Would you like a drink, Mama?" asked Faye. "I'm going to have lemonade, if it's made."

"Yes, thank you," Athena smiled back at her.

"I just can't move yet. Who would think croquet would be tiring?"

"Well, the way you two play…" Athena faked a look of disapproval.

"You don't think it's meant to be a wrestling match?" laughed Faye.

"Probably not the original intention. Plus you had a run this morning."

"Only three miles. And we walk as much as we run these days."

Luther joined them, leaning on the back of Faye's chair.

"I won today, Athena, three games out of four!" he said with a grin.

"Congratulations!" said Athena.

"I beat you on the race home this morning!" Faye lifted her eyebrows and wrinkled her nose at him, which he promptly kissed.

"How about I get drinks for everyone?" asked Luther.

"That would be lovely, dear," said Faye. "I'm stuck to this chair."

The front door opened and Pam appeared, carrying a tray of lemonade-filled glasses.

"Thank you, Pam," said Luther. "You beat me to it."

"You're welcome, Mr. Luther," smiled Pam, placing the tray on the wicker table between Athena's rocker and Faye's chair.

"Why don't you and Gloria get glasses and join us?" offered Faye. "One of these days it will be too cold out here."

"Thank you, Miss Faye, but we're working on supper already," Pam slipped back into the house.

"Good grief," exclaimed Faye, softly "Sometimes I feel like we're at Tara!"

"Not really," Luther sat in the chair next to Faye's. "Pam is white, and she is paid."

"I remember when Serafina and Malayna would sit with us," said Faye.

"That was mostly in the kitchen. They were taking care of you," Athena said a little sadly.

"You were with us too, Mama," Faye argued.

"Mostly when your father wasn't at home," Athena looked off into the distance.

Suddenly Faye jumped up, and stood by the porch rail, waving.

"Look! Someone's on the creek!" she cried. "It looks like kids!"

They could just see three figures in a rowboat. Tentatively, a teen-aged girl in the middle of two boys waved back. One boy was white; the other two children were black.

"Hello!" called Faye.

The boat moved out of sight behind some trees, the girl still waving, and Faye sat back in her chair.

"We haven't seen anyone on the creek since summer," said Athena.

Faye noticed that her mother looked a little sad.

"Mama, you never made this place feel like Tara," Faye said. "I was just venting. I can't believe how little some people have changed in the South, and it makes me angry. I'm sorry. You're not part of the problem."

"I'm too old to make a difference these days," Athena tried to smile reassuringly. "It can be depressing how long it takes people to change."

"You made a difference here," said Faye proudly. "Serafina and Malayna told me so. They thought the world of you."

"Speaking of those two, I need to call them and see how they're doing," Athena said.

"Maybe Luther and I could bring them out for a visit," suggested Faye.

"Maybe," said Athena, "You could ask."

Chapter 38

"Pass the gravy!" yelled Rachel. Whit remembered she was Dillon's daughter, about 14, with long dark hair to her shoulders and freckles across her nose.

"What?" asked Grandma Mary Ellen pointedly, her voice quiet, but easily heard over the hubbub.

"Pass the gravy, please," said Rachel, grinning at her grandmother.

The table was crowded with people around it, and food on it. Whit was on Mary Ellen's right with Emmalise next to him. Dillon was directly across, a tall man with black hair and a stern expression, keeping an eye on his two present children and Whit. Next to Dillon sat his beautiful wife Kristina, an older likeness of Rachel with straight brown hair past her shoulders and freckles adding youth to her face. She smiled at Whit, as though she was trying to reassure him that her husband wasn't dangerous.

Emmalise had brought Whit to her mother's house early, thinking correctly that it would be easier for Whit to meet her siblings and their families a few at a time. Walking into this group around the table would have been an intimidating start.

Tara had met them at the door, looking much better than the last time Emmalise had seen her, groggy from being awakened. Today, she was bright-eyed, and smiled readily at Whit, shaking his hand.

"Mom's in the kitchen," she said, adding unnecessarily. "Cooking."

"Let's go introduce you," Emmalise said to Whit. Tara led the way.

Mary Ellen was at the stove, stirring a large pot of noodles. Her long, straight brown and gray hair was pulled back in a ponytail, out of her way. Emmalise hugged her mother, and Mary Ellen turned away from her work to hug her back.

"This is Whit, Mom," said Emmalise.

Whit put out his hand, but Mary Ellen pulled him into a hug. Then she held him at arms' length, and looked him up and down. She smiled, as though she had seen something good.

"Very nice to finally meet you, Whit," she said, looking pointedly at Emmalise.

"We haven't been dating for that long, Mom," Emmalise objected.

"Never too soon," Mary Ellen said.

"Anything I can help with?" Whit asked. "I like to cook."

"Not today, thank you. I've got it all under control," Mary Ellen responded, smiling at him again. "Uh oh, I hear trouble!"

Sure enough, Mikey ran full speed into the kitchen, and grabbed his grandma around her legs. She bent down and wrapped her arms around him.

"Mikey, I have someone for you to meet," Mary Ellen turned him around to face Whit. "This is your Auntie Emmalise's friend Whit."

Mikey looked up at Whit, who put his hand out for a high five.

"Hey, big man, jump for it," Whit grinned, as Mikey jumped up and slapped his hand. Mikey took off again, and ran into his dad's legs, as Mitch and Jana walked into the kitchen, Jana carrying Petey.

"Auntie Emmalise has a boyfriend!" yelled Mikey to his parents.

"Well, good," said Mitch. "You slow down, buddy. Don't knock over your mom and Pete."

"I'll take him," said Tara. "Aren't you going to say hi to me, Mikey? Let's go to the front room and find some toys."

"You're Jana and Mitch, right?" said Whit, sticking out his hand to shake Mitch's.

As they shook, Jana smiled at Whit, and moved around him to kiss Mary Ellen on her cheek. Mary Ellen kissed Petey on the top of his head.

"OK. Everyone out! There's not enough room out here," Mary Ellen shooed them into the living room.

"I'm gonna get a beer before I go," said Mitch. "Want one, Whit?"

"Sorry, Mitch, I ran out," Mary Ellen said cheerfully. "There's plenty of sweet tea, and soda."

"Dr. Pepper?" asked Mitch, opening the refrigerator. "Yes! Anyone else want anything? Honey?"

He looked at Jana, and she said, "Sweet tea. Thanks."

Whit and Emmalise asked for ice water. Mitch said he'd bring it in.

When they walked into the front room, they saw a tall, young black man seated on the floor with Mikey and Tara, making towers and tunnels out of wooden blocks. Mikey was crashing plastic trucks into them.

"Mikey, see if you can keep the truck on this road," Tara suggested. She and the young man stood, and she introduced him, "Whit, this is Tyrone, or Ty. Ty, meet Whit."

They shook hands, then Whit and Emmalise sat on the couch. Ty was lanky, with a boyish, handsome face and a firm handshake. He gave Whit and Emmalise a smile, and returned to the floor with Tara, encouraging Mikey to build a garage, and play more quietly. Mitch came in and handed them their waters, touched Ty on the shoulder and said 'hi' with a grin. He sat in an armchair next to Jana's, and offered to hold Petey. Jana smiled at him gratefully, and handed over their son, who seemed to be waking up.

"Hey, Whit, I hear you're a private eye!" said Mitch, putting Petey over his shoulder.

"I am," answered Whit, "but it's nothing like TV or movies. And you're a lineman?"

"More on-the-ground installation these days," said Mitch. "They took me off the poles, at least for a while."

"Do you like baseball, Whit?" asked Jana, not too subtly changing the subject.

"Sure, I'm a Reds' fan," said Whit.

"Hey, me too!" broke in Ty.

"Looks like I'm the only Cardinals' fan," said Mitch, putting Petey on the floor with his brother.

"Go Cardinals!" yelled Mikey, and handed Petey a small plastic truck.

"Guess I'm not alone," smiled Mitch, ruffling Mikey's brown curls.

"I know we don't count, but the women here are all Cardinals' fans," teased Jana.

"Oh, sorry," said Mitch. "That's true. You're outnumbered!" He looked at Whit and Ty.

"I'm winning over Tara," said Ty, "as soon as I take her to a Reds' game."

"That's a good idea," agreed Whit, glancing at Emmalise.

"I love live baseball," said Emmalise. "What about the Kentucky Wildcats?"

"We're all Wildcat fans," Mitch said, looking around.

They were discussing different college and professional players, when Dillon and his family arrived, immediately followed by Frank, the shortest and stockiest of the Pine men, and the only one losing any hair. Whit was introduced and shook hands all around.

Dillon didn't smile, but Frank was friendly, and joked with Mitch a lot. Dillon's son Scott was 12, lanky, and dark-haired like his dad, with big, dark eyes like his mother, and her smile, only shyer. He and Rachel joined Tara and Ty on the floor with the little ones. Kristina explained that their oldest son Aaron was at play practice and couldn't come. He was cast as Nathan Detroit in the school musical Guys and Dolls. Dillon tried not to smile, when she mentioned that.

"Does he know who Frank Sinatra was?" asked Mitch with a grin.

"He does now!" answered Kristina. "He was blown away when we showed him the movie. He mentioned it to their director, who showed it to the whole cast."

"I can hear him practicing that accent in his room at night," said Rachel.

"And singing in the shower," added Scott.

"He sounds great!" defended Dillon.

"Says the tone-deaf guy," laughed Mitch.

"True. True," Dillon agreed, "but I know what sounds good!"

Mary Ellen called them into the dining room for dinner. The table was filled with food: baked chicken, mashed potatoes, gravy, noodles, green beans, mixed lettuces with cut-up fresh fruit, and rolls, all homemade. They each found a seat, as if there was a pre-ordained order, and began helping themselves, and passing whatever serving dish was nearest each person. For a while, there wasn't much talk, except high praise for the meal.

"You did yourself proud, Mom!" said Frank, and everyone agreed, shoveling food into their mouths. Gradually, consumption slowed, and talking increased.

"I'll bet you have some good stories, Whit," Mitch tried again. "Being a PI sounds like a crazy job!"

"Stories I can't tell, Mitch," Whit answered. "Client confidentiality. Also, a lot of computer work. Repetition. It can get boring, believe it or not."

"Not sure I do, Whit," said Mitch a little belligerently, but smiling, like he was joking.

"Ouch!" Mitch yelped. Jana, sitting next to him, smiled evilly and said, "Mixed company, Mitch."

"Did you ever shoot anyone?" piped up Rachel, and the whole table fell silent.

"What?" she said. "Why can't I ask that?"

Dillon looked thunderous, and Kristina opened her mouth to quiet her daughter, but Whit answered first.

"No, Rachel, thank God, I haven't," he said in a quiet voice that everyone heard. "I rarely carry a gun. I'm not a policeman, and I just don't do those kinds of cases. I do a lot of background checks on people applying for jobs. I interview witnesses for attorneys. It isn't the kind of job that's shown in movies and TV shows. It can be interesting, but it's private. That's why it's called 'private' investigator."

He said the last line with a smile, that diffused the various emotions around the table. Conversations gradually picked up again. Emmalise lay her hand on Whit's thigh and smiled when he looked at her. Mary Ellen was smiling at him too.

"Grandma! What's for dessert?" piped up Mikey.

"Dessert?" Mary Ellen tried to look innocently puzzled. "Didn't you get enough to eat?"

"Nope," said Mikey, still looking at her expectantly.

Mary Ellen relented, "Chocolate cake!"

Mikey cheered, and everyone else looked happy too. Tara and Emmalise rose, and began clearing the table. Tara motioned for Kristina and anyone else who offered to sit down. Frank asked Dillon how his family's vacation to Nashville had gone. Kristina, Rachel and Scott chorused, 'Great!', and Dillon smiled. Soon everyone was sharing travel and vacation stories. Conversation slowed again as the cake was served.

Jana and Mitch were the first to leave with a sleeping Petey and a tuckered out Mikey. The others trickled out gradually with excuses of long trips, school or work the next day, and they all shook Whit's hand, or gave him a personal good-bye. Dillon gave him a handshake, nod and a very slight smile. Ty was still there, sitting on the couch with Tara, holding her hand, when Emmalise and Whit rose to leave.

"Let's do that Reds' game next season," Whit said to Ty and Tara.

She smiled, and Ty said, "Sounds good."

"That was an incredible meal. Thank you for having me," said Whit to Mary Ellen.

"You're welcome anytime, with or without the whole family," answered Mary Ellen. She was hugging Emmalise at the time, let her daughter go, and hugged Whit.

"You're the only young man she's brought over," she whispered to him, loudly enough for everyone to hear.

"Mom!" objected Emmalise.

Tara laughed.

As they pulled away from the house, Whit smiled, "So... I'm the only one, huh?"

"Don't get a big head!" Emmalise warned. "I have dated other guys. Quite a few!"

After a few moments, she added, "A few, anyway. I'm picky."

Two or three minutes passed. She put her hand on his thigh, and said softly, "Yes, you're the only one."

Chapter 39

Mac slowed her buckskin Sprint to a walk, and Sam's horse followed suit. Sam was trying out Ranger, a mostly black Paint gelding that Gabe was training for him.

"Good run!" Sam grinned at her.

"It was," Mac agreed, rubbing Sprint's neck. "I want to do that as much as possible, until I can't."

"The doctor did say it was OK to ride," said Sam. It was almost a question.

"He did," Mac reassured him. "I can do any exercise that I normally do. I just figure that eventually my belly won't fit behind the saddle horn!"

"Ranger did great today!" Sam enthused. "I can't imagine that he needs much more training."

"Every time you're with him, you're training him," said Mac. "He'll learn bad habits and good habits from how you respond to him. I'm sure Dad will want to work with him a little more, and show you a few things too."

"Did I do anything wrong today?"

"No," Mac smiled, "you look good. You always have to be aware when you ride. Of Ranger, his reactions, where you are, what you're telling him.I'll warn you, if I see a problem. Besides, you'll love the things Dad can teach him to do, and you'll have even better control. Let's turn around here. It's a different spot than last time."

"Why does that matter?" asked Sam.

"So they won't expect it. If we always turn for home at the same place, they'll start anticipating it, and turn without being told."

"Tricky, aren't they?" Sam chuckled.

"A little lazy. Always ready to go home and eat!"

"Me too!" grinned Sam.

They turned their horses back toward their home, keeping them at a walk. Ranger tried to trot, but Sam circled him a few times, and Ranger settled into a calm walk beside Sprint. As they came over a rise, they could see their hill with a four-stall barn built into the back of it. The stall doors opened into a fenced-in exercise area. Beyond that were about eight acres of pasture, and eight more for growing hay. Mac and Sam looked at each other and smiled. They both felt joy and fear at their happiness, and determination to protect it.

Just then Sam's cell phone played "Old Time Rock and Roll", muffled slightly inside his jacket pocket. Neither horse startled, being desensitized to the sound. Sam pulled the phone out, saw Sheriff Dade's name, and answered. After just a few words, Mac saw his expression change to grim concern. He answered, "On my way." And to Mac, he said, "Car accident up on Ridge Road."

They urged their horses into easy lopes, and quickly covered the distance to the barn. Sam leaned from his saddle to give Mac a kiss, and handed her his reins.

"I'll call," he said, dismounting. Mac did too and led the horses into the barn. Sam ran around to the side entrance to the garage, and into the house. He picked up his badge, holster and gun, and switched hats, but didn't change into his uniform. He hadn't driven a squad car home, because he wasn't supposed to be officially on-call, so he climbed into his Honda, and started the engine. He drove to the stop sign at the end of their road, and his phone rang again.

"Sam," said Sheriff Dade, "I don't need you at Ridge Road. I've got two deputies working the scene, and our forensics officer going over the car. The ambulance has come and gone, on its way to the UK Hospital in Lexington. Sam, it was Gideon Printes. Looks like he ran himself into a tree, possibly attempted suicide. Can you meet me at the Printes place to tell the family?"

"Yes, sir," said Sam, absorbing the shock. "How bad is he?"

"The EMT's couldn't tell me much," said Dade, "He was unconscious with a head wound, when a good Samaritan found him. He called the ambulance first, then us. The ambulance came from Versailles, and just beat me to the scene. He was still unconscious, but alive, when they pulled him out, and loaded him. I'll meet you on the north side of Belleriver, end of Main Street. I'll get an update from the hospital, if there is one."

Sam turned north, drove past the Quinn ranch, and headed into Belleriver. It didn't take long to drive through the small town. As he drove, he wondered if it would be better for Gideon Printes to live or die. What they had learned was going to come out sooner or later, probably sooner. He didn't want Printes to "get off easy", but he felt mixed feelings for the Printes family, for all of the families. This case had become much more complex, sensitive, and terrible than he could have foreseen. Soon he saw the sheriff parked to the east side of Main Street. He pulled over behind him, walked up to the passenger side of the department vehicle, and climbed in beside his boss. Sheriff Dade was talking on his cell phone. He clicked it off, as Sam sat down.

"He's in emergency care," said Parker Dade. "At least he's alive. Let's take both cars to the Printes's. We may need to drive them to the hospital."

Sam led the way out of town. They drove about seven miles on country roads, turning north and east, until they reached the long, U-shaped drive that fronted the Printes home.

It was close to 5:00 p.m., still sunny, and they could see figures seated on the side of the verandah closest to the creek. Oak, maple, sycamore and walnut trees were beautifully spaced around the house, and along one side of the drive. Inside the U was an elegant expanse of green lawn, cut short, that looked like an outdoor vestibule for the large plantation-style home. Sam and the sheriff parked and walked around to the side of the house. Two people rose to meet them. Faye Wynn reached for her husband's hand, as she said, "Hello, Sheriff Dade." She paused, and turned back to look at her mother, whose face had faded to white. The three of them stared at the two officers in expectant fear.

"Good afternoon, Athena, Faye, Luther," said Sheriff Dade, then got right to the point, "I'm afraid Gideon has been in an accident, and is in the University of Kentucky Hospital in Lexington, in emergency care. I don't have any details yet, but he is alive."

Athena closed her eyes briefly. Faye let go of Luther's hand to kneel by her mother and take both her hands. Luther moved behind Athena's chair.

"He's alive, Mama," whispered Faye.

"We must go to the hospital," Athena said in a surprisingly strong voice.

"Of course," said Luther, ready to help her to her feet.

Sam and Parker stared incredulously at the small, thin woman in the large rocking chair. She looked light enough for a small breeze to knock her off her feet, but she was standing firmly, and accepting the presence of Faye on one side and Luther on the other, but not needing their support.

"We can give you an escort, and get there faster," said Sheriff Dade.

"Thank you, Parker," answered Athena. "That would be helpful."

Five hours later, Sam was still at the hospital. He and the sheriff had decided to work shifts, if necessary. Parker had promised to call Emmalise to let her know what had happened. It was difficult to watch Athena Printes, sitting very still for the first two hours, holding her daughter's hand. Luther sat on Faye's other side and held her hand. Sam stood by a window across the room and tried to watch them unobtrusively. The few times they spoke, it was in whispers, and Athena always gently shook her head. Sam imagined Faye was trying to get her mother to eat or drink something. Eventually, after a brief conversation with his wife, Luther left. He returned in twenty minutes or so, with a cardboard tray holding three drinks, and a bag of what turned out to be packets of crackers, and a plastic container of grapes. Faye finally convinced Athena to eat some crackers, and drink a little of the hot tea. Faye and Luther ate some crackers and grapes, sipped their drinks, and soon returned to their previous positions, sitting still and holding hands.

Sam texted Mac that he would be late. He made do with a Snickers bar and a bottle of water from vending machines for supper. He didn't want to be gone long from the grieving family.

Finally, a little before 10:00 p.m., a doctor came to the waiting room, and pulled a chair up in front of Athena, her daughter, and son-in-law. Sam was startled when Athena looked at him over the doctor's shoulder and motioned for him to come closer. The doctor was short and thin, with a handsome, but haggard face, and long grey hair, pulled back in a ponytail at the base of his neck. He sat with his elbows on his knees, looking directly at Athena the entire time he spoke.

"I'm Dr. Spicer, Mrs. Printes. Your son is recovering from surgery and will soon be in the ICU. He has bleeding in his brain, and we had to relieve pressure from swelling. His other injuries are numerous, but could heal in time. Cracked sternum and five ribs. Broken right femur, and he will need a knee replacement. Both wrists are fractured. What we cannot tell yet is how extensive his brain injuries are. We induced a coma to allow the swelling to decrease. You may see him very briefly, but he will be unconscious for at least 48 hours."

"Will he live?" asked Faye softly.

"I don't know. I'm sorry," responded Dr. Spicer.

"I want to stay with him," Athena said firmly. "After I see him, I will stay out here."

"I can't allow that, Mrs. Printes," Dr. Spicer laid his hand over hers and Faye's. "I can tell that you are a very strong woman, but he will absolutely not be awake for 48 hours, maybe longer. You may certainly return tomorrow, but you must go home tonight. You need to sleep and eat. You must keep up your strength, all of you."

He glanced at Faye and Luther, who nodded; then he looked again at Athena. She looked at him with great sadness, but nodded, as well.

"I'll send a nurse to get you, when you can see him. Officer, I'm sorry, but you shouldn't go in. He won't be answering any questions tonight or anytime soon."

"I understand," said Sam.

Later that night, sitting on their new couch, Sam told Mac what had happened at the hospital.

"I went with them to the ICU, even though I couldn't go in the room with them. I could see them by his bed. Luther gave Mrs. Printes a chair, so she could be right beside the bed. She held Gideon's hand, and bent over next to his head, as though she were talking to him, whispering. I couldn't hear anything. Faye and Luther didn't look as though they heard what she said, either. Gideon's head and face were almost completely covered in bandages. She kissed his hand, sat for a moment, and then they left."

"Poor woman," said Mac. "Even if she knows what he did, he's still her son."

"According to Parker, Emmalise said the same thing, when he called her tonight."

"I imagine Emmalise is frustrated, not being involved in the case anymore," Mac commented.

"None of us are, for a while, anyway," said Sam. "I doubt that Parker will want to talk to Mrs. Printes, while Gideon's life is in danger."

Sam reached for Mac, and she leaned back on his chest, lifting her legs up and stretching out.

"I love that this couch is big enough for both of us," she said with a smile.

Sam rested his other hand on her still flat belly.

"Big enough for three of us," he said.

Chapter 40

For the next two weeks, Faye brought her mother to the hospital, while Gideon remained in an induced coma. His broken bones were repaired and cast, except for his ribs, which had to heal on their own. Athena sat next to his bed, holding his hand. Faye stayed in the room with her mother, only leaving to get them snacks, or to go to the bathroom, or to take Athena there. Luther arrived each evening after his store closed to sit with them. For hours at a time, Faye would read aloud biographies of famous scientists, because she knew Gideon was interested in both history and science. She first read a biography of Isaac Newton, and then began one on Nikola Tesla. Every now and then, Athena would make a comment, or ask a question, so Faye knew that at least her mother was listening part of the time. Before they left each evening, Athena would lean over and whisper into Gideon's ear for a few moments. One night on their way home, Faye asked her mother what she was saying to him. Athena continued looking out the car window, but reached for Faye's hand.

"Just that I love him, no matter what, and to come back to us."

On the second Thursday following Gideon's crash, Emmalise and Whit were having dinner together at her apartment. Emmalise had been quiet for most of the meal, but she finally spoke.

"Sam Kincaid called me today. He said Sheriff Dade had asked him to call everyone involved in the investigation. He said that Gideon Printes is still in an induced coma, and the sheriff doesn't want to talk to Mrs. Printes, until we know whether he'll live or not. She is quite elderly, in her 90's, so he doesn't want to make this harder for her. At least not yet."

"I can understand that," said Whit. He waited, sure that she had something on her mind.

"I really wanted to confront him," Emmalise finally said, looking across the table at him, "and I don't think that's going to happen."

"It doesn't seem likely," Whit replied.

"Also, now that we know what his father did, I feel like something should be done about that."

"We don't actually have proof, and he isn't alive to be punished. We don't even know if the kids he hurt would want to come out in the open with their stories. We can only identify two of them for sure."

"I know. I know. It just seems so unjust and unfinished."

She sighed, shook her head slightly, stood up, and began clearing the table.

"Would you like some ice cream?" she asked.

"No, thanks, not now," Whit said. "Let me do the dishes."

Emmalise leaned against the counter, watching him, and absentmindedly stroking Gwinnie's head, the cat sitting on the counter, and purring. The cats' lack of boundaries had bothered Whit at first, but Emmalise said they would get on the counter anyway, when she was gone, so she just washed her counters a lot. At the moment, she was obviously still thinking about the case.

"If Gideon dies, what do we do?" she finally asked.

"I don't know. I think we'll all need to meet again and talk this over. Does it do any good to tell his mother that her son is a murderer? If he's dead, there's no one to prosecute. Maybe someone else will have an idea of how to proceed, but I think it's ultimately Sheriff Dade's decision."

Whit scrubbed the last pan and stacked it carefully on top of the dishes in the drainer. Emmalise did not have, or particularly want, a dishwasher. She also liked to air dry her dishes, and would put them away the next day.

"If he dies, at least it will be a kind of punishment, even if it was his choice," Whit said.

Emmalise nodded.

"It would be a kind of closure for James James's family, assuming Sheriff Dade tells them what we know," she added.

"You've done everything you could," said Whit.

"I know. And I was lucky that Sheriff Dade let me be so involved," said Emmalise.

She sighed, and slipped her arm around Whit's waist, as he did the same.

"Can you stay tonight?" she asked.

"Of course."

They sat on the couch, and the cats jumped on the arms to see how the humans settled.

Emmalise picked up the remote, turned on the television, and began flipping channels. Abruptly she stopped and looked at Whit.

"I just realized; I'm being so selfish. This isn't half as difficult as having your sister taken, and not being able to find her!"

She dropped the remote, leaned into Whit, and hugged him.

"I'm so sorry," she said into his shoulder.

"It's OK," he said, hugging her back. "It's two different situations. I've had time to get used to not knowing. I don't like it, but it is what it is. It's been much harder on my parents."

He picked up the remote and began searching.

"By the way," he said, "My folks want to meet you. Are you ready for that?"

"Sure," said Emmalise. "I guess it's my turn."

"Well, it won't be a huge family gathering yet. I'll see what they'd like to do. Oh, look! Die Hard is on again!"

"That's always good," said Emmalise, leaning back against him, "and distracting."

"Distracting?" Whit kissed her firmly, then fiercely. He lay back and pulled her legs up on the couch next to his. Soon no one was watching the movie. The cats were politely asleep.

When the doorbell rang three times in quick succession, Malayna rose to answer it, rolling her eyes.

"I know who this is," she said. "You have certainly started something, Aunt Serafina."

Serafina smiled, and leaned forward in her chair, as though she could hear or see better that way.

As expected, Malayna opened the door to Mary Sue Tomlinson, their across-the-street neighbor. Mary Sue had the expression of a supplicant, and was holding a cardboard box in her arms.

"Hello, Mary Sue."

"Hello, Malayna. May I come in? I have something to show you both."

Malayna stepped aside, and Mary Sue carried the box into their living room. She placed the box on the floor and sat in the chair across the coffee table from Serafina.

"I wanted to thank you again for taking me to church with you last Sunday," said Mary Sue. "The congregation was so welcoming, and I loved the sermon, and the hymns."

"You are so welcome," smiled Serafina. "Macedonia Missionary is a church with heart."

"Mr. Dodson and Mr. Mesmer were particularly welcoming," said Malayna, as she came back into the room with a mug of tea for Mary Sue. She looked up at Mary Sue under arched eyebrows, as she bent over to hand her the mug.

"Yes," Mary Sue, giggling softly, an unexpected sound from her. "They both offered to pick me up this coming Sunday, but I said I would be riding with you again. Is that all right?"

"I think that's wise," said Serafina, chuckling.

"What did you want to show us?" asked Malayna.

"I'm afraid I've come to you for help again," said Mary Sue. "At least advice. I know nothing about animals, and this little fellow was under my steps, crying, when I came home from work today."

She was bending over the box, pulling apart the folded flaps. She reached inside and pulled out a very fuzzy, tiny black and white kitten.Serafina reached for it immediately, and held it against her ample chest, smiling and petting its little head with her forefinger.

Malayna sighed, "We agreed long ago not to have any pets, Auntie."

Mary Sue said, "I don't want you to keep her, well, just part time. I've already taken her to the vet. She's only four weeks old, so still needs to be bottle fed, until she learns to lap from a bowl. She should be fed every six hours, and being at work all day, I'll miss one of her feedings. So, I wondered if you could keep her during the day, just for a couple of weeks."

"Of course, we can," said Serafina, giving her niece a look. "What's her name?"

"Magpie," smiled Mary Sue, "because she's black and white, and peeps like a baby bird."

"That fits," Serafina handed the kitten to Malayna, who took her gently, petted her twice, and then handed her back to Mary Sue, who shook her head.

"Just a minute. I'll just go get her extra litter box."

She hurried out the front door and returned barely a minute later. The litter box had obviously been on the front steps. She was also carrying a small basket of cat toys.

"I'll bring her milk in the morning, when I bring her back, if that's all right. I leave about 7:00 a.m. I hope that isn't too early."

"We'll put the litter in the downstairs bathroom," said Malayna, stroking the kitten absentmindedly. "I think that will be appropriate."

"We had lots of cats and kittens at home and at the Printeses, but they were all outdoor cats, so we haven't had any experience with raising an orphan kitten," said Serafina.

"Dr. Appleberry gave me the immediate information I need, and a little booklet," said Mary Sue, "I plan to do a lot of reading online, and I'm sure I can get books from the library."

Malayna handed the kitten to Mary Sue and asked her to sit down again. She did, letting the kitten loose in her lap. Magpie immediately half-slid, half-jumped down Mary Sue's pants legs, and took off, scampering around the chairs and tables. The ladies watched in delight, until the kitten leaped on the floor length curtains and began to climb.

"Oh, no, Magpie," cried Mary Sue, jumping up and extracting the kitten's claws from the drapes. She put her back in her lap and tried to hold her down.

Malayna left the room abruptly, and Mary Sue looked at Serafina worriedly.

"I'm sorry. I don't want her to destroy your lovely home," said Mary Sue.

Malayna returned with a string, pulled a mouse toy from the basket, and tied it to the string. She threw it on the floor at Mary Sue's feet.

"Now put her down," said Malayna, tugging on the toy, so the cloth mouse moved in short, jerky jumps.

Magpie began chasing the toy, as soon as Mary Sue put her on the floor. She pounced on the mouse, wrestled with it, let it go, and chased it again.

"Diversion," said Malayna.

"Brilliant," said Serafina. The three women smiled.

Chapter 41

Gideon Printes blinked slowly; then his grey eyes focused on Athena. She saw them fill with pain, and close. His hand tightened slightly on hers, and relaxed again.

"Gideon?" whispered Faye, leaning over her mother's shoulder.

"It's all right," said Dr. Spicer. "He may have just gone to sleep. He'll come around again, and stay awake longer next time. All of his vital signs are good. Just let him rest."

"Why didn't he stay awake?" asked Faye.

"The drug-induced coma leaves some patients groggy, and they need natural sleep," Dr. Spicer explained. "Try not to worry. You should get some rest yourselves, or a good meal. Come back in a few hours, and see if he's awake then."

Faye looked at Luther with tears in her eyes. Her hands rested gently on Athena's shoulders.

"Mama," she said, "why don't we do what the doctor says. Let's go get a bite to eat and check back in a couple of hours."

Athena looked at her daughter, how exhausted she looked.

"All right, Faye. That's a good idea. Thank you, Dr. Spicer."

They ate at Carson's, a nearby restaurant that had an unusual amount of parking. Since it was mid-afternoon on a Monday, the lot had plenty of room. Athena had declared that she was hungry, and Faye found good reviews on Yelp, so they decided to by-pass the hospital cafeteria. Faye ordered a salad, but Luther and Athena ordered the pulled pork meal. Luther had closed the store to be with them, and explained that it hadn't been busy anyway. Faye was disappointed that Gideon hadn't talked more, but Athena seemed to be in good spirits. She cut her large sandwich in half, and offered part of it to Faye.

"At least have some of my fries," Athena encouraged her daughter. "I will not be able to eat them all. Try not to worry, Faye. When he's ready, he'll talk to us."

Faye watched her mother eat more than she had since Gideon had been in the hospital. Eventually, Faye ate some of the French fries, and a few bites of the sandwich. She felt better, especially seeing her mother doing so well. They discussed preparing a room for Gideon's return, so that caring for him would be easier.

"Probably the blue guest room would be best," said Athena. "It's next to the second floor bath, practically a suite, and right above the kitchen. With the back stairs, it will be easy to bring up meals. We can have a day nurse and a night nurse, men, if possible."

"I'll start looking, Mama," Faye said. "I'm sure we'll have a few days to find good people. I doubt the doctor will release him right away."

When they returned to the hospital, they were surprised and delighted to see Gideon with open eyes. Athena hurried to her chair beside the bed, and took his hand. Faye pulled up a chair next to her, and smiled at him.

"Hello, brother!" she said.

"Hello, sister," he answered. His eyes moved to his mother's face, then his brother-in-law's. "Mama, Luther. Why am I in a hospital?"

"You were in a car accident, dear," said Athena.

"You've been in a coma for two weeks, Gideon," explained Faye, "but you'll be all right now."

"Really?" answered Gideon in a soft, slightly hoarse voice. "I don't remember."

He still had a tube in his nose, but apparently, they had removed the one in his mouth.

"You don't need to remember," Athena said, "or try to talk. Just rest."

Gideon's eyes blinked slowly a few times, and closed. He squeezed Athena's hand again, and did not release the pressure. Athena looked at Faye and Luther.

"I'm going to stay with him tonight," she said firmly. "I feel quite revived after that meal. You can get me a bottle of water, and then I want you to go home."

As Faye started to object, Athena continued, "I couldn't be in a safer place. I promise I will call you if I get tired, and want to come home. Please. I'll feel better if I stay this one night."

Luther left and came back with a cold bottle of water. Athena smiled at them, as he and Faye left reluctantly. A few minutes passed, while Athena held Gideon's hand, and sat quietly. She felt his grip tighten.

"It's all right, Gideon. They're gone," she said softly, just above a whisper.

His eyes opened.

"Mama, I have to talk to you," Gideon said.

"I know, dear. I have much to tell you too, but let's wait until this place settles down for the night. I don't want us to be interrupted. Can you take a nap for awhile?"

Gideon obediently closed his eyes, and was soon asleep. The nurse checked on him twice, first to see if he was awake, and might want to eat. Athena told her he had opened his eyes, but gone back to sleep. The same nurse, Lisa, popped in again, took his vitals, brought in a fresh cup of ice water, and said some encouraging words to Athena. About 7:00 o'clock, the nurses changed shifts. The night nurse, Bethany, asked how Gideon was, and whether Athena wanted anything. Eventually, the floor grew quieter. About 11:00 p.m., when Athena knew they would have an hour or two of isolation, she rubbed Gideon's arm, until his eyes slowly opened.

"We can talk now, son."

"Mama, I shot and killed a man. He worked for us over twenty years ago. I almost killed a young woman, just a few weeks ago," Gideon's eyes filled with tears, and he sobbed, "I thought I was protecting you. Us. The family."

Athena leaned forward, closer to his face, still holding his hand tightly.

"Oh, sweetheart, he wasn't worth protecting. Your father. I'm so sorry. He did terrible things. I found out too late, but I wish I'd told you and Faye after he died. I could have saved you from all of this."

They talked for over an hour, mainly Athena, with tears running down her cheeks. Gideon spoke briefly. He cried too, but could speak clearly after his mother told him everything.

"I won't ask you to forgive me, son. I don't deserve it. I won't ask you to forgive your father either. I haven't. Try to forgive yourself, Gideon. I do, and I love you."

"I love you, too, Mama. I wish I could ask James James for forgiveness, and Emmalise Pine. I don't deserve it, but I am so, so sorry."

Gideon closed his eyes again, and sighed deeply. He and his mother remained silent, still holding hands. After a while, they both slept.

At six in the morning, Faye Printes received a call from Nurse Bethany that her brother Gideon had passed away in the night, and her mother was waiting for her. When Faye arrived, Athena let go of her son's hand, and opened her arms for her daughter. Faye rushed to her, and they held each other fiercely.

"You knew, Mama," Faye said. "How did you know to stay? I thought he was doing better."

"I didn't know, dear. I just had a feeling I should stay. I thought he was going to recover, too, but I think his heart was broken."

"Why? What could have been so wrong?"

"We'll talk about it all. I'm very tired now, and we have a lot to do."

His funeral was three days later, a cremation with no religious or memorial service, except for the family. His obituary was simple, listing his education, place of work, memberships in local organizations, and surviving family members.At the end, it stated that a foundation for memorials would be available at a later date.His partners and staff in the law firm were baffled, but acceded to his family's apparent wishes.

Two days after the funeral, Sheriff Dade received a call from Athena Printes, asking him to meet with her at his convenience. He went out to the Printes home that afternoon and met alone with Athena in her suite for over an hour. When he stood to leave, he had an envelope in his left hand. He took Athena's outstretched hand in his right, bent over and kissed her gently on the cheek. She smiled and thanked him for coming.

That night the 94-year-old mother followed her son in death, breaking Faye's heart. Faye found an envelope with her name on it on Athena's bedside table. Faye did not read it, until after the private cremation service and the open wake held at the family home. Most of Belleriver's inhabitants attended, as well as old friends from Versailles, and Gideon's co-workers and acquaintances. Many sent flowers, or memorials to their own favorite charities, not knowing what else to do. Sheriff and Mrs. Dade attended, as well as Deputy Kincaid and his wife. Luther introduced them to Faye, with whom all of the names and faces barely registered. Judge Turner came with a former teacher, Miss Tippet. The judge told Faye that he had known her mother in her youth and early marriage, and that she had been a wonderful woman. Faye nodded and smiled at him. Miss Tippet expressed deep condolences, and Faye was touched by her sincerity.

That evening, alone in her bedroom (Luther was helping the staff clean up), Faye read her mother's letter. When Luther came upstairs, he found Faye holding the letter to her heart, and crying silently. He wrapped his arms around his wife. She handed him the three handwritten pages to read.

"She left me a job to do," Faye whispered into his shoulder.

That same evening, Parker Dade called Emmalise, and asked her and Whit to meet with the investigative group at his home on Friday evening.

Chapter 42

By 7:15 Friday evening, all members of the investigative team were sitting around the Dade dining room table. Parker Dade sat at the head with Emmalise Pine on his left, and Sam Kincaid on his right. The rest of the chairs were filled clockwise with Whitman Pierce, Judge Wainwright Turner, Lorraine Tippet, Serafina Washington, Malayna Brookes, Clare Dade, and Mackenzie Kincaid. Mrs. Dade had provided everyone with drinks, and placed plates of snacks in the center of the table. After introductions, conversation had stopped, and everyone looked expectantly at Sheriff Dade.

"It's twenty-three years, almost to the day, when Miss Tippet introduced me to a ten-year-old girl who had witnessed a murder," he began. "Emmalise was very brave to report that murder, but she hadn't seen enough to identify the killer or his victim. She was looking down from a hay loft, through a crack between boards, trying not to make a sound. She saw only that the white man wore a suit; the black man overalls and a blue work shirt; and the black man handed his killer a small red book. She heard what they said, heard the shot, and saw the victim's body being dragged away. I was a deputy then. As you know, we investigated, but found nothing except some of the victim's blood that wasn't washed away. We didn't find a body, and have still not found one. We do still have the blood locked up in evidence storage. Several weeks ago, Emmalise came to see me again. She had heard a man speak on the news. She could identify him as the murderer, because she has hyperthymesia, and can remember every moment of her life since she was about six."

"That's not always a good thing," said Emmalise with a slight, crooked grin.

Everyone either smiled or chuckled softly.

"So she came to see me again," continued the sheriff. "Eventually, this group of people here became involved in the investigation of the murdered black man. Each of you either knew or discovered some part of what happened. And we have shared it with each other. We still didn't have a body, but we almost certainly found out who the victim was: James James, who did yard work and odd jobs for the Printes family in the spring and summer of 1993. He went missing abruptly that fall. We found his mother, sister and brother still living, and wondering what happened to James. We came to believe, as Emmalise had told us, that Gideon Printes shot and killed James James. We even had some ideas about his motive. I have sent a DNA sample from James's hair given to me by his mother, and the blood found soaked into the wooden barn floor to the Kentucky State Police Central Lab. I have not received the results, but will in the next month, and I have no doubt they will match. I talked privately with our DA, and he still did not think we had enough to indict Gideon Printes. Now Mr. Printes is dead, cremated, and beyond our earthly justice. I do, however, have something more to share with you all."

Parker Dade paused, and tapped some papers that lay on the table in front of him. He took reading glasses out of a case that sat next to the papers, and put them on, adjusting them on his nose. He held up some typed sheets in one hand, handwritten sheets in the other.

"This is a typed copy of this letter that I was given by Athena Printes before she died. I asked Sam to type it, just so that I could read it more easily."

He looked at each person seated at the table, then looked down and began to read.

"Dear Sheriff Dade,

I must confess, for myself and Gideon. I do not believe in religion anymore, and I have my doubts about God existing, and if he does, what kind of god he is. So I am choosing to confess to our local law enforcement for which you stand. Besides, I know you tried to solve a murder with no body many years ago, and again more recently. You deserve to know, as does Ms. Emmalise Pine, the young witness, and anyone else who helped you come so close to charging my son with that murder. Gideon has died, so you cannot arrest him. I will soon follow, although I doubt you would arrest me for my part.

I was 17 when I married Oscar Printes, who was 30 years old. I was much too young. Oscar was handsome and charming. He seemed like a man of the world to me, so knowledgeable and experienced. He charmed my parents too, but they did try to dissuade me, arguing my youth and the great difference in our ages. I didn't listen, obviously. Our marriage was fairly happy for the first two years or so. But my miscarriages and the death of baby Alyssa left me devastated. Oscar did love me in his way, and tried to comfort me. In those days, people did not talk about such problems, not within the marriage or without. I think Oscar grew tired of my depression, as well as the failure of his charm to bring me out of it. He took me to doctors in Lexington and Louisville, who were encouraging, but impersonal, emphasizing my "wifely duty". Finally our wonderful cook, Serafina Washington, recommended a midwife. Her name was Lucy Abbott, a strong woman from Belleriver, and she was the only forthright person to whom I spoke. She agreed with the doctors that there was nothing physically wrong with me (she said she couldn't speak for my husband; the doctors hadn't mentioned him). She said bluntly that some couples were not blessed with children; it was up to the good Lord, and to keep asking Him. Being able to talk with her, as well as her practical suggestions with sex and marriage, helped me to keep trying with Oscar. I did pray, ferociously. I still had my faith then. I resumed all wifely functions with hope and energy. I tried to help anyone I heard of, or came across who was in need, which was both distracting and fulfilling. When I was pregnant with Gideon, I insisted that Lucy be with me for his birth. She was wonderful. Gideon was born perfect, and two years later, Faye. I was beside myself with joy. Oscar was proud of his beautiful, precocious children. The next fifteen years of my life were lovely. There was one moment of fear and insight, when I brought Malayna into the house as a Nanny for Gideon, and later, Faye. She was Serafina's niece, only 14 years old, but I was still weak from Gideon's birth, and she was a wonderful help. One night, I saw Oscar approach her in the tiny room she had next to Gideon's. I saw him touch her face and shoulder, and say something to her. He heard me come into Gideon's room, and turned to me at once. My heart, my entire body went cold, but I thought it was a man's need and weakness, because I hadn't been available for Oscar in that way. I could see that Malayna was afraid, so I had a lock put on her door, and resumed having relations with Oscar as soon as possible. He never bothered her again, as far as I know. He was gone a lot to his other farms. He was a distant father to the children, but a genial host to our guests, and seemed to be an attentive husband to me, at least when he was at home. I ignored my fears. Malayna and I raised Gideon and Faye, and had great fun doing so. Fun may seem like an odd term for parenting, but one or both of us was with them constantly. They were bright and entertaining, and between us, we could guide them well, I think. When the children were 12 and 10 years old, Malayna left us to attend college and become a teacher. The children were in school, and I could easily take care of them with Serafina still our cook and housekeeper. Those two women were my helpmates, and friends, and like aunties to Gideon and Faye. I am so grateful for them, and I love them more than I can say."

At this point, Parker looked at the two women, who Athena was praising. Both had tears in their eyes, and reached for each other's hand. They nodded at him, just slightly, and he continued to read.

"My marriage was shattered, when I found the little red photo album. I had a part-time maid, but I helped with the housework, particularly our rooms. Oscar was traveling again, and I was putting away some clean clothes in his bureau. The side of a drawer was loose. I thought it was coming apart and would need to be repaired, but it slid open to reveal a small compartment. I found the red book, and, of course, looked at it. I was horrified. It was filled with Polaroid photographs of young black children. Most were in their under-clothes, but three were nude. They all looked either frozen or terrified. They were simply standing, or seated, not in suggestive poses, but I knew what they were. I was sick, devastated, more than heartbroken. I don't know why I didn't confront Oscar. I suppose I thought he would simply deny it, and say they were a form of art or something. I put the book back, and never spoke of it to him. Of course, our relationship changed.

Not only did I not love him; he disgusted me, but he was still the father of our children. I did not want them to ever know. They were 15 and 13, respectively, at the time. At first I allowed Oscar to continue to have relations with me. Since I couldn't respond to him as I had, I have no idea what he thought. Eventually, I told him that I was having the change of life, and we remained in our separate bedrooms. This is more than you want to know, I'm sure, so I apologize if I am embarrassing you. Still, I want to be honest and confess completely. So I must tell you that I killed Oscar, through gradual lead poisoning. It was not difficult to find lead paint on old boards, furniture, his own childhood toy soldiers; and I ground the paint chips into fine powder that I could add to his food undiscerned. I had no idea how much to give him at one time, but I used very small amounts, in the hope that he would suffer. He did. His blood pressure went up; he had pain in his joints and stomach. He developed gout. I wondered if his doctor would suspect the poisoning, but Oscar was overweight, and such a heavy drinker and smoker, that his symptoms were attributed to any one or all of his bad habits. It took a little more than ten years, but he died in 1985, officially of heart failure. I think he was in pain often enough during those years, that he abused very few, if any more, children.

I must also tell you that Gideon confessed to me, and I to him, before he died. Gideon had found the photo album as a child, left out in his father's room. Gideon was only 10 or so, and was puzzled by the book. He did not ask either of us about it. He told me that James James, a part-time workman on our property in 1993, somehow found the red photograph album. James said he found it in an old shed, so Oscar must have moved it at some point before he died. James asked to meet with Gideon off our property to return the book to him. Neither of us now believes that James was attempting blackmail, but perhaps wanted to ask Gideon the story behind it. As soon as he saw it, the images flooded into Gideon's mind, and he panicked. He shot James, and buried the body on our property. Near the river, he said. He said he couldn't bear Faye or me finding out what his father was.

What he did next is probably worse. He suspected that the only people who might know about Oscar's abuse were Serafina and Malayna. He found out their neighbor worked in a law firm. He approached her to spy on them for him, and paid her. He made it sound like it was for their welfare. Who knows what she believed, but she needed the money, and was naturally nosey. He also kept tabs on Emmalise Pine over the years. The police investigation into the murder of James James couldn't keep quiet that a little girl said she witnessed a murder. When he learned that Emmalise had returned to the Sheriff's office recently, as well as visiting Serafina and Malayna, he panicked again. He said he felt terrible after he hit her and the dog with his car, but he left the scene, and didn't see if she was hurt. Even when he found out that Emmalise and the dog weren't badly injured, he crashed into depression and self-hate, which led to his suicide attempt.

Soon I will know if there is an afterlife, and where my son and I are in it.

I have left a similar letter and the photo album for Faye to have, when I am gone. To try and make some reparation, I have made arrangements with my lawyer to set up a foundation for abused children, which I will ask Faye and Luther to oversee. All of Gideon's inheritance, and much of mine will provide the initial investment. I'm hoping those heartbreaking photographs will help Faye to find some of the children Oscar abused, or their families. When she is finished with the search, she can finally destroy the album. In a way, I have left her with a terrible burden, but I don't think Faye will see it that way. She is strong, and has always wanted to help people. She is the best part of my life.

In hope for atonement,
Athena Walker Printes"

Parker Dade slowly lay the pages down on the table. After a moment, he removed his glasses, and looked at everyone seated around the table.

"I thought all of you deserved to know as much as I do," he said quietly.

"Under the circumstances," said Lorraine Tippet, "I think this is the most that we could hope to know."

Emmalise nodded, but couldn't speak for the lump in her throat. Whit squeezed her hand under the table.

Epilogue

The following April and May brought a spring of dramatically mixed weather to the area around Belleriver, Versailles, and Lexington. Sunny, warm days were followed by days of heavy rain and thunderstorms. Rivers and streams rose and fell accordingly, but there was no serious flooding.

Serafina, Malayna, and Mary Sue continued to share the raising of Magpie, even after the kitten reached an age where she could have been left at home, while Mary Sue went to work. Mary Sue kept on attending their church. Right before Christmas, she confessed to her two friends how she had spied on them. They told her much of the story, which upset her terribly, but they forgave her. By that April, Mary Sue was "seeing" Clemson Mesmer two or three times a week for dinner, or a movie, or a visit to her home to get to know Magpie. The rejected Barry Dodson tried to ask Malayna out, but she smiled, patted his arm, and told him she was "much too old for that nonsense!"

Lorraine Tippet and Wainwright Turner were still sharing each other's company. The Judge had hopes of more than a platonic relationship, but Lorraine was firm. He told her she didn't know how stubborn and persistent he could be. Lorraine changed the subject to The First Conspiracy, a book they had both read recently, concerning a plot to kill George Washington.

Mac and Sarah both had healthy baby girls, a little over two months apart. Sarah's was two weeks late, and Mac's was one week early. Both were close to 7 pounds, but Aoife (Eefah) Quinn was 19 inches long with thick blond curls, and Rowan Kincaid was 22 inches long with a definite reddish glow to the fine brown fuzz on her head. Their dads were very proud, and were absolutely sure their little girls could do anything, and be anything. Mac and Sarah simply insisted that the men help with diaper changes.

Faye resigned from her job, and took over the Walker-Wynn Foundation full-time. Luther did assist her with research and some decisions, but he kept his store open. He felt that Faye was more than up to the job. Her first bequest was for June Franklin's grandchildren to further, or supplement, their educations from elementary school through college. She also gave generous gifts to James James's mother, sister, and brother to use as they saw fit. She offered the Foundation's lawyer and her own help, if they wanted to invest the money. That spring, Faye was just beginning the search for the adults the children in the Polaroid photos became. Faye let Emmalise know what the Foundation was doing, for which Emmalise was grateful.

Emmalise and Whit were still dating. In fact, Whit was at her apartment far more than his own, and finally asked if he could move in with her. She agreed. Guinnie and Lance were delighted, although they tried not to show it.

After one of the many spring rains followed by a dry spell, the three young people that Faye, Luther, and Athena had seen boating down Turtle Creek were at it again. It was a mild, sunny day with a light breeze. The creek had been up and down several times in the last three months. With the end of the school year keeping them busy, this was the first time they'd decided to try the creek again. It turned out to be perfect. The water was deep enough for their rowboat, and running smoothly, but not too fast. It didn't take much effort to move the boat along, so they took turns rowing. All three were fifteen years old, and had been friends since grade school. One boy was white, one black, and the girl was black, as well. Both boys were in love with her, which she knew, but had not yet found it to be a problem. For now, they were friends, and no one wanted to ruin that. They passed the house, where people had waved at them from the porch last fall. No one was on the porch now.As they moved on, thick bushes and trees lined the banks. One stretch had weeping willows whose delicate branches trailed over and into the water. In a few places, the bank had been worn away by the water, exposing twisted roots. Suddenly the girl, who was in the bow, pointed toward the bank and said, "Look!" The boys looked, not seeing what she meant at first. She urged them to row closer. As they approached the branching roots, and the water-carved dirt of the bank, they gradually made out what she saw. What at first looked like white roots or branches among the willow roots became bones. One of the boys grabbed a root to steady their boat, and hold it still. They looked at each other in shock, but no one screamed. Most of an obviously human skeleton was embedded in the bank, horizontally placed, parallel to the water's surface. It was tangled in roots, and willow branches hung gracefully in front of it. Still, they could clearly see the entire length, with one arm pulled down toward the water, as though the fingers were trying to touch the surface. Half of the skull was exposed in profile, looking upward toward the tree. It looked posed, so carefully placed that it didn't seem real. The girl reached in her back pocket, and pulled out her cell phone. Looking at her friends, she said, "I think we'd better call the sheriff."

Acknowledgements

First of all, I am very grateful to everyone who helped me with this book. I have multiple editors/proofreaders: my sister Mary Anthonis, my children Kate and Ben Travers, and friends Deena and Mike Rodino. They have all been completely supportive as I wrote this second mystery. Mary Anthonis also designed the eerily appropriate cover.

This is a work of fiction. The town of Belleriver and its surrounds are from my imagination. Any mistakes in real Kentucky cities or locations are mine alone.

About the Author

ANN TRAVERS grew up in Indiana, migrating to central Illinois for college, and chose to stay and raise a family. Teaching was her passion. She taught Art and English in public and private schools at every grade level for more than thirty years. In addition, her knowledge of horses, and horsemanship, provided her the ability to also be a riding instructor. She returned to writing in retirement, and has completed one other mystery, "His Brother's Eyes." Ann currently lives with her husband, six cats, and two horses.